The Ether

"*The Ether* is a thrilling fictional adventure about a very real battle that is happening right now—the battle between good and evil. If this book had only been an imaginative, spiritual adventure story I would have still loved it, but it is so much more—it's a book about the fight to discover the strength and true purpose that lies within each of us."

Crystal McVea –author of *New York Times bestseller Waking up in Heaven*

The Ether

VERO RISING

BOOK ONE

LAURICE E. MOLINARI

Titles by Laurice Elehwany Molinari

The Ether Series

Vero Rising (Book One)

Pillars of Fire (Book Two)

Screenplays

My Girl (Columbia Pictures)

The Brady Bunch Movie (Paramount Pictures)

The Amazing Panda Adventure (Warner Bros.)

Anastasia (Fox Animation Studios)

Bewitched (Columbia Pictures)

ZONDERKIDZ

The Ether
Copyright © 2014 by Laurice E. Molinari

This title is also available as a Zondervan ebook.
Visit www.zondervan.com/ebooks.

Requests for information should be addressed to:
Zonderkidz, 3900 *Sparks Drive, Grand Rapids, Michigan* 49546

This edition: ISBN 978-0-310-73561-8 (softcover)

Library of Congress Cataloging-in-Publication Data

Molinari, Laurice E.
    Vero rising / Laurice E. Molinari.
      pages   cm. — (The ether)
    Summary: "While living a seemingly ordinary life, a 12-year-old boy
discovers his true identity of a guardian angel and must begin his intense
training under the guidance of the archangels while still living his suburban
life" — Provided by publisher.
    ISBN 978-0-310-73555-7 (hardcover)
    [1. Guardian angels — Fiction. 2. Angels — Fiction. 3. Identity — Fiction. 4.
Schools — Fiction. 5. Animals, Mythical — Fiction. 6. Good and evil — Fiction. 7.
Family life — Maryland — Fiction. 8. Maryland — Fiction.] I. Title.
    PZ7.M7337Ver 2014
    [Fic] — dc23   2013034796

All Scripture quotations, unless otherwise indicated, are taken from The Holy
Bible, *New International Version®, NIV®*. Copyright © 1973, 1978, 1984, 2011 by
Biblica, Inc.® Used by permission. All rights reserved worldwide.

Any Internet addresses (websites, blogs, etc.) and telephone numbers in this book
are offered as a resource. They are not intended in any way to be or imply an
endorsement by Zondervan, nor does Zondervan vouch for the content of these
sites and numbers for the life of this book.

Zonderkidz is a trademark of Zondervan.

Editor: Kim Childress
Cover illustration: Randy Gallegos
Interior design: David Conn & Ben Fetterley

Printed in the United States of America

16 17 18 19 /QG/ 20 19 18 17 16 15 14 13 12 11 10 9 8 7 6 5 4 3 2 1

For Naz, who taught me the power of words from a young age … 'til we dine at the Bumbingba restaurant.

CONTENTS

1

THE LEAP
OF FAITH

Vero Leland had been trying to fly ever since he was old enough to stand. His earliest memory was standing on the rail of his crib, perfectly balanced like an Olympic gymnast on a balance beam. He fully expected his mother to clap when she turned around and saw him. Vero remembers stretching out his arms, intending to fly into his mother's outstretched hands. But instead of clapping, she turned and let out a heartrending shriek. Startled, Vero hit the floor with a thud and cried hard as his mother cradled him.

But what Vero's mother, Nora, didn't realize was that Vero wasn't crying in pain. He was crying tears of frustration from failing to get airborne.

After the crib incident, Vero didn't stop trying to fly. Instead, he became quite the climber. He'd climb and throw himself off the kitchen table, his parents' bed, the piano, and pretty much anything with a few feet of air below it ... until the winter of his fourth year. That's when his flying attempts reached a new and dangerous high.

It happened late one afternoon when Dennis Leland, Vero's father, was standing on a ladder and stringing hundreds of Christmas lights across the front of their two-story suburban house. Dennis was very particular about his holiday light display. Each bulb needed to hang exactly two inches away from the next, and they all had to extend fully, to just beneath the gutter. Christmas displays were taken very seriously in their suburban neighborhood of Attleboro, Maryland.

The men who lived on Vero's block had an ongoing competition, and each December the holiday displays grew more and more elaborate. Front yards were cluttered with inflatable Santas, seven-foot tall snowmen, and animatronic reindeer. One dad even convinced his wife and young children to perform a live nativity each night, complete with a real donkey and goat. However, the goat was quickly sent back to the petting zoo after it ate the plastic sprinkler heads, causing impressive geysers that drenched his family and ruined the nativity.

It was a clear but chilly December day when Vero's father climbed down the ladder to test the magnificent light show. Wearing his one-piece brown coveralls and his checkered hat with earflaps, he rubbed his hands together and said, "This is it, Vero."

With great pomp and ceremony, Dennis dramatically picked up the plug of the extension cord ... all of his hard work was about to come to fruition. But when he finally took a deep breath and plugged the extension cord into the outlet, nothing happened. The lights failed to illuminate. Vero heard him use a word he'd never heard before, followed by, "I'm gonna have to check every stinkin' light bulb one at a time."

A few minutes later, Dennis grumbled miserably as he started to climb the ladder with some extra bulbs in hand.

Vero called down to his father and said, "It's okay, Daddy. I can help." While his dad had been inside the house getting some fresh bulbs, Vero had climbed the ladder and now stood proudly on the roof. Being small and nimble, Vero thought he could walk along the steep roof and check each one of the bulbs for his dad, saving him numerous trips up and down the ladder.

Vero could tell his dad was thrilled with the idea because Dennis was standing completely still on the ladder and looking at Vero with huge eyes. But when Vero caught sight of the surrounding neighborhood below, his penchant for flying took hold of him again.

"Daddy! I could fly from up here!" Vero shouted, grinning wildly.

"No, Vero! No!" his father shouted. "Don't move! I'm coming to get you!" He took two more steps up the ladder before his boot slipped, and he fell smack on his back. Luckily, a small bush broke his fall.

"Daddy, are you okay?"

Then piercing shrieks were heard as Vero's mother ran out of the house wearing an apron splattered with powdered sugar. Her cries alerted the curious neighbors.

Mr. Atwood from next door was the first one on the scene, since he was already outside admiring his "It's a Small World" display. He didn't notice Vero up on the roof at first.

"For Pete's sake," he said. "Calm down the both of you. It's probably just a bum light bulb." Then he glanced up and saw Vero peering down at them. "Holy cow!" he yelled. "That kid's crazy!"

When Mrs. Atwood arrived moments later, Mr. Atwood wagged his stubby finger in his wife's stunned face and said, "I told you that kid was off, but you never believed me! Remember that time I found him in our tree trying to jump off a branch that was as high as the house? I almost broke my neck climbing up after him!"

"Quiet, Albert! I'm calling 9 – 1 – 1!" Mrs. Atwood yelled, cell phone in hand.

"Maybe it's all a big stunt to draw attention to his Christmas display?" Mr. Atwood muttered to himself as he watched more and more neighbors gather. "I wouldn't put it past Leland."

Vero's father, meanwhile, had regained his footing and was attempting to climb the ladder once again.

"Yes, hurry!" Mrs. Atwood shouted into the phone. "The wind is gusting. It could knock the boy clear off the roof!"

Mrs. Atwood ended the call and then turned to help Vero's mother, who looked to be in a state of shock. She took off her coat and wrapped it around Nora's shoulders. "The dispatcher promised the fire truck would be here any minute."

"Vero, please don't move ... " his mother said weakly. Vero saw she had flour on her cheek, streaked with a teardrop.

"Don't cry, Mommy," Vero told her. "I know I can do it this time."

Vero's five-year-old sister, Clover, joined them outside.

She'd been baking cookies with her mother, and she had flour in her blonde hair and down the front of her shirt. She opened her arms wide and called up to her little brother, "Jump, Vero! I'll catch you!"

Nora quickly clasped a hand over her daughter's mouth.

By now Vero's father had reached the top of the ladder. He tried to grab his son, but Vero was beyond arm's reach; so he only managed to graze Vero's foot with his fingertips.

As Vero inched away from his dad, he became unsteady on his feet, and a collective gasp rippled over the gathering below. Yet somehow Vero regained his balance, and the watching crowd breathed a sigh of relief.

It was all too much for Vero's mother who fainted. Luckily she landed in the lap of the inflatable Mrs. Claus.

Mrs. Claus is cradling Mommy like a baby, Vero thought. And that's when a shiny red hook and ladder fire truck pulled around the corner with its siren blaring.

Vero felt absolutely wonderful. He smiled broadly and stretched his arms out wide, feeling the cold rush of the oncoming wind. It was exhilarating!

The fire truck's ladder swiftly extended, and a fireman stood in the enclosed basket, ready to carry Vero back to the safety of the ground below.

Vero watched as Mr. Atwood cautiously approached the fire captain now standing beside the hook and ladder. When the fire captain finished barking orders into his walkie-talkie, Mr. Atwood said, "Captain, when this is all over, would you mind helping me out next door? I really need a lift in your basket. You see, I've got this Santa that I'd like to stick upside down in my chimney so it looks like he's diving in headfirst."

Fire Captain Conrad looked at Mr. Atwood incredulously. "Absolutely not," he said. Then he turned to the crowd and shouted, "Clear the area! We're trying to save a life here!"

Vero saw Mrs. Atwood slap the back of Mr. Atwood's head as they moved away from the truck.

"Hi, Vero," the fireman in the basket said, as the basket stopped level with the roof's peak. "Climbing onto a roof is a first for you, isn't it? We've done this in trees before, but never on a roof—at least not with me."

Vero looked at the fireman and smiled in recognition.

"Hi, Fireman Bob," Vero said.

"It's okay, Vero. Don't be afraid. I'm gonna help you just like I did before," Fireman Bob said slowly, as he reached his arms toward Vero.

But Vero wasn't scared. He looked down and saw that his mother was slowly waking up in Mrs. Claus's inflatable arms. And just as Fireman Bob almost grabbed him, Vero took a deep breath, jumped backward off the roof peak, and disappeared behind the house!

The neighbors gasped. Vero's mother immediately passed out again.

After Vero leapt off the house, the wind whipped against his face, and he felt like a bird soaring through the sky! Free-falling felt as natural to him as breathing.

But Vero's flying ecstasy was short-lived. Some powerful force—something other than the hard ground—abruptly ended his peaceful flight. He felt a sudden tightening around his chest like a yo-yo being yanked backward on a string.

Vero suddenly found himself in the arms of a man who'd somehow caught him in midair.

"Vero," the man said, "that's enough with the flying."

Vero didn't recognize him as one of the neighbors. He was an older man with longish silver-white hair, a closely trimmed beard, and violet eyes. He wore jeans and a red puffy winter coat.

"I can't always be here to catch you," the man said. "I need you to promise me you'll stop."

"But I have to fly," Vero told him.

"In time," the stranger replied, and he gently lowered Vero to the ground. "Everything in its own time. But for now, I need you to promise me you won't try to fly again until you know it's the right time."

Vero looked hard at the man. There was something familiar and likeable about him, and Vero thought he could trust him. Yet at the same time, Vero knew the man meant what he said.

"Vero?"

Four-year-old Vero nodded. "Okay, Santa," he said, and he grabbed the man's beard with both hands.

"I'm not Santa Claus."

"But you're wearing a red coat ... "

The stranger chuckled and said, "I'm too thin to be Santa Claus." As they heard the frenzied crowd rushing toward the backyard from the front of the house, the man locked eyes with Vero and said, "I expect you to keep your word."

Vero nodded again.

"All right. Now, I'm sorry about this next part, but it has to look believable," the man told him. And with that, the man twisted Vero's left ankle.

Vero screamed in pain, "That hurt!"

"I'm letting you off easy. It's only a sprain. Protocol says I should break both of them."

The panicked crowd descended upon Vero who was now sitting on the ground holding his ankle.

"He's alive!" shouted the fire captain.

Vero's father picked him up and hugged him tightly, and his mother had awakened and was right beside him. Vero saw tears streaming down his father's face, and his mom had flour-streaked tear marks across both cheeks now. Vero felt bad for upsetting them.

Clover walked up and said, "He's okay. The man just twisted his ankle."

"What man?" her father asked.

"The one sitting in that tree," she pointed.

Everyone looked at the tree. There was no man in it.

Mr. Atwood shook his head and muttered, "She's just as crazy as her brother."

2

BIRDS OF FLIGHT

Vero gave up his attempts to fly, but not because his parents installed safety bars on all the upstairs windows. Vero stopped because he didn't want to break his promise to the man who'd caught him. However, staying grounded wasn't easy.

On the family's vacation to Maine last summer, they'd hiked along cliffs overlooking the ocean, and Vero had to fight the urge to throw himself off the precipice and soar over the magnificent deep blue water below. He quickly jumped back and hugged the rock walls, as sweat poured down his face.

"Vero, what's wrong?" his mom asked.

"I ... I ... guess it's the height," Vero said. He couldn't let her know the truth.

"Wimp," Clover said. "Do you need to be carried the rest of the way?"

"Clover ... " Nora said in her warning voice.

"Keep your eyes on your feet and don't look up," Vero's dad advised. "Follow the path that way, and you'll make it to the bottom just fine."

Vero put on a good show. He did as his father instructed, made it safely to their rented cottage, and then stretched out on the sofa.

His mom felt his forehead and said, "You're a little warm."

"I'm okay."

Ignoring him, she spread a cool wet washcloth across his forehead. "Lie here for a while," she said.

Vero did as his mother instructed. As a matter of fact, because the allure of the cliffs proved to be so strong, he stayed on the sofa for pretty much the whole vacation, just watching TV and playing video games.

"If I'd known you were going to spend our entire vacation sitting in this cottage, we could have saved the money and stayed home," Vero's dad said.

He's right, Vero thought. *Just not for the reason he imagines.*

❖

Last year while on a field trip to a local amusement park, Vero's friends harassed him because he wanted to ride on the Twirly—the giant carousel swings that rise up from the ground and spin around and around.

"Come on, Vero! Let's go on the Cyclone!" his best friend Tack said.

They stood on the pavement between the two rides and

watched the Cyclone pass by overhead, spinning its screaming passengers upside down.

"I heard some kid puked on it earlier!" Tack said. "It's so
awesome!"

Vero watched the coaster spin away and said, "Nah, I
think I'll stay here. Come find me when you're done."

"I think it's lame, but whatever," Tack said. Then he
ran off in the direction of the Cyclone, with his running
shorts slipping down and his strawberry-blond hair sticking straight up. "Wait up!" Tack called to their buddy Nate
Hollingsworth.

Vero rode the Twirly thirty-seven times that day. The
attendant kept track and let Vero know what number he
was at. "I ain't never seen no kid ride it so many times," the
attendant said. His name was Gary. He and Vero became
friends that day.

"What can I say?" Vero said, shrugging. "I like to swing."

But the thing was, if he closed his eyes and spread out his
arms on that ride, the sensation of the wind rushing against
his face and ripping through his hair made him feel like he
was flying—if only for a few minutes. He didn't care what
anyone else said. And that was a good thing because Tack
made fun of him the whole ride home.

❖

Though he tried to avoid it, tried to ignore it, Vero's obses-
sion with flying got him in trouble even with his feet firmly
planted on the ground.

Vero was now banned from the local pet store. The Pet
Place had dogs, cats, reptiles, rodents, and birds for sale, and

a photo of Vero's face was stuck to every cash register with a big red line written through it. If an employee saw Vero, he was to kick him out of the store immediately.

The Pet Place problems began one day when Vero and his family were strolling the suburban strip mall, eating ice cream they'd just purchased from the parlor boasting forty-seven flavors. Vero walked past the Pet Place and was suddenly overcome with such an intense and overwhelming sensation of suffocation and sadness that he doubled over and clutched his chest in pain. He'd been lagging behind his family, so Clover and his parents didn't see him when he dropped his ice cream cone and walked through the open doors of the pet store.

As he approached the bird section of the store, he saw cage upon cage of birds—macaws, canaries, exotics, and plain old finches. Vero locked eyes with a blue and gold Macaw.

Help me.

Vero heard the voice as if the bird had spoken the words aloud. Vero knew what he had to do.

Slowly, he reached out his hand and unhinged the cage door. The Macaw bowed his head in gratitude and flew straight through the open doors of the pet store. Vero then opened the next cage, and the next, until all of the cage doors were standing wide open. At first, some of the larger birds blinked and hopped to their door, unsure of what to do next. But when Vero opened the finches' cage and dozens and dozens of birds flew out through the main doors, the larger birds finally followed—just as Vero's family walked inside the store to look for him.

Vero's parents and sister ducked and yelled as the birds escaped to freedom right above their heads. "What is this, a scene from *The Birds?*" Vero's father asked. The pet store was now pure pandemonium.

With each flying bird, Vero felt the weight on his chest grow lighter and lighter.

Vero cost his parents a pretty penny that day, as the store manager expected them to pay for the lost birds. Vero would be doing chores for more than a year before his debt was paid off, but Vero didn't care. He'd do it again in a heartbeat. But he was no longer allowed in the store.

The local paper ran a story on the incident; but when the reporter called the house, Vero's parents wouldn't let him comment.

Vero was also banned from playing any neighborhood games after dark—by the neighbor kids. One hot summer night, Angus Atwood—only child to the Atwood family and a year older than Vero—distributed the Atwood family's collection of canning jars to all of the neighbor kids for catching fireflies. But Vero refused to take one. And he also chased the fireflies away, making them nearly impossible to catch, although a few kids still caught some.

"What's wrong with you, Vero?" Clover asked, her green eyes flashing dangerously. She stomped off for home to tell on him.

After Clover left, Vero grabbed Angus's jar and threw it on the cement sidewalk, shattering it and sending shards of glass flying everywhere.

"What'd you do that for?" Angus shouted.

"How would *you* like to be trapped in a jar?" Vero shouted back.

"Who cares? They're just stupid bugs!"

The other kids opened their jars and let the fireflies escape after that, but Angus was determined. He caught a firefly in his hand and stuffed it in a jar. Angus then screwed the lid on tight and held the jar high above Vero's head.

Vero watched as the firefly desperately smashed its body against the glass, trying to escape its prison. Vero grew more distressed as the firefly's light began to dim. As Angus jumped up to catch another firefly, Vero charged him. He ran headfirst into Angus's stomach, knocking the wind out of him and the canning jar out of his hand.

The jar rolled down the sidewalk, and Vero chased after it, catching it just before it rolled into a storm drain. Then he unscrewed the lid and set the firefly free.

"My dad's right!" Angus yelled after him. "You're a lunatic!"

3

LOUSY BIRTHDAY

"Hurry up and blow out the candles!" Clover said. "I'm missing my show."

"Quiet, Clover," Nora said, sliding the soccer ball themed birthday cake closer to Vero. "You only turn twelve once."

Vero looked at Clover with sad, steely gray eyes.

Clover knew she was being mean. She didn't like doing it, but she had to. Still, she mumbled, "Sorry."

Immediately, Vero's eyes brightened. His eyes were the first things people seemed to notice about him. Typically a vivid pale gray like the wintertime sky, they changed between shades of blue, green, and gray, depending on the surrounding lighting. When Clover was small, she'd told Vero that his eyes were just like the mood ring she'd won at the state fair.

Vero's hair was dark brown, and height-wise he usually got placed in the middle row in the class picture. He'd always been skinny, and it drove Clover crazy when one of her friends would lift Vero up and spin him around because he weighed hardly anything. Her best friend Vicki especially loved to flip him over her hip when practicing her Judo moves.

But as Clover watched Vero lean over his birthday candles that night, she noticed he was sitting taller in his chair. It also looked like he'd finally started putting on some weight. She wondered if Vicki would be able to lift him anymore.

In every way, Vero looked like a normal twelve-year-old boy. But Clover knew he wasn't normal.

"Make a wish," Nora said.

"I wish this party would end," Clover said.

"Knock it off, Clover," Dennis said.

Vero sighed. He and Clover used to be so close. What happened?

Even though they looked nothing alike and Clover was a year older than Vero, there was a time when Clover insisted they were twins. She had brilliant green eyes, which was how she got her name. She was tall and slender like their mom. Her hair was long and blonde, and she usually wore it in a ponytail under a baseball cap. She was very pretty, but she didn't act like she knew it.

Clover used to laugh at Vero's jokes. They used to play soccer on the same coed team. They even sat next to each other on the school bus, where Clover told Vero stories she'd made up. Vero loved her stories about monsters and other creatures. Clover had always insisted the creatures were real—that she had seen them. Her parents would just chuckle and tell her it was nothing more than her overactive imagination. Her mom had said maybe Clover would become a writer one day.

But now the stories had stopped because Clover and Vicki rode to school with Vicki's older sister Molly. At school Clover ignored Vero whenever they passed each other in the halls. And at home, Clover hardly talked to Vero.

"She's going through a phase," Nora explained. "Her hormones are going crazy. She'll come out of it, you'll see."

But Vero wasn't so sure. He couldn't explain it, but somehow he knew that if Clover didn't come back to her old self soon, she'd be lost forever.

Vero closed his eyes, made a wish to himself, and in one breath blew out all twelve candles. He heard his parents clapping; but when he opened his eyes, he realized his wish hadn't been granted because Clover stood up from the table and said, "I don't want any cake." Then she went upstairs to her room and shut the door.

❖

His second official day as a twelve-year-old started out just as great as his birthday party. First, he woke up with his back hurting. Then the milk in Vero's Cheerios was two days past the expiration date and tasted like it. Vero ate the cereal anyway. He told his mom about his sore back over his spoiled breakfast.

"It's time for a new mattress," she said. "That's probably what it is."

"I should be the one who gets a new mattress," Clover chimed in. "After all, I'm the favorite."

"Not true," Vero shot back.

"Ask Dad."

"Dad, is Clover your favorite?"

"Mom and I don't play favorites," Dennis said from behind his newspaper. "You both irritate me equally."

Nora slapped Dennis's shoulder playfully. He put down the paper and stood up. "I've got to get to work," he said.

"You've got a Cheerio stuck to your sleeve," Nora said.

Vero smiled as he watched his mom wipe cereal off his dad's suit jacket. Vero loved to watch his parents. After fifteen years of marriage, they still liked each other. Even though she was forty, Nora still looked a lot like she did in their wedding photos. Her blonde hair was pulled back in a ponytail, and she was dressed for her morning run. If not for the faint laugh lines, she could pass for Clover's big sister. Dennis's dark hair had a bit of gray in it, and his laugh lines were a bit more prominent than Nora's.

"Have fun on your run. I'll go with you this weekend," Dennis said, and he leaned over and kissed Nora. Clover looked at Vero and pretended to stick her index finger down her throat. Vero smiled at her, his sore back forgotten for the moment.

❖

That good feeling didn't last very long. On the bus ride to Attleboro Middle School, Vero sat on a third grader's brown-bag lunch. Unfortunately, Vero didn't realize it until they'd reached the school, so the kid's lunch was smushed. When the kid started crying, Vero gave him his own lunch. So not only did he spend the day hungry, but he also had to walk around school with a huge jelly stain on the back of his pants.

The day brightened a bit when Vero got to be lab partners with Davina Acker in science. Davina was new to the school. Her family had recently moved to the area, and Vero thought she was beautiful. She had long brown hair that perfectly framed her sparkling blue eyes, and she had a warm smile for everyone.

In an attempt to be a gentleman, Vero pulled out a stool for her to sit on at his lab table. Unfortunately, Danny Konrad walked past and purposely bumped Vero. So Vero accidentally pulled the stool out too far, and Davina fell hard on the cement floor.

"Smooth move," Tack said, shaking his head as he took a seat next to Nate at the table in front of Vero's.

Vero's face burned red with embarrassment as he scrambled to help Davina stand up. "I'm so sorry! I didn't mean to … Are you all right?" Vero stammered.

Davina got back on her feet while Vero collected her books. "Yes," she answered, rubbing her backside. "But I might be sore later."

"I'm totally sorry. I only meant to … "

"I know. I'm only kidding," Davina said without any bitterness. "You were just trying to be nice."

Vero sighed with relief. Vero caught Danny's glare from across the room and quickly turned away. He definitely didn't want any trouble from Danny. Even though they were both in the sixth grade, Danny was Clover's age — he'd been held back in third grade.

Vero remembered when Clover had a crush on Danny back in second grade. She'd drawn a pink heart around his head in their class photo. She had said she loved the way his dimples showed up whenever he cracked a smile. Clover still talks to Danny sometimes, and she says he's only gotten better looking over time. But she no longer carries a torch for him.

Clover didn't say so, but Vero imagined the reason why she no longer crushed on Danny was because some of Danny's favorite pastimes included knocking cafeteria trays out of kids' hands—especially on creamed-corn days; hiding Nate's clothes while he showered after gym class and then pulling the fire alarm; he even filled a teacher's car with packing peanuts because he'd given Danny a D on his report card—though no one could prove it was him. Danny bragged about that one to all the kids, but no one would turn him in. Everyone kept their distance from Danny.

"Do you still want to be partners for lab today?" Vero asked Davina.

"Sure," Davina said, pulling out her notebook. "I wonder what today's lesson will be?"

Their science teacher was Mr. Woods, a man whose wardrobe broke every fashion rule. He wore stripes with plaids, white socks with black pants, and sandals with suits. But every lesson was exciting. The kids had learned that the crazier his outfit, the more interesting the class.

Mr. Woods entered the classroom wearing a multicolor plaid suit jacket with equally plaid pants. He was carrying a cage with a blanket draped over it.

"This is going to be a good class," Vero whispered to Davina.

"What's in the cage, Mr. Woods?" Danny shouted.

"One of the most magnificent creatures ever known to man." Mr. Woods motioned everyone to join him. "Come on, gather 'round." Vero and Davina walked to the front of the room for a better view. When everyone had found a spot around the cage, Mr. Woods whipped the blanket off with the finesse of a magician. Sleeping peacefully in the corner of the cage was an orange and yellow snake.

"Sweet!" Tack said. The rest of the class oohed and aahed. Everyone, that is, except Vero, who took a step away. He hated snakes. He hated everything about them. His shoulders suddenly throbbed painfully.

"This is a corn snake," Mr. Woods said as he opened the cage, waking the snake. He gingerly picked it up and held it between his outstretched hands. "It gets its name from Indian corn. The pattern on the snake's body resembles the pattern on the corn cob."

Vero took another step back.

"Don't be scared," Mr. Woods said. "The corn snake is nonvenomous and is actually rather docile. He's only aggressive when he coils his body around his prey, constricting it, so it can no longer breathe. You can take turns holding him."

He held the snake out to Missy Baker whose blonde hair was always green during the first few weeks of school because she spent all summer in the pool. Her greenish hair provided a nice contrast to the snake's orange and yellow body. The snake slithered up her arm and traveled onto Danny's arm as he stood next to her.

"Hey, I think he likes me," Danny said.

Nate picked up the snake. It coiled around his hand.

"Hey, Nate," Tack said. "That snake has your beady eyes."

"Very funny," Nate said.

"Snakes get a bad rep," Mr. Woods continued. "The corn snake is very tame and makes a great pet."

Vero didn't agree with him, but he kept his mouth shut. He wanted to get a good grade in the class.

Mr. Woods removed the snake from Nate's hand and said, "I want everyone to have a chance to hold him." He placed the four-foot snake on Davina's forearm. She giggled as the snake crawled up her shoulder and around her neck. Davina didn't even flinch. She was perfectly comfortable with the creature.

"See? He's very sweet. I've raised him since birth," Mr. Woods said.

As Mr. Woods was talking, the snake looked up from Davina's chest and seemed to stare at Vero. Vero held its gaze.

"Next person," Mr. Woods said. As he stepped forward to remove the snake from Davina's shoulders, Vero swore the snake flicked its tongue and smiled at him. Then it began to squeeze Davina's neck. Davina gasped for air, unable to speak. Mr. Woods desperately tried to pry the snake off of Davina, but it constricted tighter and tighter. And all the while it stared right at Vero.

Davina's face started turning blue. Kids were screaming. The classroom erupted into chaos.

"Someone get a knife!" Mr. Woods shouted.

Vero knew a knife could accidentally cut Davina. Suddenly, a cold resolve consumed Vero, and it was unlike anything he'd ever experienced. Vero stepped forward, grabbed the snake behind its head, and pinched—hard! The snake let out a violent hiss, but Vero continued to crush the snake's head in his hand until it finally loosened its hold on Davina.

Then Vero furiously unraveled the reptile from around her neck and hurled it against the wall with such force that the snake slumped to the ground, unmoving.

Missy Baker was crying and shaking and rubbing her arm where the snake had been slithering only moments earlier.

Nate was leaning against Mr. Woods's desk, looking like he might throw up. Tack was balancing on top of a lab stool as if he'd seen a mouse scurry across the floor. And the rest of the class was staring at Vero like he was an alien who'd just stepped out of his spaceship. But the danger was past.

Mr. Woods crouched next to Davina who was sitting on the floor, coughing and holding her neck.

"I'm so sorry," Mr. Woods whispered. His face looked ashen. "I . . . I had no idea . . . "

She could have died. She almost died. Despite his courageous performance a moment ago, Vero's hands were shaking as he bent down until he was face-to-face with Davina. He was dimly aware of the rest of the class crowding behind him.

"Are you okay?" Vero asked.

Davina nodded. "I think so," she said, her voice scratchy. She smiled and took Vero's hand.

Suddenly Danny was there too, and he frowned at Vero. He reached down for Davina's other hand, and together they pulled her to her feet.

Davina smiled and said to Vero, "I'd say this more than makes up for you pulling my stool out from under me."

Mr. Woods picked up the limp snake and said, "Davina, I want you to go to the nurse's office, so she can take a look at your neck." His voice had regained its usual tone, but Vero saw his hands shake as he finished putting the snake's lifeless body back in its cage. "Missy, please walk with Davina. I'll meet you there in a few minutes."

As Vero watched Davina leave, Tack walked up behind him and whispered, "Dude, there's got to be an easier way to impress girls."

4

❖

BABY DOE

Everyone credited Vero's heroic defeat of the snake to "hysterical strength" brought on by an adrenaline rush. Vero had heard stories of people getting super-human strength in times of trouble, like a mom who lifted a car off her child, and a woman who swam across a raging river while dragging her unconscious husband to the shore. So Vero accepted the explanation.

After the excitement over the snake incident had passed, life in the Leland house settled back into a state of normalcy. They lived in Attleboro, Maryland, a suburb outside of Washington, DC, in a development that had been farms and orchards twenty years ago. Those original properties were torn down to make way for Vero's neighborhood, a planned development filled with nearly identical homes. The homes were so similar, in fact, that if a resident walked into his neighbor's house, he never needed to ask for directions to the powder room because it was in the same exact place as in his own home. More than once neighborhood kids had gotten confused and entered the wrong house after playing outside. The Lelands lived in a very *normal* neighborhood, and they lived very *normal* lives.

Nora drove a minivan and took her turn in the neighborhood carpool, driving kids to the weekly soccer games and Saturday afternoon movies. She'd been a nurse before becoming a stay-at-home mom, so she was the go-to mom whenever someone needed help bandaging a banged-up knee or bringing down a high fever. And she never refused anyone. Vero felt lucky to have her as his mother — most days.

Dennis worked as an analyst at the World Bank. He sat in an office all day and analyzed applications for international loans. The World Bank lent money to underdeveloped countries so they could build bridges or schools or clean up pollution. Vero's dad studied the requests, researched them from every angle, and made recommendations. His reports carried a lot of weight.

Dennis drove a government car, a generic-looking black vehicle that got traded in every three years. The kids were never allowed to eat in his car because candy wrappers or leaky juice boxes on the floor of a government car would be unpatriotic.

The Lelands took camping trips and beach vacations and mall outings, hosted birthday parties, attended school plays, supported various sports teams, played late-night pajama Twister games, and just about every typical family thing one could imagine. The family was so normal, in fact, that some psychologists might suggest that Vero's mom was overcompensating — trying to hide the fact the Vero was anything *but* normal.

Vero came into Nora's life one fateful night when she was working in the ER. A horrendous storm system had wreaked havoc across the area, as vicious winds knocked telephone poles onto cars and houses, the torrential rains flooded low-lying areas, and power outages occurred across the region. It was her regular night shift, and the ER was overrun with victims of the storm. Shortly after she arrived at work, an elderly man was wheeled in on a gurney.

"A metal sign broke loose and sliced open his head!" the paramedic yelled. "Vitals are not good!"

The man was unconscious and had lost a lot of blood. Nora assisted the doctor as he tried to save the old man, but the heart monitor announced that he had flatlined. All of their efforts to revive him were unsuccessful. The doctor declared the man deceased and moved on to help another storm victim. Nora was with the deceased man when an aide walked into the room.

"I'm here to take him down to the morgue," the aide said, and he draped a sheet over the body.

"Wait, please," Nora said.

As she pulled the sheet away from the man's face and tenderly closed his eyelids, the elderly man's hand suddenly grabbed her wrist! The aide screamed and jumped away from the gurney, sending a tray full of medical supplies crashing to the floor.

The dead man did not release his grip. He opened his eyes and mouth, letting out an unearthly moan. And through the moan, Nora heard him say, "Name the baby Vero. Raise him as your own."

Having heard the loud crash and the aide's shrieks, the

doctor rushed back into the room and saw the dead man clutching Nora's wrist.

He checked the old man's heartbeat to make sure they hadn't made a mistake. They hadn't. He was truly deceased. There was no sign of life coming from the old ticker. The doctor pried the man's fingers from Nora's wrist.

Oddly enough, Nora wasn't nearly as upset as she should have been. She should have been screaming her head off just like the aide. But it had happened so fast, she didn't have time to comprehend it all.

"It's common for a body to jerk or have involuntary movements as rigor mortis sets in," the doctor said.

"I've never seen *that* happen before!" the aide shouted. "And I heard the guy moan! Explain that!"

"Bodies can moan as gasses escape," the doctor answered calmly.

"It was more than a moan, Doctor," Nora said. Then she turned to the aide and asked, "Did you hear what he said?" She was putting together her thoughts, which didn't make much sense.

"No, I did not! I most definitely did not. It was just a moan!" the aide yelled.

"He said something about a—" Nora began, but the aide cut her off.

"They don't pay me enough to put up with this! I quit! I'm out of here!" And the aide stormed out of the hospital for good.

Nora took one last look at the elderly man and pulled the sheet back over him. As she walked to the nurse's station, she began to question whether or not the old man had said anything. Her mind had to be playing tricks on her.

So when she reached her desk and saw an infant lying on her chair, she wasn't sure the baby was real. That is, until the chair began to cry. Then Nora knew she'd better not sit on it.

❖

All of the other nurses had been helping patients, so no one saw the baby arrive. The security cameras hadn't picked up a single image of Vero being dropped off. One moment he wasn't there, and the next he was.

Pediatricians on call that night gave the baby a complete physical from head to toe. He was perfectly healthy and rather cute. The hospital's social worker granted temporary custody to Nora until the child's parents could be located, or until a judge determined a permanent home for him.

"We'll just call him Baby Doe," the social worker said as she filled out the paperwork.

"His name is Vero," Nora told her.

"Vero?" the social worker asked. "Where'd you get that one?"

Nora grabbed the pen from the woman's hand and met her eyes with an unwavering gaze. She said, "I found him, and his name is Vero."

Seeing the conviction in her eyes, the social worker took back her pen and wrote VERO on the forms.

Nora loved Vero from the first moment she held him. The two bonded even before they left the hospital that night. As Nora stepped outside the hospital doors, she noticed it was oddly calm outside. The storm was now a memory. Clover was only a year old at the time, so Nora strapped Vero into

Clover's car seat before setting out for the all-night grocery store. Vero would need diapers and baby formula.

The store was completely empty except for a young man standing behind the cash register. He wore headphones and listened to music on his iPod to pass the time. After all, it was 5:30 in the morning, and the sun was not yet up. Nora read the labels on the various kinds of formula while baby Vero slept in the built-in baby seat on the shopping cart.

Out of the corner of her eye, Nora saw a figure, a man dressed in a long black trench coat that resembled a hooded robe. The hood was pulled far over his head, obscuring his face. When the man began to knock diapers off the shelves as he approached her, that little thing called intuition kicked in. Nora picked up Vero and sprinted down the aisle.

She turned back toward the entrance. Nora screamed at the cashier who was banging imaginary drums to some song on his iPod. He couldn't hear her, and she couldn't leave through the front of the store without running smack into her pursuer.

The huge double doors to the storage room caught her attention. She plowed through them. The storage room was filled with rows of shelves that were stocked to the ceiling with wooden pallets filled with all different sorts of foods and goods. Nora ducked behind a massive crate containing boxes of cereal, and silently prayed that Vero wouldn't make a sound. She peered around the corner of the crate and saw that the man in black was now surveying the warehouse.

He's abnormally tall, Nora thought.

It seemed like a stroke of good luck when the man went down another aisle. She exhaled with relief until ketchup bottles, soup cans, and products of all kinds started flying off the highest shelves in every direction and crashed to the floor. Vero began crying. Nora held him tightly to her chest and stepped out into the open. The man saw them.

"Stay away from me!" Nora shouted.

The man let out a chilling laugh as he slowly approached her. With her back against the locked loading-dock gate, Nora had nowhere to turn. The hooded man had cornered her like a trapped animal.

Instinctively she knew he was after Vero, and this man wouldn't hesitate to take her life in order to get what he wanted. "Please," Nora begged. "Don't hurt the baby!"

But her pleas fell on deaf ears as the dark figure loomed toward her. He reached out his hand to grab her, his face still hidden by his hood. Nora clutched Vero with all her might. She would die protecting him. She would die without seeing the face of her killer.

"God help me!" Nora shouted. "Please help us!"

Suddenly, the massive metal gate behind her blasted away with an immense *BOOM!* A blinding white light filled the room, and the figure instantly recoiled with a howl of intense agony. The light blinded Nora as well, so she didn't see the hooded man vanish. She also didn't see the baby in her arms staring directly into the brilliant light, smiling serenely. He wasn't even blinking.

❖

"Are you okay, lady?" the deliveryman asked Nora as he pushed the metal gate open.

Nora was standing by the loading dock, still clutching Vero to her chest, and feeling totally bewildered. The radiant light was gone. It had been replaced with the regular morning sun that now streamed throughout the warehouse, coaxing Nora back to her senses.

"Yes, I think so," Nora said meekly.

The deliveryman's bright violet eyes and friendly smile helped put her at ease.

"He looks just like you," he said with a nod toward Vero. "But you should probably be getting him home to bed, no?"

"I don't understand ... there was a man in black chasing us ... and then you ... "

"I didn't see anyone," he said. "I just got here for my morning shift and found you standing there when I opened the warehouse door. But when I was driving in to work, I heard we had a decent-sized earthquake this morning. Unusual for DC, but not unheard of. Crazy times, huh? First that storm last night, and now an earthquake."

The deliveryman surveyed the damage as food and other goods were strewn all over the warehouse floor.

"I pity the poor sap who has to clean up this place," he said, shaking his head. But then he looked directly at Nora, his violet eyes piercing her own. "Really, you should be getting that boy home now."

"Y-y-yes," Nora said. "Home." She was stunned, confused. *What had just happened?*

"Can I help you to your car?" the deliveryman asked with a smile.

Nora blinked and came back to herself. "No, thank you. I'll get my groceries, and then I'll head home. Thank you again."

"No problem, ma'am."

Right before she went through the double doors and

reentered the main grocery store, she looked back at the man and said, "I didn't catch your name ... "

But he was outside unloading boxes from a produce truck.

No one besides Nora had seen the man in black. Nora didn't dare tell a soul what she'd experienced that night—not even her husband. She knew if she did, any judge would label her crazy, and she'd never be allowed to adopt the baby. So it was her secret to keep.

Weeks later, a judge formally permitted Nora and Dennis to adopt the baby, and he became Vero Leland.

As for Vero, he grew up knowing he'd been adopted. Nora told him that his biological parents had dropped him off at a hospital because they couldn't provide for him. And then Nora and Dennis became his parents, and Clover became his sister. There was never a need to question anything.

5

BACKSEAT
DRIVER

Vero was smart in school. Good grades came easily to him. He barely had to study, and yet he got all As on his report cards. Mrs. Cleary, his language arts teacher, was most impressed with his reading and writing—especially his essays. She assigned him the more difficult books to read. At the Lelands' parent-teacher conference, Mrs. Cleary presented Vero's essay on Milton's *Paradise Lost*.

"This poem is usually assigned in the twelfth grade, but I wanted to see if Vero could handle it," Mrs. Cleary began. "*Paradise Lost* tells the story of the fall of the angel Lucifer and his descent into hell. Of how he turned against God, was cast out of heaven, and spread his ills into the garden of Eden, persuading Eve to take a bite from the forbidden fruit."

"Yes, I remember reading that in college," Vero's dad said.

Vero sighed and rolled his eyes at the pride in his dad's voice. Vero looked at the clock, willing it to go faster.

Mrs. Cleary continued, "It's the original story of good versus evil. God was good. Lucifer was evil. There's no debating that. However, readers of the poem often debate Eve's sin. Some feel anger toward the very first woman because all of mankind was forced to live with the consequences of her choice. On the other hand, some feel sympathy for her. Eve was deceived, tricked by the serpent, and at a time when deception was unheard of. They feel she was simply a pawn in the great war between heaven and hell. I expected Vero to take one of these two viewpoints in his essay."

Nora squirmed in her seat. Vero thought she looked uncomfortable. He wished Mrs. Cleary would hurry up and get to the point.

"But Vero saw Eve's sin from a completely unexpected angle," Mrs. Cleary said. She began reading Vero's essay aloud, and Vero felt his cheeks burning. "It was the archangel Uriel's job to protect the garden of Eden. Uriel was the one who failed to prevent Lucifer from gaining access to the garden in the first place. Man's fall was actually the result of Uriel's poor job performance. If an archangel, a heavenly being, could be deceived by the serpent, then poor Eve never stood a chance. A human, especially one only recently created, could never be a match for the master of deception. So the archangel should have been aware of Eve's vulnerability and stayed extra vigilant."

Mrs. Cleary handed the paper to Vero's father. "Brilliant," she said.

Dennis beamed with pride. His entire face lit up. But

Nora didn't have the same reaction. She actually looked a bit sick.

"Vero's insight is far beyond that of his peers. It's a joy to read his papers. How did you ever come up with your idea?" Mrs. Cleary asked Vero.

"I don't know," Vero shrugged. "It just made sense to me."

"And he's modest too," Mrs. Cleary said, admiringly.

Nora suddenly stood up and declared, "He copied it off the Internet!"

Everyone else looked taken aback.

"No, I didn't ... " Vero said. "I swear."

"Mrs. Cleary, please give him the F he deserves," Nora said.

"Nora, don't you think you're overreacting?" Dennis said.

"Enough!" Nora shouted with a ferocity that silenced them all. "There's no way Vero could have such knowledge of these things! He may have fooled you, Mrs. Cleary, but not me. I'm done with this conversation!"

Nora pulled Vero out of his chair by his upper arm and dragged him out of the classroom. But not before Vero saw Mrs. Cleary turn to his dad with a bewildered expression on her face.

Dennis shrugged and said, "I'm sorry, but my wife has a hard time hearing that Vero is anything but normal."

❖

"You just gotta stop getting such good grades," Tack said to Vero as they were changing clothes in the boys' locker room the next day.

"You sound like my mom," Vero said.

"Your mom doesn't want you getting good grades?" Tack asked, wide-eyed.

"Yeah, yesterday at my parent-teacher conference, she accused me of stealing an essay off the Internet. And no matter how much I tell her I didn't do it, she won't believe me. She won't even go there," Vero said. "It's like she wants me to dumb myself down. It's weird."

"Did you steal it?"

"No!" Vero shouted.

"Okay, chill ... but I think she's on to something. Getting good grades the way you do, everyone's gonna think you're a dork. It was okay being a super-genius when we were little, but now girls like jocks."

"Whatever you say, Tack." Vero snorted as he watched Tack shove an entire Hostess Ding Dong into his mouth.

"Whaa?" Tack asked, with a mouth full of chocolate. After he'd swallowed, he said, "I need the energy to run the hurdles."

Vero shook his head as Tack adjusted his extra-large sweatpants. Up until last summer, Tack had always been the pudgy kid. And he and Vero had been best friends since preschool.

It all started one afternoon during naptime when Tack accidentally rolled on top of a sleeping Vero. The preschool teachers panicked when they did a head count and couldn't find little Vero anywhere. They searched the classroom closets, bathrooms, and even inside the school's piano, but Vero was nowhere to be found. They immediately feared the worst: Vero had wandered off the schoolyard.

When Tack woke up and complained that his mat was lumpy, the teachers found Vero squashed underneath him.

Vero was perfectly fine; but from that day on, Tack had to sleep in a corner away from the other kids. And then he and Vero became inseparable.

They grew up sharing each other's lunches — with Tack typically eating the lion's share. They raced across the monkey bars, played with Tonka trucks in the sandbox, and spent hours on the seesaw. Tack would sit on his end with such force that Vero went flying into the air — which Vero loved, of course.

When Vero had a difficult time learning how to swim, Tack swam with him for hours to help Vero stay afloat. When Tack got sick and missed days of school, Vero brought his homework to him. (Although Tack didn't always appreciate that gesture.) When Tack's dog Pork Chop ran away from home, Vero posted flyers and searched the whole neighborhood until Tack's beloved English bulldog was finally found.

As they grew older, Vero remained much smaller than average, and Tack was the complete opposite. So whenever the other kids would tease Vero for any reason, Tack would stand behind him, pounding his right fist into his left palm. That usually sent the bullies running.

Standing next to his best friend, Vero appeared short but gangly, with long arms and legs. Vero's mother was constantly trying to fatten him up with protein shakes, while Tack's mother began padlocking the refrigerator between meals.

But during the past summer, both Vero and Tack had grown significantly. No one would call Tack fat anymore, maybe just big boned — although they wouldn't dare say *that* to his face either.

Tack's real name was Thaddeus Kozlowski. He got his nickname "Tack" from his older sister Martha. When their parents first brought Tack home from the hospital, Martha took one look at her little brother and declared he was as short and fat as a thumbtack. And it stuck. Since that moment, Thaddeus was called Tack.

Over the years Martha has tried changing her story, saying the reason for his nickname is because his brain is the size of a tack. But that simply wasn't true. It requires real intelligence to come up with new excuses for why you didn't do your homework, or how the latest zombie video game was beneficial for your hand-eye coordination. All of these things needed a certain amount of smarts, which Tack possessed in excess. But as his math teacher, Mrs. Grommet, told his parents, "His intelligence is utterly misguided."

As bad as Tack's grades were, Marty, Tack's father, was more disappointed that Tack would not be carrying on the family tradition. All of the Kozlowski men were dowsers. And after having three daughters, Tack's dad was thrilled when Tack finally came along because the dowsing gift was passed down through the male genes. But so far Tack hadn't shown any abilities in this area.

Dowsers have an innate ability to locate water, minerals, and oil underground. Using a Y-shaped rod or twig, Marty would explore an area, and the dowsing rod would twitch when it was over the target. A really gifted dowser didn't even need a rod or twig. Tack's Great-Great-Uncle Morris had never used any tools for his dowsing back in Poland. He just felt it in his bones. Tack, on the other hand, had shown no aptitude for the gift.

For years Marty took his son to the beach every summer

so Tack could practice finding metal under the sand. The only time Tack ever found anything happened two summers ago when he stepped on a melted Hershey's Kiss. Hardly impressive.

In years past, a dowser could make a good living finding wells for homes and such. But with modern technology and geologists, dowsers weren't in high demand any longer. While dowsing could be lucrative from time to time, the income wasn't enough to support a growing family. So Marty owned a hardware store in Attleboro, K & Sons Hardware, which he'd inherited from Tack's grandfather. And Tack helped out in the store from time to time.

Tack shut his locker door and locked the padlock (purchased from the family hardware store).

"Why are you running hurdles?" Vero asked. "I thought you wanted to do shot put?"

"That was before I grew taller," Tack said. "When I go over those hurdles, it'll be spectacular. Everyone on that track is gonna eat my dust."

Vero checked his laces.

"Why don't you run in the lane next to me?" Tack asked. "Maybe you'll pick up some pointers."

"Maybe," Vero said.

Minutes later, the boys were warming up for gym class during second period. As he stretched, Vero could see his breath in the air. It was unusually cold for an early spring day. The gray sky made it feel like snow might even be on the way.

There were eight lanes drawn on the track, each with ten hurdles set up at eight-meter intervals. A pit formed in Vero's stomach and he felt nervous for his friend. Tack had never run hurdles before.

"Are you sure you want to do this?" Vero asked.

"Why? Afraid I'm gonna beat you?" Tack replied with a smirk.

"Fine!" Vero said. "You wanna race? It's on!"

"Bring it!"

"Get on your starting blocks!" Coach Randy yelled.

Tack and Vero chose to run in lanes four and five, and boys from gym class filled the other six lanes. Coach Randy stood on the outside of the track while the runners lined up at their starting blocks. A cold wind suddenly blew through, catching everyone off guard. Coach Randy grabbed the top of his ball cap to keep it from flying off his head. He was never seen without his ball cap. Kids joked that his cap was guarded more securely than the Crown Jewels of England.

Vero turned his head to the left and glanced at Tack.

Tack mouthed, "You're going down."

Vero ignored his friend's taunt and faced forward again. Out of the corner of his eye, he saw Davina standing off to his right on the sideline. Their eyes met, and Vero's stomach flipped. He quickly returned his gaze to the ground in front of him and tried to focus on his feet.

"Runners, on your marks!" Coach Randy shouted. "Get set ... "

The starting gun shot into the air.

The runners took off. Vero and his classmates sprinted down the oval track toward their hurdles. It was a close start. Vero and Tack kept pace with the other sprinters, and everyone was neck and neck. Tack cleared the first hurdle with surprising ease. He looked over his shoulder and smiled smugly at Vero.

Seconds later, Vero reached the first hurdle in his lane. He began to leap, but what happened next sent a hush over his classmates. Vero didn't clear just the first hurdle—he cleared the second one too! He soared over *both* hurdles in one bound! Everyone was astonished. Coach Randy's mouth dropped open. And Vero was as surprised as everyone else. When his feet came back to earth, Vero continued running.

Now Tack looked ahead and saw that Vero had somehow passed him. As he came to the next hurdle, Tack watched as Vero cleared the third and fourth hurdles in a single leap! Tack was so surprised that he lost his concentration while he was still in midair and landed smack on top of the hurdle— it hit him right in his unmentionables!

Tack doubled over in pain and rolled into the next lane, which caused that runner to fall, which then created a dom- ino effect. Runner after runner tripped over their hurdles and then each other until no one was left standing. That is, no one except Vero who crossed the finish line in first place. As he looked back and saw the mass of injured runners and hurdles lying on the track, Vero didn't feel as good about his victory.

The rest of the gym class students were agape.

And Coach Randy did a little victory dance. "State Championship, here we come!" he shouted.

❖

"You should have *told* me you could jump like that," Tack said to Vero. He was now lying down in Nurse Kunkel's office with an ice pack across his unmentionables. "That was such an unfair advantage."

"I'm sorry," Vero said. "I didn't know I could do that."

"You can tell me the truth. I'll still be your friend," Tack said.

"What?"

"You're secretly taking ballet, aren't you? That move you did out there ... I've seen girls in my sister's ballet class do that one. But they can't do it nearly as good as you can. I think it's called a 'granny jet' or something."

"It's a *grande jeté*," Vero said in a flawless French accent.

"So you *have* been taking ballet!"

"No, I haven't!" Vero insisted. "I swear! I know what a *grande jeté* is because my family goes to see *The Nutcracker* every Christmas."

"*The Nutcracker.* Very funny," Tack said. "Well then, where did you learn to jump like that?"

"I don't know," Vero said. "It's not like I practice doing it or anything."

"The hurdles, the snake ... you've been acting weird lately," Tack said. "And it's like you're getting smarter. You're reading all of these big books, and you seem to understand them so easily when I can't even pronounce their titles!"

Vero couldn't disagree. And he didn't mention that his desire to fly had returned with a vengeance, and his back hurt all the time. But it was true: Vero *was* feeling different, and it was getting more and more difficult to hide these changes from people.

As Nurse Kunkel handed Tack a fresh icepack, she asked Vero, "Have you been checked for scoliosis?"

"What's that?" Vero asked.

"Curvature of the spine. From the way you're hunching over, I'd say you might want to have a doctor examine you. Has your back been hurting lately?"

Vero nodded and said, "My parents said it's probably because my old bed is so lumpy. They're gonna buy me a new mattress."

"Bend over and let me take a look," she commanded.

Vero flashed Tack an uneasy glance. He'd only come to the nurse's office to help Tack.

"Come on, hurry up," Nurse Kunkel said in her no-nonsense way.

So Vero bent over at the waist, letting his arms dangle in front of him as Nurse Kunkel had instructed. He tried not to shiver as she ran her cold hands underneath his T-shirt and along his spine. From his upside-down vantage point, Vero could see the nurse's enormous white orthopedic shoes behind him. But what he couldn't see was the look on Nurse Kunkel's face when she saw his protruding shoulder blades. Startled, she jerked her hands away, staggered back, and fell onto the cot where Tack was lying—and landed right on top of Tack.

Tack let out a high-pitched "Help!"

Nurse Kunkel immediately tried to stand up. But she was a large woman, so it wasn't easy. She was the exact opposite of one of those inflated punching-bag clowns, where no matter how hard they're punched, they bounce back up. In this case Nurse Kunkel couldn't lift herself off the cot. In her many attempts to get back on her feet, she steamrolled all over Tack, left and then right, but still couldn't prop herself up. Finally, she just rolled off the cot and fell onto the floor with a loud thud followed by silence.

Vero exchanged nervous looks with Tack.

"Is she dead?" Tack whispered.

"Of course I'm not dead, you idiot!" the nurse shouted from the floor. "Now help me up!"

Vero and Tack each grabbed one of Nurse Kunkel's hands and somehow hoisted her to her feet.

On any given day, the buttons on the front of her nurse's uniform were stretched to capacity, and they were known to occasionally shoot off her dress like bullets. There was a rumor that a button nearly took out a kid's eye when Nurse Kunkel leaned over to take his temperature. As Nurse Kunkel pulled herself and her uniform back together, Vero and Tack noticed that this latest incident had cost her three buttons.

"Thank you. I'm fine," she snapped, attempting to smooth her wiry hair. Face flushed, she turned to Vero and said, "You've got something worse than scoliosis. No wonder your back's killing you."

"What? What's wrong with me?" Vero asked.

"Kyphosis," she said.

Vero had no idea what Nurse Kunkel was saying.

"Hunchback syndrome," she continued. "It's one of the worse cases I've seen."

The nurse gave Vero's back another look, and Tack made sure he wasn't behind her this time.

"Hmmm ... when you stand up, I can't see it. That's very strange," she said. "Nevertheless, here ... " She quickly scribbled something onto a pad of paper, ripped off the page, and shoved it into Vero's hand. "Give this to your parents. *Tonight*. You don't need a new mattress. You need to see a doctor ASAP."

Vero reluctantly put the note in his back pocket. Tack looked at him with a worried expression on his face. Vero knew exactly what Tack was thinking—just another weird thing to add to the list.

❖

Word of Vero's hurdle-jumping exhibition spread like wildfire throughout the school. Kids and teachers gossiped about him in the hallways, locker rooms, and cafeteria. Coach Randy begged Vero to join the school's track-and-field team, but Vero refused. He was afraid to draw any more attention to himself.

Later that day, school was dismissed early due to an unexpected snowstorm that started right after gym class, for which Vero was extremely grateful. He'd silently prayed for a huge snowfall so he wouldn't have to go back to school for a few days—or even weeks.

As students boarded the school buses for the ride home, Tack, who was still recovering from his hurdle mishap, was lying across one whole bus seat. So Vero had to look for another place to park himself. The bus was overcrowded with kids whose parents normally would have picked them up but were now unable to leave work early or couldn't drive in the bad weather. Even Clover was on the bus. She wasn't allowed to ride with Vicki's older sister in any kind of treacherous weather.

When Vero reached the next-to-last row of bus seats, he spotted his sister sitting with Vicki. He could possibly squeeze in with them, but Clover shot him a most unwelcoming look and then turned her face toward the window. It was a clear sign that she wasn't happy with all the recent talk about him in school, and she wasn't going to make room for him in her bus seat.

His only option was to head back to the front of the bus and sit directly behind the driver.

After checking the snow chains on the tires of the bus, the driver got on and started the engine. He then stood up and faced his passengers.

"Listen up!" the driver said. "It's starting to come down hard out there, so no messing around. Everyone stays in their seats and keeps quiet. Got it?"

No one answered.

"Got it?" he repeated.

"Yes, Mr. Harmon," the kids answered in unison.

Mr. Harmon was actually Wayne Harmon, a baby-faced nineteen-year-old who was not much older than the students. He got the bus driver job right out of high school because his uncle owned the bus company. And even though he'd gone to school with some of the kids on his route, Wayne insisted they address him as "Mr. Harmon."

The bus slowly pulled away from the curb. As Vero sat by himself, he glanced behind him at the other kids. They were busy texting, laughing, or swapping food from their leftover lunches. Vero was beginning to feel more and more isolated. He felt as if he were watching the scene on the bus through an invisible divider, like that piece of plastic that separates the backseat of a taxicab from the front.

Vero was sitting on the bus, he could feel the wheels vibrating on the road beneath him, yet somehow he felt as if he were elsewhere.

Vero turned back around and stared out the windshield. The snow was coming down hard. He'd always loved the snow. There was something so peaceful about it. He'd learned in Mr. Woods's class that no two snowflakes are alike, and it seemed so impossible. Of all the snowflakes that have fallen throughout the history of the planet, how could that be? But the scientists stood by their claim — the intricate ice crystals were full of endless possibilities.

Mesmerized by the falling snow and the swish-swish rhythm of the windshield wipers, Vero's enchantment was suddenly broken when an oncoming car crossed into the bus's lane. The car's driver wrestled to gain control of the steering wheel, but the car still careened toward them with no chance of stopping in these icy conditions.

Vero noticed another man in the car was leaning over the backseat. He appeared to be fighting the driver for control of the steering wheel. The falling snow obscured Vero's vision, but the face of the man in the backseat appeared distorted, unreal, with exaggerated facial features — a large snout-like nose and a massive forehead made his eyes appear sunken. As the car got closer, Vero saw what looked like a gruesome burn scar etched across his face. And his eyes! *Were his eyes glowing red?*

Vero jumped to his feet, pointing and shouting about the approaching car. Everyone on the bus grew silent. Vero felt Clover's eyes on him from the back of the bus. Somehow — he didn't know how — he could feel her hostility toward him.

"What's your brother doing?" Vicki elbowed Clover.

Clover sunk lower in the seat.

"He's headed straight toward us!" Vero shouted again.

"Sit down!" Mr. Harmon shouted back.

The car continued to slide closer and closer to the bus.

And now it was close enough for Vero to see the rage glowing from the monstrous red eyes of the backseat driver.

"Don't you see it?" Vero's voice was edged with panic, but Mr. Harmon seemed oblivious. "I said, sit down!"

A head-on collision was imminent. "Look!" Instinctively, Vero reached over Mr. Harmon's shoulder and yanked the steering wheel — just like the man in the backseat of the car was doing.

Suddenly, the entire windshield flashed white. A feeling of tranquility seized Vero, and somehow he knew they were safe. Then the whiteout disappeared, replaced by the steadily falling snow. Mr. Harmon brought the bus to a screeching halt at a stop sign. He opened the bus door, stood up, and pointed to the open door.

"Get out! You can walk home from here!"

"But I just saved your life! I saved *everybody's* lives! He was gonna drive his car right into us! See? That car over there!" Vero pointed to the car in the opposite lane, which was now stopped at the stop sign on the other side of the intersection.

"That car swerved over the center line for less than a second!" Mr. Harmon shot back. "It wasn't a big deal. You were the one who was going to cause an accident! It's bad enough that I'm driving in a complete whiteout. I don't need you yanking the steering wheel away from me!"

"But ... you didn't see ...?"

"Get off my bus! Now! Or I'll have some of the football players escort you off."

Mr. Harmon grabbed Vero's backpack and threw it out into the snow. Vero knew he wasn't going to win this fight, so he walked down the steps and into the snowstorm. The car that he'd been certain was going to hit them just moments before, accelerated cautiously through the intersection. As it drove past him, Vero saw the driver casually talking on his cell phone. There was no sign of the misshapen man in the backseat.

As the bus pulled away from the stop sign, Tack and Clover watched Vero through their bus windows with mortified expressions on their faces. Angus pointed at Vero, shook his head, and laughed. Vero knew exactly what Angus was thinking: *Wait 'til my dad hears about this!*

6

THE SNOW ANGEL

That night in his dream, Vero walked down a dark alley in a large, unknown city. Despite the recent rain, the alley was dirty and dingy. Vero stepped in puddles that had nowhere to drain. A light flickered on and off over a doorway. Large hairy rats climbed into an open dumpster in search of a meal. A yellow mutt with wiry fur hobbled over to Vero and knelt down, allowing Vero to stroke his head. Vero noticed the dog was missing his back left leg.

Suddenly, the dog's ears perked up, and Vero heard the faint sound of distant music. Vero scanned the upper apartment windows but saw nothing. Nor was anyone standing on the metal fire escapes above him. The dog got up, sniffed the air, and started walking farther down the dark alley. He looked back at Vero and barked, prompting him to follow.

Vero walked deeper into the eerie darkness, growing

more and more apprehensive. He wanted to turn back but felt compelled to find the source of the music. In spite of the eerie blackness surrounding him, Vero noticed a vast number of stars in the sky overhead, and their glimmering lights comforted him despite the deep shadows of the alleyway.

Vero's three-legged guide turned a corner, and Vero lost him. He called out to the dog, but it had disappeared. Boxes and garbage lined the street ahead and stood in haphazard piles in dim corners, leaning against decrepit brick walls covered with spray-painted symbols. The music was louder here. Vero tentatively jostled the piles of boxes in turn, eliminating each as the possible source of the enthralling music.

When Vero moved a big box out of his way, he saw Clover sitting on the sidewalk with her back against a brick wall. He gasped at the sight of her. Her clothes were torn and dirty. She seemed to be out of breath, and her hair was wet with sweat.

Despite her appearance, Clover smiled at Vero. Instantly she transformed into the old Clover — the sister who'd been his closest companion. His confidante. The sister he loved. Yet this version of his sister was older. She had aged. Clover reached out her hand, and Vero helped her up.

Still the music persisted. Clover motioned for Vero to follow her, and as they walked on, the music grew louder and became more distinct. Vero could make out the sounds of a lyre and a flute. An exquisite voice sang, and Vero was charmed by its melody. Vero thought of the irresistible sirens of Greek mythology that lured unsuspecting sailors to their deaths, powerless to resist the bewitching songs. He, too, felt captivated by the music, drawn to it.

Vero and Clover turned a corner and came upon a crowd

of people crammed into a tiny alley, their faces were hidden as they stood gazing upon something. He felt compelled to get a glimpse of it as well. The source of the music.

Clutching Clover's hand, Vero made his way through the throng of onlookers. He tapped a man's shoulder so he would let them pass, but when the man turned and was no longer obscured in shadow, Vero saw that he had the face of a lion. But Vero didn't feel threatened, just curious—curious enough to pause his search for the source of the music, which was definitely coming from whatever object all of these people were staring at.

The man turned his head toward Clover, and his face transformed into that of an ox, then an eagle, and finally a human, with striking violet eyes and a peaceful, welcoming expression. It reminded Vero of a program on his laptop where he and Tack once took Clover and Vicki's school photos and morphed them into animals.

"Who are you?" Vero asked, but before the man could answer, Vero's alarm clock woke him up.

❖

Unlike the Clover in Vero's dream, the real-life Clover was in a foul mood that morning.

"He's ruining my life!" she shouted across the breakfast table to her parents.

Vero stared at his sister, trying to catch a glimpse of the old Clover who was nowhere to be found. And now after he'd spent some time with the old Clover in his dream, Vero realized he missed her even more. He felt a deep ache combined with an almost overwhelming disappointment.

"What!" Clover barked, when she noticed Vero was staring at her. "It's true!"

"If I didn't grab that steering wheel, we would have had been in a head-on collision," he explained again.

"Every single person on that bus—including me—said that car was never any threat," Clover said. "I was mortified!"

Dennis and Nora exchanged glances.

"It doesn't make any sense," Dennis said.

"I know what I saw," Vero said firmly.

But Vero held back some information, like that second driver in the backseat. Vero knew that if he were to divulge that information, they'd lock him up for good in the nearest loony bin.

"Come on, Clover. Aren't you exaggerating just a bit?" Nora said in a slightly accusatory tone.

"No!" Clover snapped. "You always accuse me of having an overactive imagination. But not this time! He's off! He needs help!"

Clover glared at Vero, wishing she could get inside his head. Sure, she'd probably never live this one down, and she may forever be known as Crazy Vero's Big Sister. But she knew Vero was hiding something.

"Vero, the principal called and said you'll need to meet with a counselor before he'll allow you back on the school bus," Nora said gently.

Vero saw the pain in his mother's face, and he felt guilty for having caused it. He nodded, hoping his compliance would take a little of that pain away.

"Okay, that's that," Nora said, fighting back tears. "Now, since today is a snow day and there's no school, we'll make it a cleaning day."

"Oh great," Clover groaned.

For once, Vero didn't mind wiping down kitchen counters, mopping hardwood floors, or even scrubbing toilets. He was grateful for the distraction. His mind needed a rest, and at least he wasn't at school.

His first job was to clean out the toy closet. As Vero pulled out his old Hot Wheels cars and Legos, he accidentally stepped on the World War II Corsair model airplane he'd built with his dad. As he picked up the broken airplane and ran his fingers over it, he was surprised that he wasn't more upset. Vero had a fleeting thought that the crushed model was just a relic of childhood. *Strange.*

"Vero!" Clover called from downstairs. "Mom said you're supposed to collect all of the laundry and put it in the washing machine!"

Vero placed the remains of the model airplane on a shelf. He couldn't bring himself to throw it away.

Vero grabbed the laundry bag off the washing machine and went from bedroom to bedroom looking for stray socks. He hesitated at Clover's bedroom door. She no longer allowed Vero access to her room, but gathering laundry was an exception.

Lucky me, Vero thought.

Clover's room looked the same as he remembered it. Posters of pop idols and boy bands hung on the walls. The lava lamp she'd received from their grandmother sat on Clover's nightstand, forming new blobs of purple bubbles. Her stuffed animals were scattered across the window seat, looking very much neglected. He looked at her ceiling fan and saw that little bits of dried toilet paper still covered the multicolored blades.

He remembered a day he'd spent with a ten-year-old Clover—three years ago now. It had been raining for days, they'd been cooped up inside, and they were bored out of their minds. Of course, this was when Vero was still allowed in Clover's room, so they'd been hanging out and trying to think of something to do.

"I just thought of a cool game," Clover said. She disappeared for a minute and returned with two straws and a roll of toilet paper. She handed Vero a straw and said, "Quick, turn on the ceiling fan."

Vero pressed the remote, and the blades began to spin.

"Now take some toilet paper and wet it." Clover handed him a roll of toilet paper.

Following Clover's lead, Vero ripped off a tiny piece and chewed it.

"We're gonna make spitballs and shoot 'em at the fan. You've got to lie on your back and hit the moving target to get any points. The red blade is five points, the blue is three, and the others are one point each."

"Cool," Vero said, and he and Clover spent the rest of that rainy afternoon shooting spitballs at the fan.

Vero smiled at the memory as he emptied Clover's hamper into the laundry bag. He looked on the floor of her closet for any stray items. Then he got down on all fours and searched under the bed. As he reached for a white T-shirt, something caught his eye. Clover's dream journal. Vero hadn't seen that in a long time.

Ever since she was little, Clover had kept the journal by her bed and would quickly jot down what she remembered about her dreams right when she woke up.

Vero couldn't help himself. The temptation to read it was

too strong. He sat on the bed and opened the book. Turning to a random page, he read about a dream in which a boy on the football team kissed Clover. Vero rolled his eyes. He then flipped to another page and read how a different boy on the soccer team kissed Clover. In the next dream, Clover got voted "most popular girl" by her class. Vero began to think these weren't dreams, but rather wishes. He tossed the notebook aside, bored.

The journal hit the side of her nightstand and landed open on the carpet. Vero bent to close the book and shove it back under her bed, but then he saw a sketch that made him pause. There, on the open page of Clover's journal, was a drawing of the same creature from his dream — the one with the four distinct faces of the man, the ox, the lion, and the eagle! Vero was stunned. It couldn't be possible, but there it was, drawn in Clover's style. Then he looked at the entry date. It was last night — the same night as his dream! *How could that be possible?* Somehow he and Clover had shared the same dream.

"You'd better not be in my bedroom!" Clover yelled from the hallway.

Vero quickly shut the diary and threw it under the bed just as Clover walked into the room.

"I'm getting the laundry," Vero stammered.

"Well you got it, now get lost."

Vero stood for a moment just staring at her. He didn't move.

"Clover ... "

"What?" she snapped.

Vero wanted so badly to ask his sister about her drawing, her dream. He needed her to confide in him once again. But he couldn't bring himself to ask. He picked up the laundry bag and headed for the door.

"Um, nothing ... "

As Vero left his sister's room, Clover slammed the door shut behind him. His parents' bedroom door was shut when he walked past, but Vero could still hear their voices through the closed door. He paused to listen.

Mom: "I thought I could do it, but I can't. I won't send him to a psychiatrist!"

Dad: "The school didn't give us a choice in the matter."

Mom: "Then I'll homeschool him."

Dad: "And take him away from his friends? Nora, he's seeing things that aren't there. And when he was little, he was always trying to throw himself off of high places. I love him just as much as you do, but we need to find out what's going on with him."

Vero's heart sank. *Am I mental?* First Tack and Clover, and now his parents thought he was crazy. So the reckless car heading toward the school bus—was that just a hallucination? And the drawing in Clover's diary—was that also imagined?

Because he'd been adopted, Vero had often wondered about his biological parents. Now an image of a man and woman wearing straightjackets came to mind. Vero dropped the laundry bag, raced down the stairs and straight out the back door. He needed to get away from it all.

Vero ran into the backyard, trying to clear his head. His life was spinning out of control. Tears burned the corners of his eyes, and he fought to catch his breath. Twelve-year-old boys shouldn't cry. He was too old for this, but he couldn't stop the tears from leaking out of his eyes.

What's wrong with me? Am I crazy? He thought of the creature he'd seen in that car. Was he completely losing it?

He looked up at the low-hanging clouds as fresh snow started falling in big, fat flakes. The sight of the snow calmed him for a moment. He took in some deep breaths, and then slowly he became aware of the cold and realized he wasn't wearing a coat or boots. He'd been so distraught when he first came outside that he hadn't even noticed the frigid weather.

Looking around, he saw that the day's snowfall had turned everything completely white. The snow had interrupted daily life in the suburbs, and out here, at this moment, the stillness triumphed. The world felt eternally quiet.

Vero collapsed onto his back and stared up at the cold sky, as if it might hold some answers for him. He remembered his rooftop adventure all those Christmases ago, the feeling of standing on the roof, the certainty that he could jump into the crisp, clear sky and soar. And what about the man who had caught him? Did Vero imagine him as well?

Vero forced that notion away and thought of winter days long ago, when he and Clover played in the snow for hours and made snow angels across the lawn. Vero smiled to himself and then swept his arms and legs back and forth, like he and Clover used to do. The repetitive motion soothed him.

The longer Vero swept his limbs, the more tranquility embraced him. He closed his eyes, and his old urge to fly came back so powerfully that Vero fell into a trance. For the first time in a long time, the pain in his back was gone and a content smile spread across his face.

Vero had no idea how long he stayed there in the white stillness. Time seemed to stop, until, "*Squaaak!*"

A black raven flew overhead. *Was that a tail hanging from its backside?* Vero was suddenly very aware of the wet, cold snow.

"*Gawwk!*" the raven cawed again.

Were its eyes glowing red? Vero pushed himself up from the snow, and the raven flew away. Vero's body now felt heavy. He stood up and gazed down at his depression in the snow, his snow angel, with a mix of awe and fear. The wings were at least six feet long, with feathery details that Michelangelo himself could have painstakingly fashioned! Yet Vero had absolutely no recollection of making them.

Mental. He dashed into the garage, grabbed a shovel, and frantically dumped shovelful after shovelful of snow over his splendid angel. Ruining it felt like a sin, but he couldn't have anyone seeing this. He could only imagine what the Atwoods would say if they happened to peer over their fence and see it.

When he finished hiding the evidence, Vero leaned against the shovel to catch his breath. Then he looked up at Clover's window just in time to see her face disappear behind her curtains.

7

THE FALL

Now, Vero, can you describe what you saw on the bus that day?" the stout, frizzy-haired counselor asked.

Vero sat on a sofa across from Dr. Weiss, who put her stubby legs up on her chair and proceeded to sit cross-legged. She picked up a yellow legal pad and a pen from the coffee table. Her brightly colored walls with murals of rainbows, stars, and cute furry animals were trying their best to relax him. But for Vero, no matter how many Skittles or M&Ms she offered him, Dr. Weiss was still a psychiatrist who had the power to lock him away in a nuthouse.

"Just take your time and tell me everything that happened."

Vero hesitated. He knew he had to be careful about his choice of words because so much depended on it.

"We got out of school early because of the snow ... " he began.

"Do you like snow, Vero?" she interrupted. "I love it. I always have."

"I like it except for when I have to shovel the driveway," Vero said.

Dr. Weiss laughed. "Good point."

"I got on the bus and sat behind the driver," Vero continued.

"Do kids pick on you? Is that why you sat behind the driver?" Dr. Weiss asked.

"No, I don't usually sit there. There just weren't any other seats open because of the snow," Vero fought to keep his voice civil.

But being a psychiatrist, Dr. Weiss seemed to notice the annoyance in his voice, and she instantly backed off. "Okay," she said, sitting back in her chair. "Then what happened?"

"We were driving, and the snow started hitting the windshield really hard. That's when I saw the other car coming into our lane."

Vero paused. *Should I continue?*

Dr. Weiss scribbled some notes across her legal pad. "And?"

"That's it," Vero said, deciding that he'd better stop there.

"I think you're not telling me everything."

Vero shook his head. He wasn't going to give her any more.

Dr. Weiss picked up the phone on the coffee table and spoke into it. "Could you bring Sprite in here?"

Before she'd replaced the receiver, the office door opened and a female Jack Russell terrier puppy bounded into the room. Sprite ran to Vero and immediately began tugging on his shoelaces. Vero laughed, picked her up, and held her on his lap. Sprite began licking his face.

"Isn't she cute?" Dr. Weiss asked as she reached over to pet the dog's head. "She's such a good girl." And that's when Dr. Weiss went in for the kill. "Vero, in order for me to help you, I need to know what you saw on that bus."

The puppy made him feel more at ease, and Vero dropped his guard. "The driver of the car was wrestling for control of the steering wheel. He was trying to yank it away from the scary guy ... "

But Dr. Weiss didn't hear the words *scary guy* because at that very moment, an ambulance sped past the window with its siren blaring.

"What? What did you say?" Dr. Weiss asked.

The surprise of the siren startled Vero and Sprite. The puppy jumped off his lap, and the moment was over.

"Who was the driver wrestling with?" she asked.

Vero knew that lying was wrong, but he couldn't tell her the truth. It was kind of like when Great-Aunt Sophie's hairdresser burned a huge bald spot on the top of Sophie's head. When she asked Vero if she still looked pretty, he told her yes. It was a lie, of course. But the way Vero saw it, to tell the truth in that instance would just be mean.

Now with his sanity being questioned, Vero decided this was another time when he would need to stretch the truth. "I said he was wrestling with the steering wheel." Then Vero looked at the floor and managed to produce some real tears to make his story more convincing. "The car slid a little bit into our lane. Just like everyone said. I made the whole story up."

She handed him a tissue. "Why, Vero? Why did you do that?"

"Everyone was being mean to me. I had a bad day at school, and Tack, he's my best friend, he was mad at me and wouldn't let me sit with him on the bus. And then my sister ignored me. I was mad at both of them. So when the car slid across the center line, I thought that if I pretended to save everyone, then Tack and Clover would think I'd saved their lives and be nice to me again."

Dr. Weiss handed Vero another tissue, gave his forearm an encouraging squeeze, looked him square in the eyes, and said, "That was excellent sharing, Vero." Then she winked at Sprite and said, "And *you're* getting a steak bone tonight."

⬥

Vero glanced at the clock. It was exactly 11:30 a.m. Right now the kids in his class would be headed to the cafeteria for lunch. It was a bright, clear day, so they'd probably go outside and pelt each other with snowballs after they finished eating. He, however, was stuck sitting in the waiting room while his parents met with Dr. Weiss.

The receptionist was out for lunch. Vero had already leafed through all of the magazines, so he walked over to the aquarium and watched the fish swim back and forth, back and forth, over and over again. He envied the simplicity of their existence. Their entire lives were limited to the space within those four glass walls. Every day it was always the same — no surprises. The fish knew exactly what to expect — something Vero deeply craved.

Vero decided to use the restroom. He picked up the bathroom key from the receptionist's desk. The key was attached to a Rubik's Cube by a little chain, so no one could put it in his pocket and accidentally take off with it. Vero walked out of the waiting room and down the hallway to the men's room.

The doors on all three stalls were closed, so Vero bent down and looked for feet underneath. Empty.

A minute later, Vero was washing his hands in the sink when a rattling sound came from one of the stalls. Startled, he splashed water on himself.

"Ah man ... " he said aloud. He turned around, but the restroom was still empty. His heartbeat picked up a beat. But then he noticed an exposed heating unit overhead, just like the one in Tack's house.

That was it, Vero thought. The heater in Tack's house was ancient and made the same sound when it was running.

Vero looked down and saw that the front of his pants were wet. "Great," he said. "Now it looks like I peed my pants." He could just imagine the worried glances that would fly between his mom and dad and Dr. Weiss. *Maybe he's worse than we thought.* He searched for some paper towels, but there was only an electric hand dryer. He turned the drying nozzle so it pointed toward the floor and tried to contort his body underneath it. He was about to press the On button when a loud banging started from inside the end stall. Vero whipped around, his chest tight with fear, and his wet pants forgotten.

"Who's there?" Vero asked, but he knew no one had come into the restroom.

No reply.

Get out! Something inside urged him. *Now!*

Vero turned to run out, but he slipped on the wet floor and fell — hard. With his head pressed to the concrete floor, he now had a clear view under the bathroom stalls. This time he saw two sets of feet that hadn't been there before — and they weren't human!

Am I hallucinating? Do I need to be locked up in a loony bin?

What he saw were two sets of ugly, claw-like feet that resembled talons. He'd just hit his head on the floor, so could he be unconscious? Dreaming? Then the stall doors opened, and Vero saw the rest of the creatures who were attached to the clawed feet. He was in trouble.

They were covered in scales and fur and sharp claws for their hands and feet, a tiny slit for a mouth, and where there should have been a nose was only a flat space. But the worst part of their appearance was their eyes—or, actually, *eye*. Each creature had a single eye.

One of them turned its hideous head, and Vero saw that the eye went clear through, so it could see backward and forward at the same time!

Vero jumped up and sprinted for the door. Both creatures got down on all fours and bounded after him. Vero grabbed the door handle. A vague image of his mother flew through his mind, and he heard her say, "Use a paper towel whenever you leave a public bathroom, so you don't pick up more germs."

Sorry, Mom.

He needed to get out of there now! But before he could leave the room, a sharp pain ripped through his leg. One of the creatures had clawed him and was attempting to pull him back. Not waiting to see what would happen next, Vero kicked the creature as hard as he could in its grizzly face and dashed into the hallway.

He meant to run back to Dr. Weiss's office, but he sprinted the wrong way down the hall. He ran as fast as he could. He knew he needed to get outside, but he'd never been inside this building before. He ran straight into a dead end. He quickly turned around and, to his horror, saw the two creatures blocking him in, taunting him, and slowly, methodically approaching him from the other end of the hallway.

Vero stood frozen with terror.

Suddenly, they leapt toward him. Their bodies were turned backward as they flew the length of the hallway — the bloodshot eye in the back of each creature's head guiding them.

Please help me.

From the corner of his eye, Vero saw an emergency exit door, and he pushed through it mere milliseconds before the creatures were upon him.

Vero dashed up a staircase, winning some distance as the creatures struggled to open the door with their claws. But they soon followed, screeching in rage.

As Vero ran, he realized he was jumping whole staircases in a single bound — just like when he'd run the hurdles. He was so light on his feet that he quickly found himself at the top of the emergency staircase and bounded onto the roof of the office building. Though he had just cleared nine stories in a blink, Vero felt no need to catch his breath. He rapidly scanned the roof, looking for some way to escape. He was trapped.

The creatures appeared on the roof. Feeling no need to rush since Vero had nowhere to go, they steadily approached him, smiling evil, hideous smiles.

And that smile stretched their slitlike mouths clear across their faces, revealing rows of sharp, yellow fangs. When Vero glimpsed those fangs, he knew he couldn't win.

"What do you want?" Vero asked desperately.

The creatures' loud replies contained no words, only strange clicking and hissing sounds.

Vero slowly backed away until he was almost standing at the edge of the roof, and still the creatures pressed him. Then his foot got caught on a metal pipe that was part of the air conditioning system, and for a single moment, Vero balanced on the edge. But he was too far gone.

As he plunged off the side of the building, he flailed his arms wildly and somehow managed to catch hold of a ledge with his right hand. Then he swung his left hand up and dangled there, breathing heavily, nine stories above the concrete sidewalk below.

His whole life, Vero had believed he could fly. And he'd fearlessly jumped off of anything he could climb. But now, Vero wanted to cling to that edge with all his might. He closed his eyes against the dizziness.

Help me! Please!

From the rooftop above him, Vero heard an ear-piercing shriek, then the sound of metal clanging on metal, like the sound of clashing swords.

As Vero squinted into the sunlight above, the horrid face of one of the beasts appeared over the edge. Vero's heart pounded as he dangled from the ledge and looked into the eye of the beast. He saw the decaying, putrid teeth, and a drop of saliva fell from its gnarled tongue onto Vero's cheek, burning it like acid. But Vero did not let go. He could hear a scuffle on the roof above and beyond his line of sight.

The creature snarled viciously and opened its mouth, preparing to attack. But suddenly its head jerked back violently and out of Vero's view. Then a shrill wail sent a chill straight through him, and it was followed by an enormous thud. Vero felt himself slipping. He closed his eyes, preparing to fall, when a man's head peered out over the ledge.

"Grab my hand!" the man shouted.

The man stretched his hand toward Vero. Vero hesitated. Could this be one of the creatures in disguise? But his violet eyes looked familiar.

"Take it if you want to save your life! They're going to come right back!"

At this point Vero realized he didn't have much of a choice. So in an act of complete blind faith, Vero removed his right hand from the ledge and reached up to grab the man's hand. The man smiled warmly, and Vero felt relief— until the man abruptly withdrew his hand.

That day, Vero Leland fell nine stories and hit the pavement with a bone-crushing thud. He was dead.

8

HOME

Tack once told Vero a joke.

"What's the last thing that goes through a bug's mind when it hits the windshield?"

Vero shrugged, not knowing.

"His butt!" Tack laughed.

A lot of things went through Vero's mind before he hit the pavement. Thoughts flew through his mind in flashes, in fractions of seconds, in completely random segments:

He wondered how much pain he would feel when his body broke into pieces.

He thought of his last birthday and realized there would never be another soccer ball cake or thirteenth birthday.

He thought of the bathroom key attached to the Rubik's cube. What had happened to it during his struggle with those creatures?

His last thought was of his mother and the heartbreaking look on her face when she was given the news of his death.

Then blackness.

❖

"Come on, get up," Vero heard the voice and felt someone nudge his shoulder. He opened his eyes, and a face gradually came into focus.

"You!" Vero cried. "You tricked me!" It was the man from the ledge.

"Now before you jump to conclusions," the man said, "there are two sides to every story."

"Not in this case," Vero argued. He sat up and touched his chest, his shoulders, his head. "You let me fall!"

"If you'll recall, I said to take my hand if you want to live, and now here you are."

"What the . . . ?" Vero found no blood, nor cuts or bruises. His bones appeared to be intact. "Am I dead?"

"Well," the man answered. "That's not an easy question to answer."

"I fell from up there." Vero pointed to the top of the building.

Vero was more confused than ever, but one thing became very clear to him — he knew the man standing before him. He recognized the tightly cropped silver beard, which was the same color as his shoulder-length hair, the strong jawline, and those bright violet eyes.

"You caught me when I jumped off the roof that Christmas."

The man nodded. "See? I said you could trust me."

"You twisted my ankle!" Vero said. "And now you dropped me off a nine-story building! Who are you? And what's going on?" Vero jumped up and began pacing frantically, still checking his arms, his head, his ankles.

"I didn't have a choice, Vero. I had to make it look real. I couldn't have them find out who you are."

Vero froze. "Who am I?" he asked. He gazed into the man's eyes trying to decipher something, anything that might explain how he was still walking and talking instead of being road pizza.

"Not now. We've got to get out of here."

The man held his hand.

"I'm not falling for that again."

"Look, Vero, it seems you and I got off on the wrong foot . . . no pun intended," he began. "But you need to—"

"You just killed me! That's a bit worse than getting off on the wrong foot!" Vero yelled. "And now you won't even tell me if I'm dead or not!"

"Do you see those two creatures anywhere? The ones who were about to rip off your head?"

Vero looked around. The creatures were nowhere in sight.

"Yeah, you can thank me for that," the man answered. "Now come with me."

Vero shook his head and backed away from the stranger. He ran to the front of the building where just an hour before he'd arrived with his mom and dad to see Dr. Weiss. Vero pulled on the door handle, but no matter how hard he tugged, the door wouldn't open. He kicked the door.

"Open!" he screamed. Then he kicked the door again.

"You're wasting my time," the man said.

Vero didn't care. He ran the length of the building to Dr. Weiss's window, where he could see his parents deeply engrossed in conversation with the doctor, talking about him.

"Mom! Dad!" Vero screamed and wildly flailed his arms, but not one of them so much as glanced Vero's way.

The man followed Vero and watched him pound on the glass. "They can't see you," he said.

"Then I *am* dead." The awareness was brutal.

The man placed his hand on Vero's shoulder. "Now will you come with me?"

Vero looked at the man, at his outstretched hand, and Vero grabbed hold of it.

❖

The buildings, the trees, cars and people, everything before Vero's eyes melted away in a flash and was replaced by a lush green field that had no end. Effervescent wildflowers dotted the fields with colors so bright that Vero wished he had his sunglasses. Instead, he shaded his eyes with his hand and tried to take it all in.

In the distance Vero saw clusters of magnificent trees with leaves that closely matched the colors of the brilliant wildflowers. Red wasn't just red, and blue wasn't just blue. It was as if someone had taken a rainbow and wrung it through their hands, pouring the colors out upon the earth. The sky above was a blue so deep that it was nearly violet, and he felt warmth emanating from it, yet he saw no sun. It was as if he was being embraced by the sky. And the longer Vero stood there, the more he felt like this place wasn't so foreign after all. He felt comfortable with his surroundings, a sense of belonging.

"Is this heaven?"

"No."

"But if I'm dead, there are only two places you can go." A real fear overtook his thoughts. "So if it's not heaven, then is it . . .?"

"It's the Ether."

"That's what I'm asking. Either what?"

"Not either. *Ether*. E-t-h-e-r." The man spelled it out. "The upper air. It has existed since the beginning. It's what ancient Greek philosophers described as that which is not known or understood but is essential to life. The Ether cannot be tested or proven in a lab, yet it is all around us."

The man looked at Vero with a steadfast gaze, his violet eyes intense. "You know this place, Vero. Close your eyes and let it wash over you. It's calling to you."

Vero closed his eyes and took several deep breaths. The man picked a wildflower and placed it in Vero's hand. As Vero opened his eyes and looked at the flower, he instantly understood the complexity of its nature and its simple beauty all at once, as if he could see right through it.

Vero felt as if he were seeing things clearly for the first time in his life. He looked at his surroundings. The trees, the grass, the sky, it all beckoned to him.

"Where are you, Vero?"

Vero didn't hesitate.

"Home."

❖

"It's been a long time since you were here," the man said.

"I guess. I don't remember much," Vero replied.

"True knowledge unfolds in its own sweet time, and we don't want to overload you all at once."

Suddenly, a rustling in the tall grass caught Vero's attention, and he saw gazelles calmly grazing next to a pair of lions a few feet away. A male and female monkey happily swung from tree branch to tree branch. Two hippos sunned themselves along the banks of a mighty river. Vero gazed across the scene before him. Animals of all kinds roamed in every direction.

"Why are there two of all the animals?" Vero asked.

"You've gone to Sunday school, so you should know the answer," the man replied.

"You mean these are the actual animals ...?"

The man nodded.

"But they get along with each other."

"When they lived in such tight quarters on the ark, they learned to get along if they were to survive ... a lesson humans have yet to learn."

Without warning, the male lion bounded out from under a tree and darted over to Vero. Vero froze. His legs wouldn't move. As the lion approached, Vero protectively covered his face with his arms. But then, the ferocious lion fell to his feet, bowing his head to Vero. Vero's eyes went wide with disbelief.

"He's friendly," the man encouraged him.

Vero hesitantly stretched out his hand and stroked the lion's head. The lion rubbed his body against Vero like a cat.

Suddenly, the light above began to swirl into the shape of a circle, growing bigger and bigger. It spun so wide, it looked as if the sky had opened up. The swirling lights began to take form. They were angels, thousands and thousands of angelic beings flying at high speed.

Vero's mouth dropped open at the sight of the grandiose creatures with colossal wings. He felt their strength and power. He longed to join them, to be in their company.

Vero fell to the ground. He felt as if someone had punched him hard in the back, followed by overwhelming relief. He rose to his feet and stood, magnificent alabaster wings jutting out between his shoulders. The sky closed up, and the angelic beings disappeared from sight. Vero turned to the man.

"Am I . . . ?" Vero began.

The man quickly cut him off.

"Yes, Vero. You are a guardian angel."

9

THE ETHER
AND BACK

As Vero sat on the ground, his wings smoothly retracted inside his back with a slight popping sensation, almost like when Vero cracked his knuckles.

"Did I just do that?" Vero asked.

The man nodded.

"Where did my wings go?"

"They're hidden once again until you learn to handle them better. It takes time. But soon you'll be able to control them as easily as you move your arm."

With his left hand, Vero reached around and felt his back.

"My shirt's not ripped!"

"It mends itself each time."

"Are you a guardian angel too?" Vero asked the man.

The man shook his head and sat down next to Vero.

"I'm an archangel ... Uriel." He looked at Vero expectantly, one eyebrow raised over his violet eyes and a slight grin on his face.

Uriel? Then it dawned on Vero, and he blushed guiltily.

"Yes, your paper on *Paradise Lost*. You pinned the whole expulsion from the garden on me."

"Well, I meant ... uh, I didn't mean you were like drinking on the job or anything like that ... "

"Gee thanks," Uriel's words dripped with sarcasm. "It's not so easy recognizing the Wicked One. He's the master of deception."

His words rattled Vero back to the memory of the two frightening creatures that had chased him earlier.

"So who was chasing me?"

"Those were two of the Wicked One's minions. He sent them after you."

"But why me?"

"Because you're good. The Wicked One hates anything good. He wants to destroy all that is good."

"But now that I'm dead, he can't come after me, right?"

"Yes, he can," Uriel said. "And you're not really dead."

"But I fell from a nine-story building!" Vero protested. Vero thought of his mom and dad back on earth, probably wondering and worrying over where he was. Then Vero thought of Clover, her face in the bedroom window, the rainy days spent indoors, her mortified look as the bus drove off without him. The thought of Clover all on her own brought a well of emotions bubbling to the surface until Vero felt tears forming in his eyes. Vero held his face in his hands, embarrassed.

Uriel knelt before Vero and removed his hands from

his face. Vero lifted his head and met Uriel's gaze. His face seemed softer.

"Vero, you are made of the Spirit. And nothing of the Spirit can ever die."

◆

Uriel stood beside Vero as he stroked the lion's head; his eyes were fixed on the puffy clouds above. Vero watched as they molded into the shape of a lion. Then just as quickly, they changed into a single cloud that resembled Clover's face. The clouds then shaped themselves into a huge question mark. Uriel chuckled when he saw the perplexed look on Vero's face.

"Uriel, how ...?"

"You're doing that with your thoughts," he explained.

"I was thinking it was so cool that I was petting a lion. But then I wished Clover could also pet him, and then I wondered how the clouds knew what I was thinking. Everything here is amazing. How can this not be heaven?"

Uriel chuckled. "You obviously haven't seen heaven."

"Seriously?" Vero must have looked as astonished as he felt because Uriel laughed again. "Don't get me wrong. These parts of the Ether are wonderful; but Vero, this is our battleground. The Ether is where we fight our spiritual battles."

"I don't understand," Vero said.

"The Ether is the spiritual realm that surrounds the earth. Lucifer and his evil followers also dwell here. They do everything in their power to destroy man, or at least what's good about man, and we do everything in our power to stop them."

"So where's your sword? Don't angels have swords?" Vero asked.

"Only when needed." Uriel began walking across the field. Vero followed.

"But guardian angels protect people, right?"

"Yes," Uriel replied.

"Is that what I'll be doing from now on?"

Vero watched as a flock of angels flew overhead.

"You will be trained first," Uriel explained. "You won't become a full guardian until you have completed your training. Then, once your training is complete, you will choose your destiny."

"I thought *this* was my destiny?"

"An angel is who you are. However, your destiny will be determined by the decisions you make."

"But ... "

"Vero, you were created with the gift of free will." Uriel stopped walking, grabbed Vero's shoulders, and looked very intently into his eyes. "At some point, we all have to choose between the light or the darkness."

"But I'm an angel, and angels are always good."

Uriel dropped his hands from Vero's shoulders. "Lucifer was once the most glorious of angels and loved by God. But when he fell, one-third of the angel ranks went with him. One-third chose to live outside the Light."

Vero pondered what Uriel said. The idea of the angels falling into darkness terrified him. What if that was his destiny? Would he really need to make that choice?

"Don't be frightened," Uriel said, placing his hand over Vero's heart. "A pure heart will never lead you astray."

Uriel removed his hand. "Now it's time for you to go back."

Vero raised his eyebrows, "Back where?"

"To earth, of course."

"I'm not staying here?"

"You will return for your training," Uriel said. "But for now, you are to go back to your family. Don't you miss them?"

Suddenly, a wave of homesickness swept over Vero. He looked to Uriel, crestfallen, "I know I was adopted, but I guess now my mom and dad really *aren't* my family anymore—"

"Your family is the people you love," Uriel cut him off.

"Do I have angel parents?" Vero asked.

"No, angels don't have children. Just as God is everyone's Father, so it is the same for us."

"But what if I no longer fit in down on earth?"

"Why wouldn't you?"

Vero spread his arms wide and said, "Because after all of this, do you think I can just sit down with my family and have a normal dinner? Should I ask Clover to pass me the milk and add, 'Oh, and by the way, I just happen to be a guardian angel'? Is that what you expect me to do?"

"Don't ever tell *anyone*," Uriel said sternly. "I stopped you once already in the psychiatrist's office. I sent that ambulance when you were about to mention the malture in the car."

"You did that?" The psychiatrist's office seemed like another lifetime ago.

Uriel nodded, "We can never appear to humans in our angelic form unless God allows us."

"What's a malture?"

"Maltures are Satan's creations—the evil fiends that tempt humans."

"How could Lucifer create anything?" Vero asked.

"Well, he can't create anything good. These maltures are an extension of his own evil and hatred. They have no souls."

Vero thought about the bus that day and what he'd witnessed. "That guy in the backseat of that car—he was a malture, wasn't he? One of them was trying to crash that car into the bus!"

Uriel nodded. "Yes, he was. I saw him too. And you did well, Vero ... you have all the right instincts."

Vero smiled for what felt like the first time in a long time. *I'm not crazy,* he thought.

"You instinctively protected and saved those kids—exactly what a guardian angel is supposed to do."

Suddenly Uriel's eyes took on a faraway look. He was seeing something else.

What is it? Vero wondered.

Uriel turned to Vero. "I have to go," he said. "One of your fellow guardian angels is slacking off on the job and about to cause a ten-car pileup on a bridge."

"But I have a million more questions!" Vero protested.

"Just recall the last normal thing you were doing before all of this happened, and then I'll be in touch!"

Colossal wings shot out from Uriel's back. Uriel's wings were more elaborate than the other angels' wings, with outer feathers adorned in gold. A golden glow embraced Uriel as his wings created a gust of wind, knocking Vero to the ground.

"Don't worry, Vero, we'll be watching you."

Then the wind stopped blowing, the glow disappeared, and Uriel was gone.

Vero stood and looked out over the animals grazing in the lush fields. He closed his eyes and turned his face up to the sky, feeling the warmth of the light upon him. He wondered whether he would ever return to the Ether. Would he wake up in the morning and realize it had all been nothing but a dream?

Vero tried to remember where he'd been before the craziness began. He pictured his mother and father sitting in Dr. Weiss's office; but when he opened his eyes, he was still standing in the Ether. He closed his eyes once more and saw himself falling from the rooftop. He felt something wet on his cheek and opened his eyes. The lion was licking his face like a faithful dog. Vero stroked his mane.

"I have to go," he told the lion. "Hopefully, I'll see you again."

Vero gave it one last shot. This time when he closed his eyes, he saw himself standing in the men's room holding the Rubik's Cube attached to the key. When he opened his eyes, he stood before the stall doors and the sinks. Fear gripped him as he remembered the hideous maltures. But when Vero looked under the stall doors, there was nothing there — no hooked claws. He surveyed the bathroom and saw no sign of his previous struggle. Everything was in order, including himself — no bruises, cuts, or scrapes. Even his ripped pant leg from where the malture had clawed him was now perfectly mended.

Vero walked out of the bathroom and down the hallway. He opened Dr. Weiss's office door. The waiting room was still empty — except for the fish swimming around in their protected little world. He returned the Rubik's Cube key to the receptionist's desk and collapsed in a chair, completely exhausted. He glanced at the clock and saw the big hand click to 11:31. No time had passed since he'd been to the Ether! *How could that be?*

He heard his parents' voices inside Dr. Weiss's office.

They were on their way out. And they had no clue that while they'd been discussing his mental state, Vero had been attacked by two maltures, fallen off a roof, died, gone to the Ether, discovered he was a guardian angel, and returned to earth good as new.

As his parents opened the door, sweat trickled down Vero's forehead. Would they suspect anything?

His mom walked out and glanced at Vero with an odd expression on her face. Vero felt his heart drop into his stomach. *She knew!*

But then she smiled warmly and said, "Vero, tie your shoelaces before you trip."

"I was thinking we could go get some burgers for lunch," his dad announced.

Seeing his parents standing there wearing their sensible shoes and winter parkas, their ordinariness deeply moved Vero, and he realized that ordinary was something he would never be again. He hugged both his parents, afraid to let them go. He feared that if he did, he'd be letting go of the only life he'd ever known.

"It's okay, Vero," his dad reassured him. "You're going to be all right."

But his words were of little comfort. Vero's father had no idea that the boy he embraced wasn't even human. And he certainly wouldn't be able to protect his son from those maltures, should they ever return. All of it terrified him, but what scared Vero most of all was a question—would his parents still love him if they knew the truth?

Dr. Weiss walked into the waiting room with Sprite nipping at her heels.

"Hey now, don't take it so hard," Vero's dad said as he ended the hug. "Dr. Weiss says you'll be fine."

"We're happy you told the whole truth," Dr. Weiss said, patting Vero's back.

Vero caught his mother's gaze. Her worried expression told him she knew there was more to the story.

10

THE BULLIES

After his return from the Ether, Vero didn't want to be around anyone. He was still trying to make sense of everything that had happened there, so he told his parents he didn't feel well. They let him stay home from school the next day. And the next. And even the next. He also kept his distance from Clover—who probably didn't even realize he was doing it—and he avoided Tack as well, except for a few online rounds of golf on the latest edition of *The PGA Tour.*

Vero watched TV and played video games to dull his senses, but they proved to be only momentary distractions because his thoughts would always stray back to the Ether.

The Ether had been beyond glorious. It was so amazing, in fact, that it was now difficult for him to be confined inside a two-story house. He knew the walls of the house no longer defined his home—his true home was the infinite space of the Ether.

His parents loved him so much and had given him a wonderful home all these years, but he was beginning to feel like one of those birds in a cage at the pet store. The word *confused* couldn't even begin to cover it. Vero was a mess. He eventually retreated to the privacy of his bedroom and spent most of the day lying on his bed and staring at the ceiling.

His dad assumed he was upset and embarrassed by the bus incident. Being a nurse, his mom knew he had no fever or sore throat. She worried there was something else going on with him. But after a week of seclusion, both parents agreed he should return to school.

School now felt like an exercise in futility. Vero knew he would learn more in five minutes with Uriel than all his teachers could teach him during an entire year of school. To make matters worse, Coach Randy continued to hound Vero about joining the track team. But he refused. With the bus incident still fresh in everyone's minds, Vero didn't want to draw any more attention to himself.

Most kids avoided him, staying as far away as possible. When Vero walked down the hallway, it was like Moses parting a Red Sea of students. One day poor Nate scurried past him so fast that he wasn't watching where he was going and smashed his head on the open door of a metal locker.

When Vero tried to help him up, Nate stuttered, "No ... no ... I'm ... uh ... all good."

"It's awesome that you have that kind of power," Tack told Vero during lunch period.

Vero and Tack were sitting at a table in the cafeteria with noticeably empty space all around them. Vero glanced around the room and met eyes with Danny, who then moved both his fists like he was grabbing a car steering wheel. His friends, Blake and Duff, laughed and pointed at Vero.

Blake and Duff were big for their ages. They looked more like high school seniors than eighth graders, scruffy beards and all. Lately they seemed to follow Danny everywhere. But Vero rarely had to deal with them because Tack was usually at his side. No one wanted to mess with Tack who was equally big for his age, minus the beard.

Vero turned back to Tack. "You wanna trade places?"

"In a heartbeat," Tack answered. "That's *real* power when everyone is afraid of you."

Vero gave him a look.

"Okay, well, at least you're not being shoved into garbage cans or getting wedgies in the locker room anymore."

"Thanks," Vero said. "That makes me feel so much better."

As Danny continued to mock Vero from across the cafeteria, his elbow accidentally knocked over his drink. Water spilled all over the table and onto Blake's lap. He jumped up and headed for the restroom to get cleaned up. Duff followed him out the door, but not before sending Danny a menacing look over his shoulder.

"See? It's Karma," Tack said. "Danny made fun of you and look what happened!"

Davina quickly swooped in with some napkins to help clean up the mess. With her trademark smile, she picked Danny's cup off the floor and handed it to him. But her hand lingered near his for a split second too long, at least in Vero's opinion.

"Thanks," Danny said. His face lit up when Davina sat next to him.

Across the cafeteria, Vero watched with a jealous eye as

Davina and Danny spent the rest of the lunch hour talking and laughing.

"Some Karma," Vero muttered to himself.

❖

By the end of the day, Vero was more than ready to leave school. Even though he was officially allowed back on the bus, his dad thought it might be better if he waited a few more days. So the buses all left without him. But by four o'clock, his father still hadn't arrived.

It was bitter cold outside, so Vero was waiting in the lobby, incessantly looking out the window for his dad's car, while constantly sidestepping the janitor's mop. It would be so great if he could just use his wings and fly home. It was totally unfair of Uriel to send him back to earth and expect him to act like nothing had ever happened.

"Forget this," Vero said. He shoved the door to the school open and trudged outside. The wintry air swept across his face and instantly invigorated him. He felt powerful. With a fierce determination, Vero walked around the side of the brick building. Scanning the area to make sure he was alone, he placed the palms of his hands against the wall of the school to brace himself. He knew the force of his wings could knock him to the ground. Vero closed his eyes tight, mustered up all his strength, and willed his wings to appear.

Nothing happened.

"Come on!" he shouted.

So he tried even harder and with a fiercer resolve. Sweat dripped down his face despite the frigid air. Still no wings.

He let out a yowl of frustration and banged his fist against the bricks.

"Hey, nut job! What did that wall ever do to you?" Danny yelled from behind him.

Could this get any better?

Vero turned around and saw Danny and his two buddies, Duff and Blake, standing there. All three of them were smiling darkly.

"Hey, wacko! He asked you a question!" Duff called.

Vero didn't respond. He started walking back toward the school entrance. He *did not* want to deal with these guys right now. But before he'd taken but a few steps, Blake grabbed Vero's shoulder and spun him around.

"It's rude to walk away when someone's talking to you. Didn't your mother teach you any manners?"

"Look, I'm just waiting for my ride."

"Well, I don't think they're coming," Danny said, looking around. "Even Mommy and Daddy don't care about you."

Vero felt his blood pressure rising. "No!" he shouted back. "Everybody knows that's *your* parents!"

A dark look passed over Danny's face, and Vero knew his words had stung. For a brief instant, Vero felt bad for Danny.

"Get him!" Blake said to Danny.

"Don't let him get away with that!" Duff shouted.

Before Vero could make a run for it, Danny's fist cut him hard across the jaw.

Vero staggered backward into Duff, who caught Vero and shoved him back toward Danny, who then hit him again — this time in the nose. Blood trickled down Vero's face. Duff and Blake laughed.

"I don't think he's learned his lesson yet," Blake said.

Danny seemed to hesitate, but Vero was done with this abuse. He was a guardian angel! A powerful being to whom lions bowed down! Vero made a fist and was about to strike Danny with his full strength when an unseen force prevented his arm from moving.

What? Not fair!

Danny took advantage of Vero's hesitation and slugged him hard in the gut. Vero doubled over and fell to the ground, cutting his forehead on the corner of a cement flowerbed.

"Bull's-eye!" Duff shrieked as he high-fived Blake.

Vero curled up on the ground, winded and in pain.

The bully crew walked on by, and as Duff passed him, he turned and spit on Vero.

What was that? For a split second, Duff's unusually blue eyes seemed to flash red!

Then a drop of blood dripped from the gash in his forehead.

No, Vero thought. *It was just my own blood blurring my vision.*

11

$\diamond$

FAILED FLIGHT

The last thing Vero wanted was to attract more attention, so he didn't tell anyone about his encounter with Blake, Duff, and Danny—but especially not Tack. Tack would either (a) retaliate, or (b) make Vero retaliate. Neither one was an option. Vero still couldn't wrap his mind around what had happened when he'd tried to hit Danny, or what he thought he'd seen afterward ...

Not going there.

Instead, he worked hard to regain anonymity. His life became quiet and monotonous. Vero's basic routine consisted of going to school, going home, going to his bedroom, going to dinner, and going back to his bedroom. Yet his mind was consumed with thoughts of the Ether.

When will I see Uriel again? Had it really happened?

Eventually Vero broke his routine and went to a movie with Tack one Saturday morning.

"Wasn't it awesome when that meteor hit the dam and the water flooded everything?" Tack asked as they walked out of the theater and into the lobby.

"Yeah," Vero answered, completely disinterested.

"Or when that second meteor hit the desert and created that sandstorm?"

"Yeah, great," Vero said halfheartedly.

The truth was, all Vero could think about was the Ether.

"That movie's got Oscar written all over it!" Tack said as he pressed the Down elevator button. "Oh man, look!"

Vero turned around and saw a group of girls exiting the same theater. They were giggling about something. Were they laughing at him? Then Vero noticed one of the girls was Davina.

Tack licked the palm of his hand and tried to smooth down the double cowlick that made his hair protrude at the back of his head.

"How do I look?" Tack asked as the girls approached.

Vero didn't answer. He was too preoccupied with the sight of Davina. She'd been one of the few bright spots of being back on earth.

"Is my hair sticking up?" Tack asked.

With their backs to the elevator doors, Tack and Vero watched the girls pass by. They heard the chime and *whoosh* of the elevator doors opening.

"Dude, did you hear me?" Tack asked, giving Vero's shoulder a shove. "Can't you at least acknowledge me or something?"

Taken by surprise, Vero stumbled backward through the

open elevator doors—except there was no elevator floor to catch him!

❖

When Vero opened his eyes, he was lying under a tree with delicious-looking apples, oranges, lemons, peaches, and pears hanging from its branches. He breathed in the magnificent aroma of the fruit, and he experienced instant peace.

Vero was back in the Ether.

As he was lying on his back, just marveling at the different fruits all sprouting from one tree, he felt a foot nudge his side. He quickly sat up and saw a girl with a slight build towering over him. She looked to be about his age. And she was pretty. Her skin was olive, her eyes were bright, and she had curly auburn hair—the fiery color of autumn leaves.

"You can eat some of those, if you want," she told him, absentmindedly twirling a curl around one of her fingers. "None of the trees are off-limits here."

The girl picked a peach off the tree and handed it to Vero. It was the size of a soccer ball, and Vero had to hold it with both hands.

"I don't know whether to dribble it or eat it," Vero said.

Then, right before his eyes, a tiny bud blossomed in the exact spot where the girl had picked the giant peach. It quickly grew in size until it matched the one Vero held. Vero looked at the new peach in complete astonishment.

"Pretty cool, huh?" the girl said. "Go ahead, try it!"

Vero looked at the peach and then back at the girl suspiciously. "Who are you?"

"My name's Ada. Ada Brickner."

"Good. Before I bit into this thing, I just wanted to make sure your name isn't Eve." Vero took a bite, and peach juice dripped down his hands. It was so fresh, so perfectly ripe, it tasted unlike anything he'd ever eaten. Until that moment his favorite food had been pizza, but no more. And the peach did more than fill his stomach — it felt as if it had nourished his entire body.

"Let's go. They're waiting for us," Ada said.

"Who's waiting for us?"

"The others."

"Oh, *the others*. That clears up everything. I'd better not keep *them* waiting."

Ada didn't respond. She turned and briskly walked away.

Vero quickly followed, still holding the massive peach in his hands.

"Why didn't Uriel greet me?" he called after her.

"There are more important things he's gotta do than welcome you," she shot back over her shoulder. "I know you're new to the Ether, but the first rule you need to learn is to leave your ego back on earth."

"So are you a guardian angel too?" Vero asked as he caught up to her.

"Yes. This is my third training session. I'm from a large city, East Coast."

"What? Are "the others" more guardian angels? Am I training with a group?"

Before Ada could answer, her wings sprouted from her back, and she took off in flight, leaving Vero standing alone on the side of the steep mountain.

"Hey! Come back here!" Vero shouted.

Ada didn't look back as she flew out of sight.

Vero willed his wings to appear, but nothing happened. He wearily walked along the side of the cliff, carrying the weight of his frustrations on his shoulders. Ada could command her wings with a single thought, but he wasn't able to do that. He couldn't help but wonder how a girl could have the power, but he didn't.

He wasn't sure where he was supposed to go, and he was hoping for some sort of sign to guide him. Looking out over the horizon, he saw nothing but endless white. There was no sign of Ada anywhere.

Suddenly, Vero heard a voice say, "Jump."

Vero spun around and nearly dropped the enormous peach. But no one was there. "Who said that?" Vero yelled. His eyes searched for the source.

"Jump," the voice repeated. It wasn't a frightening voice. It sounded firm but somehow trustworthy.

Vero peered over the edge of the cliff. Clouds hung in the air below him, preventing him from seeing the bottom. If he were to throw himself off the side of the mountain, he'd have no idea where he'd land. Yet the clouds beckoned to him.

Somewhere deep inside, Vero felt the clouds would protect him.

"Jump," the voice enticed him again.

If my falls from the rooftop and down the elevator shaft didn't destroy me, Vero reasoned, *then neither should a fall from a cliff in the Ether.*

He stood with his back straight, feeling full of confidence. While still holding the peach in his hands, Vero ran full speed toward the edge of the cliff and jumped into the unknown.

Vero was exhilarated as the crisp air held him. He felt a tug on his back as his wings quickly sprouted. Finally, he was truly flying! It was a feeling of pure freedom as he soared the skies. He'd never felt happier.

The clouds began to dispel, and Vero glimpsed the land far below. Instantly he became aware of the fact that his actions defied logic. Doubt spread through him with the swiftness of a deadly virus. Soon, Vero succumbed to uncertainty, and then the sky simply dropped him. Vero hit the side of the mountain hard.

The colossal peach flew out of his hands on impact. Vero tumbled head over heels down an incline that seemed to go on forever, and then he finally came to an abrupt stop with one last "Ooomph!"

He was unhurt but dazed. And when he looked up, he was surprised to see other kids sitting on the grass in a forest glade, staring at him with what seemed to be looks of disapproval. His face flushed hot, and then, as if his fall wasn't humiliating enough, the immense peach finished its descent and landed on Vero's head, splattering juice down the sides of his face.

Ada laughed.

"See what happens when you doubt?" Uriel asked, standing over him.

With his right hand, Vero felt his back.

"Don't bother," Uriel said. "Your wings are gone."

Disappointment swept over Vero. He overheard Ada whispering to a slight boy with ears that stuck out from his head and glasses that were too big for his face.

"Are you *sure* this is the guy?" she asked in a low voice.

Vero watched as the boy nodded.

"He doesn't seem so special," she said.

What did that mean? How did these other guardian angels know about him? Vero had so many questions, but somehow he knew Uriel wouldn't be forthcoming with any answers.

Uriel went around the group and introduced each angel in turn. Vero had already met Ada. The slight kid with the huge glasses was named Pax. Kane was a dark-haired boy who was built like a linebacker. X was a tall boy with a classic, angular face, chiseled nose, and high cheekbones. His light brown skin was flawless, and his chest and broad shoulders seemed exceedingly well developed for someone whom Vero thought couldn't be much older than himself.

Vero noticed how Ada shot an admiring glance at X during his introduction.

"Stop drooling," Kane said quietly, nudging Ada in her side and giving a slight nod toward X.

Ada flashed him an angry glance, then caught Vero looking at her and turned away—but not before Vero saw her blush.

"This is Vero. He comes to us from suburban America," Uriel told the group. "And obviously he's going to need some flying lessons."

Vero hung his head in embarrassment.

"I'll help him fly," X said as he stood up. "Kane can help too." X reached his hand down and pulled Kane to his feet.

For some reason Kane was less intimidating to Vero, probably because he was about the same height. But where Vero's body hadn't filled out yet, Kane exuded strength.

"Thank you," Uriel said.

"Should we go with them?" Ada asked Uriel.

"No, you and Pax have prayers to answer."

"Come on, let's get you airborne," X said to Vero. "We can start with that small mountain."

Vero followed X's gaze to the mountain looming behind them. He felt his heart skip a beat. There was nothing small about it.

12

❖

THE PRAYER
GRID

Vero swallowed hard as he stood at the base of the mountain. It was a long way to the top. Kane and X began to climb. Vero, determined to keep up with them, followed.

"Is your name really X?" Vero asked, stepping over a large rock.

"It's Xavier. X for short."

"Where do you guys come from?"

"Large city, Europe," X answered.

"Island in the Indian Ocean," Kane said.

"So how come I can understand you? I mean, don't we speak different languages?"

"We do when we're on earth," X said. "But in the Ether we can all understand one another. The more advanced angels can communicate by thought. They don't even have to open their mouths."

"That way, words can never distort," Kane explained.

"They can read my mind?" Vero asked.

"Yeah, but it's no big deal unless you've got something to hide," X told him.

Vero thought about that for a moment and felt a twinge of guilt. Not all of his thoughts were good. He often wished Clover's friend Vicki, who constantly teased him for being so skinny, would wake up one morning with a face full of pimples. He also hoped some bigger guys would beat up Danny so he'd know what it felt like to be bullied. And he wished Clover, his own sister, could feel the meanness she regularly inflicted upon him.

"Of all of us, Pax is the only one who can read minds," X said. "But even he can do it only sometimes."

"As we advance more toward our spiritual selves, we'll get better at it," Kane added.

X stopped climbing and turned to Vero. "Try it again."

Vero was so caught up in his thoughts that he hadn't realized they'd reached the top. It was just like when he'd climbed nine stories when the maltures were chasing him, and he'd hardly broken a sweat. It wasn't until Vero looked over the edge that he began sweating.

"It's pretty far down. I really don't feel like falling again."

"You have to believe you can do it," Kane told Vero. "That's the secret to flying."

"It's a matter of trust," X chimed in. "When a mother bird throws her baby bird out of the nest for the first time, it has no idea how to fly. It's never done it before, but it trusts its instincts."

"But a baby bird has wings! Birds are supposed to fly!" Vero shot back.

"Well, so are you," Kane said.

Vero's mind flashed to when he was younger. He saw himself standing on the pitch of his roof, totally fearless. Back then he'd wanted so badly to fly. But now eight years later, having been in a human body and suppressing the urge to fly for so long, he'd forgotten his true nature.

"We'll catch you if you fall," X said.

Vero remained hesitant. It wasn't that he was afraid of flying; he was scared he wouldn't be able to do it. What if he couldn't? What if he failed completely? Would they make fun of him?

"Sometime today ... " Kane said.

But Vero didn't move.

"Maybe that mother bird is on to something ..." X said.

In one swift motion, Kane and X pushed Vero off the cliff. Vero fell into the sky, screaming, while Kane and X laughed and waved. Vero became angry. Really angry. He was sick and tired of people shoving him off buildings, down elevator shafts, and now off a cliff! He did *not* want to face-plant into the soil again.

As the ground quickly approached, Vero's anger turned into resolve. His thoughts raced. *I can do this. I CAN do this!* And suddenly, he knew he could. Vero's wings shot out of his back and took his body gracefully upward.

"Ride the wind!" Kane yelled to him.

Vero felt utterly lighthearted and invigorated. And for his trust, he was rewarded with panoramic views of the glorious world below. He saw crystal clear lakes hugged by fertile mountains. Fields of golden wheat swayed in the breeze. Herds of animals roamed over the open hills. The scene before him was far more beautiful than anything Vero had ever seen on earth.

Vero turned his head and saw X and Kane flying on either side of him.

"Sorry about the push, but you needed it," Kane said.

Vero recalled his fear when he'd learned to ride his bike without training wheels. Vero made his father promise to hold on to the back of the bike seat until Vero said he could let go. After two hours of clutching the bike, his father became frustrated and let go. Vero pedaled another ten minutes on his own before he realized his father was sitting on the front porch drinking a cool glass of iced tea. He hadn't even been mad at his father for breaking his promise.

Vero's anger at Kane and X was gone. "Ha!" Vero cried.

"Ya-hooo!" X hollered, and the three of them soared together.

Vero trailed them but quickly became distracted by the sound of rushing water. He looked down and saw not one, but three majestic waterfalls flowing into one another.

The three waterfalls were equidistant from each other and formed a perfect triangle. The water from each fell into a collective tranquil pool below. Vero lagged behind Kane and X; he felt drawn to the falls. He longed to have the water wash over him, and not just because he wanted to get the sticky peach juice out of his hair. No, he wanted to drink the water and let it cleanse his entire body.

Vero flew faster toward the falls. He was no longer shaky with the new wings. He grew excited with anticipation. The closer he got to the water, the more he felt as if his heart would leap out of his chest. It was almost within his grasp when he slammed up against what felt like an invisible glass barrier.

He suddenly remembered Tack's joke about the bug and the windshield. The impact caused him to lose his ability to fly, and he hurtled toward the ground. Kane and X flew to his side and caught him in midair. Vero regained control of himself, and Kane and X released him back to the wind.

"I told you to follow us," Kane said.

"Well, you could have warned me. What *was* that? Some kind of force field?" Vero asked.

"I guess," X said. "Not just anyone is allowed to drink those waters. You have to be invited."

Vero rubbed his head. It hurt. And exercising his wings depleted a great deal of his energy. He was wiped out.

"Can we take a break?" Vero asked.

"Down there—in the clearing!" Kane shouted.

X and Kane landed gracefully in a wide-open spot ringed by trees, which overlooked the valley below. Vero tried to imitate their landing technique, but he hit the ground with a loud thud.

"You have to flap hard and get your feet in front of you before you land," X said.

"Once again, thanks for the timely heads-up." Vero rolled back to a sitting position. He felt a slight push between his shoulder blades, and then his wings vanished.

"Why do they disappear?" Vero asked.

"Because we're not flying. But they'll come back when you need them," Kane said. "You'll also build up stamina for flying. The first couple of times really drain you."

"How long have you guys been coming to the Ether?" Vero asked.

"We started together. This is our fourth time," X answered.

"Do your earth families know you're guardian angels?"

Both men shook their heads no.

"Sometimes it cracks me up ... like the other day, my little sister's kite got stuck in a tree. I climbed the tree to get the kite, but my dad's practically having a heart attack because he thinks I'm gonna fall out of the tree and kill myself." Kane laughed. "He'd definitely have a heart attack if he could see me flying."

"I feel bad for my mother," X said. "Back on earth, I'm in a wheelchair. But Mom takes really good care of me. She has to feed me when my arms spasm, and I can't even hold a fork. Lots of times I hear her crying in her bedroom. It breaks my heart that she can't follow me here to the Ether and see me whole and know that I'm all right."

Vero thought of his own mother. It would be such a relief to tell her he was an angel, just so she wouldn't worry anymore.

"Then why do they do it this way?" Vero asked. "Why do we grow up with human families who have no idea who we really are? Isn't that sort of mean?"

"Our mission is to protect and guard humans, so we need to live among them. We need to understand their world," Kane said. "At least that's what Uriel says."

"But we live among humans for only a short time — until we finish angel training," X added.

"When is that?" Vero asked.

"I guess when we know everything we're supposed to know."

"Angels know everything, so won't that take forever?" Vero asked.

"First of all, only God knows everything," X said. "There's a ton of stuff that even the archangels don't know.

But once we have all the knowledge we're supposed to get, we leave our earthly lives for good."

"How long does that take?" Vero asked, picturing his own family.

"It's different for everyone, but most leave before they turn eighteen in earth years," X explained.

"What do you mean? I won't be with my family ever again after that?" Vero asked.

Kane and X exchanged glances.

"Yeah," Kane said. "They'll believe you died. Right now we can go back and forth between the two realms, and no one knows. But when you become a full-fledged angel, your body will stay on earth. They'll think you're dead and have a funeral for you. The whole thing."

Vero's head sunk to his chest. The thought of his parents having to bury him made him feel sick. He could visualize his mother sitting in the front pew of their church, weeping inconsolably while his father stoically held her. Even Clover would mourn his passing. Deep down, he knew his sister still loved him.

"But that's not fair," Vero protested.

"That's the way it is," Kane said.

"But Vero," X began, his voice sympathetic, "the hope is that one day, many years from now, you will all be together again."

Vero understood what X was telling him, but it still bothered him to know that his family would suffer.

Kane stood up. "Come on, we have to go," he said.

Vero and X stood up as well. Kane's wings opened and then X's. Vero touched his back. He couldn't feel any wings.

"My wings?" he questioned, pointing to his back.

"You might need to take a running start until you get it down," X said.

Vero backed up a ways and then sprinted toward the edge of the bluff. He boldly leaped off and instantly became airborne. Soon he was streaking like a beam of light across the Ether.

❖

Vero, Kane, and X flew into an area that resembled an ancient Roman coliseum, but rather than being made of stone, this structure was made out of crystals. The walls were transparent, and thousands of angels of every age sat in the bleachers. The angels were looking down at what would be the arena's field, only it wasn't a green playing field. It was a massive grid full of lights in every possible color — brilliant, vivid colors that reminded him of the Lite-Brite he and Clover used to play with.

Suddenly a burst of light shot up from the grid, and an angel caught it and flew off with it. This happened again and again, continuously, as angels caught bullets of light and then flew away.

Vero hovered close to Kane and X. "What is this?" he asked.

"A prayer grid," Kane said, leading them to three empty seats. "Uriel wanted us to show it to you."

They flew to the seats and sat down. This time, Vero's landing was adequate, if not graceful. Vero watched with fascination as the bright beams shot up like geysers into the waiting hands of the receivers.

"What are they doing?" Vero asked.

"Catching prayers," an older voice said.

Vero turned and saw an angel smiling at him with the same violet eyes as Uriel's. His long hair was pulled back in a ponytail, and his round face was friendly. Vero felt immediately at ease with him.

"Welcome back, Vero," the angel said. "It's been awhile. I'm Raphael."

Vero stuck out his hand to shake Raphael's.

"Oh, I don't do that," he laughed.

Raphael then grabbed Vero and hugged him, totally catching him off guard. He squeezed Vero so tight that Vero was momentarily winded. Raphael squashed Vero a few more times and then mercifully let him go with a playful slap on the back. But the pat was hard enough that it made Vero cough.

"You're looking good, Vero. Earth has been kind to you."

"You're the archangel Raphael?" Vero choked out.

"I don't like to be so formal. I'm just Raphael. We all got such a big kick out of your book report ... everyone except Uriel, of course. You nailed him good!"

Vero couldn't help laughing; Raphael was easy to like.

Suddenly, a bright ray of light sped toward Vero, and without thinking, Vero reached up and grabbed it.

Astonished, Vero looked at the beam that was now illuminating his palm. He had no idea how he'd caught it. It was as if his hand had a mind of its own.

"Let's go." Raphael stood, suddenly serious, and grabbed Vero's arm. They flew off together, and in a flash they were sitting on a bench on a busy city sidewalk. Vero watched yellow cabs zip past them as they tried to speed through red lights. Impatient drivers laid on their horns. People crisscrossed sidewalks and streets in haste. Storefronts with elaborate window displays tempted pedestrians. Bike messengers weaved in and out of traffic. Horses pulled tourists in carriages.

"Are we in New York?" Vero asked.

Raphael pointed to a crowd of people walking past.

"They're in New York. You're not," Raphael said.

Vero was confused. How could he be sitting on a bench in the middle of the city, yet not be there?

A rather plump woman pulling a small cart filled with groceries approached the bench. She was breathing heavily when she parked her cart and sat down on Vero.

"Hey! I'm sitting here!"

Raphael chuckled. "Let me help you out."

Raphael kicked the woman's shopping cart so it rolled a few feet away from her. She leaned forward to retrieve it.

"Quick! Now!" Raphael shouted.

Vero saw his chance and jumped up and away from the woman before she could sit on him again. He looked back at the woman, studying her.

"She can't see us, can she?"

"Not at all."

"I knew she sat on me, but I didn't feel a thing," Vero said. "We're still in the Ether, aren't we?"

"Yes. And if you want proof, just close your eyes."

Vero hesitated.

"Come on, shut them tight," Raphael commanded.

Vero closed his eyes.

"Concentrate hard. Pray to see beyond the limited scope of human eyes."

Vero clamped his eyes even tighter. He tried to block out

the sounds and commotion of the busy city, but it wasn't easy. His mind wandered. He grew frustrated and opened his eyes again. Nothing had changed.

"I can't do it!"

Raphael stood before him, his playful disposition now gone. He bent down in front of Vero to block out any distractions. Vero could see a fervent conviction in Raphael's eyes as he lowered Vero's eyelids with his thumbs.

"The truth is there, and you must open your eyes and heart to it," Raphael said, coaxing him in a calm, yet resolute voice.

Vero concentrated as hard as he could. He cleared his mind of the world around him. One by one, the distractions of the city fell away. He had a single thought, and that was truth. The need to know the truth consumed him.

Raphael removed his thumbs, and Vero opened his eyes. The sight before him knocked him back against the bench. Everywhere he looked in this bustling city, there were angels—thousands of them—radiant noble angels protecting and assisting humans in their everyday endeavors.

Vero watched as an angel caught an elderly man in his arms, saving the man from a nasty spill after he failed to see an uneven sidewalk.

As a group of schoolchildren crossed a busy intersection, massive angels stood with their arms locked shoulder to shoulder, forming a solid line to prevent any cars or buses from breaking through.

Men and women wearing business suits walked into buildings through revolving glass doors, and the angels kept step with them.

As a little boy climbed a tree, an angel followed him on

the branch below, his arms stretched out to catch the boy if he should fall.

A homeless man wearing threadbare clothes lay on the sidewalk napping, and an angel cushioned his head while stroking his hair.

Two deliverymen unloaded their rig, and angels stood in the back of the truck, holding up several crates to keep them from collapsing.

A woman opened her purse to pull out a tissue, and an angel quickly spread his sheltering wings around her, preventing a devious-looking man from seeing the loose dollar bills in her purse.

Angels attended to every single person no matter how mundane the task. And the humans went about their business, never suspecting a thing.

But it wasn't only people that the angels protected. Godzilla-sized angels, taller than skyscrapers, stood around soaring buildings and kept guard at every corner. Other angels stood knee-deep in a river supporting a bridge span.

Vero was overcome with emotion. The immense outpouring of love these angels held for the humans caused tears to well up in his eyes.

Raphael placed an arm around Vero's shoulders as a mother pushed a stroller past them. Her baby girl, only six months old, sat smiling at the brightly colored mobile hanging above her. As the mother stopped in front of Vero, the baby reached out her arms and tried to grab him. At first Vero thought it was just a random act. But when the baby made eye contact with him and held his gaze, he suddenly felt exposed.

He turned to Raphael and said, "I thought people couldn't see us."

"That's true for most. But babies need to be gently eased into this world. Angels offer comfort during their transition. By the time she's a year old, she'll no longer be able to see you."

In her excitement, the baby giggled and stretched her arms toward Vero. It was the most innocent of gestures, and Vero was powerless to resist. He smiled and held out his hand, and the little girl took it in hers.

To the mother it looked as though her baby was grabbing for the mobile.

13

❖

A CAB IN RUSH HOUR

Vero walked with Raphael down the busy city street, dodging throngs of people and their angels, trying to make sense of it all. Some angels acknowledged them, but most stayed focused on the humans entrusted to their care. Vero's mind flashed back to the snake incident in his science class.

"There's no such thing as hysterical strength, is there?" Vero asked.

"Nope. It's us," Raphael told him. "Now we'd better see what prayer you caught."

Vero abruptly stopped walking. He was completely caught off guard.

"I forgot about it," he said, feeling ashamed. Vero looked down at his hand. The ray of light was gone. "I must have dropped it."

Raphael laughed. "Do you think a prayer is like water that drips through your fingers?"

Vero didn't know what to think.

"Prayers are precious to God," Raphael explained. "None are ever lost."

Raphael took Vero's hand in his and turned it palm up. Vero's eyes went wide when a hologram of a woman appeared in his hand. She looked to be about thirty-five years old and wore a business suit. She had an anxious look on her face as she desperately waved her hand in the air. Vero felt her anxiety.

"She's in trouble," Vero said.

"Get closer," Raphael said softly.

Vero leaned into the image of the woman. He put his ear close to her mouth, and he heard her desperate plea.

"Please, Lord, let me get a cab," the woman said.

Vero jumped back upon hearing her request.

"A cab! A crummy cab is her prayer request?"

"By the time a prayer shoots up from the prayer grid, God has already decided to grant it," Raphael told Vero firmly. "It's your job to carry it out without question."

Raphael gave Vero an intimidating look that left no room for discussion.

Vero knew he had no choice. Somehow he had to flag down a taxi for the woman. It didn't seem like some Herculean task except for the fact that out of the thousands of cab drivers in New York, not a single one could see or hear him. Vero balled his hand into a fist, and the hologram of the woman vanished.

"How can I help her? Even if I stand right in front of a cab and scream at the top of my lungs, it'll just drive right through me. And besides, aren't we too late anyway? She must have asked for that cab awhile ago."

"We're not bound by time," Raphael said. "Look. There she is."

Raphael nodded his head toward a woman standing on the edge of the sidewalk.

She was waving her arms at passing cabs. Seconds ago, Vero held her in his hand, and now she was standing right before his eyes. It was amazing and freaky at the same time.

"The key is to make it happen so it appears seamless to humans—like nothing out of the ordinary. Go on now. Get her that cab."

Vero hesitated. Raphael smiled and gave him a gentle push toward the woman.

Vero approached tentatively, trying to buy some time while he figured out what to do. Unfortunately, nothing came to mind, so Vero wildly waved his arms like a mad man at every passing cab. Raphael chuckled and shook his head. As Vero jumped around, he failed to look behind him and bumped into someone, knocking him to the pavement.

"Hey! You knocked off my glasses!"

Vero turned and saw a familiar young angel sitting on the sidewalk behind him.

"Pax?"

"You're going to make me fail my mission," Pax said, as he put on his glasses.

Pax made a comical sight with his oversized glasses and his extra-large ears, but then Vero remembered Ada's comment to Pax about Vero: *He doesn't seem so special.* Was Vero somehow different from the others? More importantly, was he a disappointment?

"You need to move," Pax said.

Vero quickly stepped out of the way.

"Sorry," Vero said. "What are you doing anyway?"

"I need to keep this parking space open for the right person." Pax got up and stood between two parked vehicles on the side of the street. In font of Pax was a big SUV, and behind him was a delivery van. There was about four feet of space between the back of the SUV and the front of the van. Vero noticed that although those two vehicles were parked so close to each other, there was also three or four yards of clearance in front of the SUV and behind the van. Had those drivers parked better, there would be plenty of room for a car to fit between them.

Vero looked at the spot Pax had called a parking space. Even a motorcycle couldn't fit there!

"That's not happening," Vero informed him.

A sporty little red convertible slowed down as its driver eyeballed the space. Pax stood his ground in the spot, stared at the driver, and whispered, "Go away. It's too small. There's nothing here for you." The driver then quickly sped up, realizing she'd never squeeze her car into that tiny spot.

"See?" Vero announced. "I think you need to find a new space."

A gray nondescript four-door sedan crossed through the intersection and was headed their way. Pax sprang into action when he saw the car.

"Here he comes!" he shouted.

Vero watched as the sedan slowed down while the driver scanned the area, hopeful for a parking space. Vero felt bad for Pax because he was certain he was failing his mission.

He wondered what happened when guardian angels failed their tasks?

But to his astonishment, Vero watched as the scrawny angel placed his hands on the SUV's rear bumper and pushed it ahead four feet. He then turned and pushed on the van's front bumper with his super strength, moving it back far enough to create a parking space for the sedan. The van and SUV had rolled only a few feet, so the humans passing by on the sidewalk never detected a thing. They were too wrapped up in their own lives to notice the supernatural goings-on.

The gray car backed into the space. And then the driver got out, threw a few coins into the meter, and looked at his watch. "Thank God," he said and hurried off.

"How did you do that?" Vero asked.

Pax held his head high, proud of his accomplishment, "It's nothing you can't do."

"How old are you?" Vero asked.

"Ten."

Pax saw the look of disbelief on Vero's face.

"Yes, I'm small for my age," Pax said.

"I didn't say anything," Vero said.

"But you were going to."

Vero heard his prayer assignment try to hail another cab. "Can you teach me how to do that?" Vero asked desperately. "Please?"

Pax glanced over at Raphael, who was standing on the curb observing them.

Raphael nodded.

"Okay. Let's find a cab," Pax said.

Impressed by their nonverbal exchange, Vero asked, "Can you read my thoughts too?"

"Only sometimes," Pax said. "The first thing we need to do is find an empty cab."

Then Pax stepped off the curb and walked directly into oncoming traffic. Vero was impressed with Pax's confidence. Vero hesitated, afraid to leave the safety of the sidewalk.

Pax yelled to him, "Come on! They can't run you over! Remember, you're still in the Ether!"

The Ether was a difficult concept for Vero to embrace, and especially as an eighteen-wheeler headed straight for him. Pax wasted no time and stuck his head right up next to the windows of cabs and peered inside. He quickly moved from cab to cab. Vero waited for a taxi to stop at a light and then looked into the backseat for passengers. But they all seemed to be filled — businessmen and women on their way home, a woman who was already late to catch a plane at the airport, a man with two small children who were fighting over a piece of gum.

Vero didn't realize the light had changed from red to green. Panic gripped him when the traffic accelerated, and the next thing he knew he was being run through by trucks, cars, vans, and even bikes. So many vehicles struck him, he lost count. But not a single one of them hurt him. All Vero felt was a whooshing of wind through his body.

"I got one!" Pax yelled.

Vero saw Pax waving to him a block south of where he stood. Pax jumped into the backseat of a cab and motioned for Vero to follow. Vero ran over, but he was too slow. The cab pulled up to the curb to pick up a man wearing a business suit and holding a leather briefcase.

"Don't let him in!" Pax shouted to Vero. "You've got to stop him!"

Pax quickly locked the backseat door while the businessman tried to open it. The man tapped the window and motioned for the taxi driver to unlock the door. The driver released the unlock button, but Pax kept his index finger on the lock. The businessman tugged at the door again, but it still wouldn't open.

"The thing must be stuck," the driver said. Then he unfastened his seat belt and stepped out of the cab to examine the lock. Pax panicked.

"Hurry up! Get rid of him!" he said to Vero.

"How? I can't do anything!" Vero said. "Cars just drive right through me!"

"When we're answering prayers, we get incredible strength and can manipulate matter," Pax said. "You have the ability!"

As the driver jimmied the lock, Pax continued to hold the button down, completely frustrating the driver. Vero hesitantly pressed his index finger on the metal clasp of the man's briefcase, but it wouldn't unfasten. His finger went right through it.

"Don't be so wimpy!" Pax said. "If you *will* it, it *will* happen!"

Meanwhile, the businessman gave up and opened the front passenger door. "I'll just sit up here," he said to the driver.

"You're gonna lose the cab!" Pax yelled at Vero.

Realizing it was now or never, Vero pressed down hard on the briefcase latch. Instantly, the lid sprang open, and the man's papers flew out and were quickly snatched by the wind.

"I did it!" Vero yelled triumphantly.

The businessman ran off, chasing his papers.

"That was harsh ruining his papers," Pax said to Vero through the open cab window.

"It was all I could think of," Vero said. "You told me to hurry up."

The driver got behind the wheel, and the cab started to take off, leaving Vero standing on the curb.

"Hey! Get in here!" Pax shouted.

Vero sprinted after the taxicab.

Pax stuck his head out the window, cheering him on. "Come on! You're an angel! We move faster than New York City cabs!"

Raphael stood on the curb watching as Vero chased after the yellow cab. When a man jaywalked across the street, the cab slowed for a moment and Vero caught up to it.

"Help me get in!" he called to Pax.

Vero dove headfirst through the open backseat window. But before he could get all the way inside, the cab sped up again, so now his legs were sticking out in traffic. The cab changed lanes. A cement truck traveling in the opposite direction clipped Vero's right foot. Finally, Pax pulled Vero into the cab.

"Thanks."

"Your petitioner is up ahead," Pax said. "But there are three other people flagging down cabs, so we need to be sure the driver picks her."

"How do we do that?"

"Plant suggestions in his mind. You're allowed to influence him, but you can't direct him."

Vero was puzzled. What did that mean — influence but not direct?

"Whisper in his ear, tell him to notice that lady in the brown suit. But you can't go any further than that."

Vero looked at the man's ear. He was an older man with hair sprouting from his earlobes. The thought of whispering into his ear wasn't too appealing.

"Isn't there some other way?" he asked Pax.

"Not that I can think of."

Seeing no other option, Vero resigned himself to the task. He leaned forward. There wasn't a divider separating the front seat from the backseat, so Vero put his mouth close to the man's ear. It was worse than he'd expected. Not only had stray hairs sprouted, but also yellow crusty wax lined the outside of the man's ear canal. Vero nearly gagged, but he managed to get out the words, "Look at the lady in the brown suit." He quickly sat back.

"There. Done," he said to Pax.

Vero sat tall in the seat feeling proud of himself. Mission accomplished. But then, to his dismay, a huge moving van pulled up in the right lane and tried to pass the cab.

"Oh no!"

Vero knew the moving van would block the cab driver's view of the woman, and he became alarmed. Suddenly, he felt a tingle run through his body, giving him confidence. Was this the extra strength Pax spoke about? Vero impulsively reached over the front seat and yanked the steering wheel to make a hard right.

"You're not allowed to do that!" Pax yelled.

The cab swerved in front of the moving van. The van slammed on its brakes. Pax gripped the seat in front of him, bracing for an accident. Vero glanced behind him and saw Raphael pulling back on the rear bumper of the moving van. The van safely skidded to a stop. Pax and Vero caught their breath.

The driver of the moving van shouted a fair amount of swear words at the cab driver who looked totally bewildered. He had no idea what possessed him to cut in front of the moving van.

Raphael shot Vero a disappointed look. Vero felt humiliated. As the moving van drove off, the cab driver glanced over at the sidewalk and saw the woman in the brown suit standing on the curb under some construction scaffolding. The woman dashed over to the taxi and climbed in the back.

"Fifty-fourth and Lex, please," she told the driver breathlessly.

Vero and Pax climbed out the open window, and the cab drove on down the avenue.

"I hope wherever she's going it was worth the effort," Vero said to Pax as they watched the cab blend into the sea of yellow taxis. "It amazes me that God would bother with cab rides and parking spaces."

❖

"You're famous!" Kane shouted at Vero as he walked across the green field of the Ether.

Vero saw Kane and the other young angels walking toward him.

"No one screws up that badly on their first prayer attempt. To save one person, you almost took out two!" Kane laughed.

Vero blushed. He knew he'd messed up big time. But he was also angry about having been thrown into the situation without any guidance. He'd only just learned a few weeks ago that he was a guardian angel. No one had explained any of the rules to him. How could he be expected to know what to do? Vero felt ripped off.

When he thought he was just a regular kid, his main responsibility was to keep his room clean. Now he was expected to save lives! It was incomprehensible! The enormity of it weighed heavily upon him.

"He's only messing with you," X said to Vero.

"No, he's right. I don't know what I'm doing. I just wish someone would explain everything to me."

"It's on a need-to-know basis here. They give out knowledge one tiny morsel at a time."

"Why?"

"Because they have to make sure you're ready for it. If you're not able to understand it, lies and deceptions can seep in. It goes all the way back to the garden of Eden," X said. "Adam and Eve wanted to know everything all at once, so they ate from the forbidden tree of knowledge. Look what happened to them."

"Yeah, but there are still some things I need to know now, like how do I defend myself if the maltures attack again?"

Every head turned in Vero's direction.

"What?" he asked.

"You were attacked on earth?" X asked.

"But we're supposed to be protected from the maltures when we're there," Pax added, sounding a bit fearful.

"Uriel had to defend me or else they would have gotten me," Vero said.

"What did they look like?" Ada asked in an awed whisper.

"They were covered with fur and scales. They had rows

of sharp yellow fangs. And each one had a single eye that went all the way through the head."

Ada gasped.

"But the scariest thing was . . . you could feel hatred and rage coming out of them. Like that hated and rage made up their very essence."

Everyone was silent for a moment.

"Has anyone else been attacked by them?" Vero asked the group.

"None of us," X said.

It was hard to imagine X in a wheelchair on earth. With his striking dark features and his strong build, Vero couldn't imagine him looking frail. Yet at that moment when X talked about the maltures, Vero definitely saw fear in his eyes.

14

❖

THE TRACK
STAR

Vero heard beautiful music as he and Uriel walked through a meadow of waist-high wildflowers. Their petals swayed with the soothing rhythm. As the melody grew louder, soon the flowers' stalks also followed the beat. They were dancing! But the sight of dancing flowers brought him no enjoyment.

Sensing Vero's thoughts, Uriel said, "Have faith, Vero. The answers will come in time."

"Why haven't the others ever seen a malture?" Vero asked.

Uriel stopped walking, turned and placed both hands on Vero's shoulders, and looking Vero squarely in the eyes, said, "Do not be afraid, Vero. You are far greater and stronger than you know."

"But they attacked me!"

Uriel considered. He stared hard into Vero's eyes, making

sure he had his total attention. "The opposite of faith is not doubt. The opposite of faith is fear."

Vero contemplated Uriel's words as they resumed walking.

"When I first came to the Ether, I told you I was home. How did I know that?" Vero asked. "Have I been here before?"

"All living things spend time in the Ether before it's their earth time."

"So why didn't I remember the Ether when I was on earth?" Vero asked.

"You do as a baby, but gradually the memory fades."

"But why?" Vero asked.

"Because you must rediscover it, and return of your own free will. The knowledge of the goodness of the Ether exists in every living thing."

"But the Ether isn't heaven?"

"It's the middle ground between heaven and the lake of fire," Uriel said.

"Lake of fire?"

"Where darkness reigns."

"But everything I've seen in the Ether is wonderful," Vero said.

"You've seen but only a small part of the Ether."

Vero looked to Uriel. "What do you mean?"

"Lucifer's demons and maltures are also here in the Ether, and they would love nothing more than to dig their claws into a young angel like yourself."

Vero felt his stomach churn. "Am I special? I heard the other angels talking."

"We are all special to God," Uriel said sharply, and Vero

knew not to probe any further. "It's time for you to go back. You've learned enough for your second training."

"But wait! I still have tons of questions!"

"You feel like you haven't learned enough, but I disagree." Uriel motioned with his hand for Vero to explain what he's learned.

"I learned to fly better. I met some of the other angels. I now know what a prayer grid is—"

"I could have told you all of that," Uriel interrupted. "But what did you learn about *yourself*?"

Vero paused and looked down for a moment, then said, "I learned there's so much about myself that I don't know . . . but I want to."

Uriel slowly nodded, "Well said. And by the way, your petitioner got the job."

Vero gave him a curious look.

"The prayer you answered. The cab driver got her to the interview in time."

"Really?"

Uriel nodded.

"Uriel, one last thing . . . when I was flying past the three waterfalls, why couldn't I get close to them? Some sort of invisible force stopped me."

"That, Vero, is for another day."

Uriel smiled and then wrapped his wings around himself and disappeared.

Vero looked down at the dancing flowers. They finally brought a smile to his face.

"Mom would love to see this," he said to no one, allowing the soft petals to caress his fingers.

His mom adored flowers. It was always so easy to buy

presents for her birthday or Mother's Day. Flowers of every kind delighted her. He wished that someday his mother could stand where he now stood and dance with the wildflowers.

Vero realized he missed his mother. The last time he'd seen her, she was dropping off Tack and him at the movie theater.

The next thing Vero knew, an elbow jabbed him in the ribs causing him to stumble backward into a closed elevator door.

Vero opened his eyes in time to see a group of preteen girls headed his way.

"Dude, is my hair sticking up?" Tack was unsuccessfully attempting to flatten his protruding tuft of strawberry-blond hair.

Vero grabbed the wall to support himself. It took a few moments to regain his balance. He didn't remember the transition back to earth being so jarring.

"What's wrong with you?" Tack asked.

"Just relax!" Vero hissed.

How could Tack be so concerned about something as trivial as his hair with all that was going on around him? But then Vero reminded himself that for Tack, nothing had changed. He hadn't just been shown a completely new vision of the universe. At the moment, the most important thing in the world for Tack was that group of girls who were walking toward them.

"Since when does Davina hang out with Hollow Legs and Monkey Arms?" Tack whispered to Vero, but not nearly as quietly as he'd intended.

"Hey, Vero. Hey, Tack," Davina said.

"We heard what you called us, Tack," Sasha Wyburn said.

Sasha had earned her nickname because she could eat more than anyone else in the school—even Tack—yet she remained thin as a rail. So the other kids assumed the food must be stored in her long legs.

"Yeah, Tack," Amanda Farkas chimed in. "And I *don't* have monkey arms."

Amanda got her nickname because of her gangly arms. She was the go-to girl whenever a teacher needed a light bulb changed or something retrieved off a high shelf.

Amanda gave Vero a once-over as he clung to the wall, still trying to adjust, "What's wrong? You look like you're going to be sick."

Sasha eyed Vero, "Yeah, he does. It's probably because he just got a look at Tack's awful hair."

Tack shot Vero a silent plea for help, but Vero was too disoriented to respond.

"Let's go," Amanda said to Sasha, and they walked away.

Davina lagged behind.

"Vero, you okay?" She seemed genuinely concerned.

"Yeah, probably put too much butter on the popcorn."

"What did you think of the movie?"

Her question caught Vero off guard. He'd totally forgotten about the movie, so he said the first thing that came to mind.

"It was great. I'd see it again."

"Really? I saw that movie last weekend, and there's no way I could ever sit through it again. I thought it was so impossible," Davina said. "I couldn't wait for it to end."

Vero felt like an idiot. *Why'd I say that?* He could feel the heat building in his face.

Then Danny appeared around the corner and locked eyes with Vero.

Perfect, Vero thought. *Would Danny try to start something here? In front of Davina?*

Davina smiled at Danny and turned to leave with him.

Vero felt a twist in his gut far worse than anything Danny could ever dish out. Davina had come to the movies *with Danny*? Vero found himself wishing Danny *would* try to insult him, trip him, put him in a headlock, even punch him in the face. Anything would have been easier to take than seeing Davina smile at Danny that way.

"Danny's brother is waiting for us," Davina said to Vero. "See you."

As they walked off, Danny glanced back at Vero with a smirk.

"She's too good for him," Tack said. "Get this ... Nate said he saw Danny out at that new house they're building on Fairburn. He was shattering the windows with a slingshot."

"Serious?"

"So don't worry. He's gonna wind up in juvie hall. Then you'll get your chance with Davina."

Vero watched Danny and Davina turn the corner with a concerned look on his face.

Clover waved her hand up and down in front of Vero's face, trying to get his attention during dinner. Vero finally saw her hand and snapped out of his thoughts.

"What?" he said.

"Pass the salt."

As Vero handed the saltshaker to his sister, Clover stared at him from across the kitchen table. She knew something was different about him. Ever since she was little, Clover had shared a connection with Vero. It was so strong that she'd been convinced they were twins. No matter how many times her mom and dad explained that Vero was adopted and that she was a year older, Clover still insisted. And as they'd gotten older, Clover felt their connection had only grown stronger. So Clover knew something was happening to her brother.

Besides the hurdle jumping and the bus incident, something was different ... something life changing.

She desperately wanted to know what was happening, but she was afraid to ask.

Because whatever it was also affected her.

Clover had secrets too — secrets that kept her awake at night. Even though Vero hadn't done anything she could name, she secretly blamed her brother for what she was going through. And she punished him for it — unfairly, she knew. But she blamed him anyway.

"You're quiet tonight," Nora said to Vero as she placed a basket of dinner rolls on the table. "You feel all right?"

"It's his heart," Clover said. "It's broken because Davina Acker went to the movies with Danny Konrad."

"I don't care about them!" Vero shot back.

"Really? Tack said you were practically crying the whole way home," Clover said with a smile.

"Who's Danny Konrad?" Dennis asked with a mouth full of mashed potatoes.

"He's a mean jerk," Vero said.

"Watch your mouth," Dennis scolded him.

"Danny used to be in Clover's class. But a few years ago, he was held back. Now he's in Vero's class," Nora said. She passed the green beans to Dennis. "You might remember the Konrads. We met them at Clover's kindergarten roundup. The teacher said Danny wasn't ready for kindergarten, but his mother and father insisted the school accept him. I remember wondering what the big deal was about waiting another year, and I really felt like they just wanted him out of the house. They're divorced now."

"I think Danny and Davina make a cute couple," Clover said. She knew she was hurting Vero's feelings. Why did she feel the desire to goad him?

Vero stood up abruptly, knocking his chair to the floor. "What's your problem?" he shouted in Clover's face. "What did I ever do to you?"

Clover felt a twinge of guilt. She wanted to apologize, but then she thought of Vero's snow angel and the otherworldly raven with its fiery eyes and rat's tail, and she felt scared. And she was angry about feeling scared. She narrowed her eyes and glared at Vero.

"Vero!" Dennis said sharply. "Pick up your chair and sit down."

Vero picked up the chair, but he didn't sit down. "I'm done," he said. He bunched up his napkin and threw it at Clover before leaving the room. "You'll miss me when I'm gone!" he shouted.

Clover noticed her mom watching Vero as he walked away. *Was she scared too?*

❖

After dinner, Vero retreated to his bedroom and stared at the ceiling, wishing it would cave in and crush him. Or maybe

Mr. Atwood would miss his driveway and plow his SUV through Vero's bedroom window.

Davina and Danny. Davina with Danny. The more Vero thought about it, the less he understood.

Vero longed to go back to the Ether. He desperately wanted to get away from Clover and the idea of Davina being with Danny. But no catastrophe befell him. It was a quiet night, broken only by the sounds of his parents' muffled conversations about Vero.

Suddenly his bedroom door flew open, and Clover walked in.

Vero shot up. "What are you doing here?" he asked. "I'm surprised you even remember where my room is."

Clover ignored his comment and asked, "What did you mean by 'when I'm gone'?"

Vero wanted so badly to tell her the truth, to tell her their time together would be coming to an end soon, maybe even before he got his driver's license. He didn't want to spend his remaining time on earth fighting with Clover.

But he couldn't tell her. It was the rule. If he tried, Uriel would send a fire truck or set off a smoke alarm — just like he did in Dr. Weiss's office. So Vero shrugged and said, "Nothing. I didn't mean anything by it."

Clover studied him. She knew he was lying, but they no longer told each other their secrets. It had become too dangerous. Clover feared her secrets would land her on the shrink's couch next to Vero. Silence was the one thing they both shared.

"Okay, fine," Clover said, and she turned to leave.

"Clover, wait!"

She spun around, keeping her hand on the doorknob.

Now that she was looking at him, now that he had her attention, Vero wasn't sure what to say.

"Um ... " *Where to start?*

"What?" Clover demanded.

"Do you remember when I was four and I fell off the roof and twisted my ankle?"

Vero could tell his question disturbed her. He saw her hands start to shake. But now that he'd started, he couldn't stop. "Do you remember the man ... the man in the tree?"

His eyes begged for an answer, for something, anything. All she had to do was give him a nod, whisper yes. Clover locked eyes with her brother, staring him down. It was a silent showdown, and it was her move.

"No," she said. "I don't know what you're talking about." Then she walked out of the room and slammed the door behind her.

Silence had never sounded so loud to Vero.

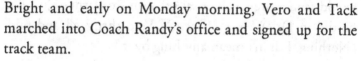

Bright and early on Monday morning, Vero and Tack marched into Coach Randy's office and signed up for the track team.

"You're going to put this school on the map," Coach said. "We've lost every single track meet since I've been here, but now that's about to change. And Tack, I think the shot put is definitely a better choice for you than the hurdles."

"Me too. I'm pretty good at it. I've been practicing in our backyard."

"Keep it up," Coach Randy said.

"I can't anymore."

Vero and the Coach looked at Tack.

"I accidentally threw the ball through Mrs. Carlotti's window next door. Broke the glass. And her cat was sunning itself on the windowsill ... "

"Did you kill it?" Vero asked, wide-eyed.

"No, but it beaned him good. Ever since then, the cat keeps head-butting the walls."

"Do everyone a favor and stay away from the javelin toss," Coach said.

❖

Vero's first track meet was against the crosstown rival, Lexington Junior High. The bleachers filled quickly with rowdy students, anxious parents, and the occasional miserable sibling who resented giving up a whole Saturday for a stupid track meet. They watched the oval-shaped field below as athletes stretched on the grass. As Vero and Tack were walking along the track, Coach Randy caught Vero's eye and gave him a double thumbs-up. Vero nodded back.

"And here we are ... our first track meet," Tack said between bites of his chocolate protein bar. "Still glad you changed your mind?"

Vero looked across the track and saw Danny sitting in the middle of the field, stretching.

"I guess we'll find out," Vero said, never taking his eyes off Danny.

"I'm glad I decided to go back to shot put," Tack said. "I figured, why not?" Tack messily shoved the rest of the protein bar into his mouth. After he'd finally swallowed, he said, "Plus, I realized I shouldn't deny my fans any longer."

Normally this remark would have gotten a rise out of Vero, but he was too intent on watching Danny scan the bleachers. *He's probably looking for Davina,* Vero thought, and his insides burned.

When Danny spotted Davina, he gave her a smile and slight wave, but then he continued searching the stands—until he caught Vero staring at him. Danny held Vero's gaze, refusing to turn away. But he didn't look like his normal, malicious self. Did he look disappointed? Nervous? Danny finally looked away first. *You should be nervous,* Vero thought.

"Runners for the boys' 400 meter to your starting positions," the announcer called.

Danny walked to the starting line.

Vero followed.

❖

"Please don't embarrass me," Clover said to her parents as they found their seats in the stands. "It's bad enough I'm giving up my Saturday for this."

"Hush, Clover," Nora said while she adjusted the camera's strap around her neck. "You should be rooting for your brother. This is the first sport he's really gotten into."

"And we are ... " Dennis shouted in Clover's face while waving a large, yellow foam hand, " ... number one!"

The foam finger accidentally grazed the head of a father from the rival school, knocking his sunglasses from his face. Dennis quickly threw the finger into Clover's lap as the man turned around and gave the hairy eyeball.

"Sorry, she's overly excited for her brother," Dennis said.

Clover threw the foam hand back at her father, then slumped down and pulled her hoodie up over her ball cap. "Vero's played soccer and baseball," Clover said. "So what's the big deal now?"

"He never scored a goal in soccer or ever got on base," Dennis said. "But he was always lightning fast. I should have known back then that track-and-field was his calling."

Clover stood up.

"Where are you going?" Dennis asked. "As fun as this is, I'm gonna go sit with my friends."

"Stay here with us. We're Vero's cheering section," Dennis said.

Clover rolled her eyes and sat back down, "Mom, please stop him ... "

But Nora wasn't paying attention to Clover. She watched eagerly as Vero positioned his feet on the starting blocks. She was as excited as her husband was, but for different reasons. After the school bus incident, Nora had been desperate to get some normalcy back into their lives. If Vero played sports, then he'd be just like all the other boys. He'd fit right in. And if he performed well, then maybe people would simply come to know Vero as the track star and forget about the whole bus incident. And then maybe Nora would be able to move beyond it and stop lying awake at night, worrying. Maybe she could convince herself that the man who chased them in the grocery store all those years ago never existed.

Bang!

The official shot the starter's gun, and the runners took off. Danny took the lead by a few paces. The crowd cheered him on. Vero lagged behind in fourth place. As Danny raced ahead of him, stretching his lead, Vero glanced into the bleachers and saw Davina cheering her little heart out. *But who is she cheering for?*

Jealousy seized Vero, and before he knew it, he was gaining on the other runners. The crowd jumped to its feet as Vero flew by the two runners in second and third place and then caught up to Danny. The two ran neck and neck. As Vero saw the perspiration streaming down Danny's face, he realized that he was barely sweating.

The scene suddenly seemed surreal, like Vero was observing it as a spectator, seeing things in slow motion as Danny pushed himself harder than he ever had in his life.

And then Vero smiled smugly and left Danny in the dust, crossing the finish line a full two paces ahead of him.

The crowd erupted into cheers as Attleboro Middle took first and second place in the boys' 400 meter dash. Without thinking, Coach Randy whipped off his ball cap and threw it high into the air in celebration, revealing his bald head for all to see.

Vero saw Tack elbow Nate and say, "Look! Coach is bald!"

Vero looked up into the stands. His dad was on his feet, waving his foam hand proudly. Vero's mom was taking picture after picture, capturing the moment. Clover's mouth was ajar. But when her dad started whistling loudly, she inched her way to the next bench down and tried to disappear farther inside her hoodie.

Then Vero saw Blake and Duff in the stands, applauding and high-fiving each other. *Why are they celebrating Danny's defeat? Nice friends.*

Vero turned and saw Danny hunched over, still trying to catch his breath. Oddly, he suddenly felt bad for the guy. He considered confronting Blake and Duff, but then he saw

Davina walk over and place a hand on Danny's shoulder as she handed him a water bottle. Vero changed his mind.

Vero went on to win the high jump and the long jump events. His long jump even set a new school record. Soon it was time for the 80 meter hurdles. By now, it was Vero's day, and he was expected to win this event. The story of how he jumped two hurdles in a single bound had been exaggerated to four hurdles. And after watching him break the school's long jump record, the crowd totally believed the rumor.

"Good luck — not that you need it," Tack said as he shook Vero's hand. "The shot put is next, so I won't be able to watch you run."

"Good luck to you too," Vero said. "Try not to hit any cats."

As Tack walked over to the shot put ring, Vero took his place in the lane next to Danny. They got into position on their starting blocks, and Danny glanced over at Vero. His menacing look was meant to intimidate, but it didn't work. After the starter's gun went off, Vero dashed ahead of everyone. As he approached the first hurdle, Vero cleared it with no problem. The crowd's exhilaration spurred Vero on, and as the next hurdle got closer, he decided to leap over it and the next one in a single jump. Vero sprung into the air. A hush fell over the crowd as he hung in midair between the two hurdles ... when suddenly ... from out of nowhere ... an errant shot put ball smashed into Vero's skull. He crumpled to the ground.

The crowd gasped as Tack looked on in horror.

15

❖

C.A.N.D.L.E.

"Yeah, you deserved that."

Vero felt the back of his head. No lump yet. He found himself sitting on the thick green grass of the Ether. It took a few seconds before he realized Uriel was standing over him wearing a scowl.

"What's the point in humiliating Danny like that? Your job is to safeguard people, not make them feel like dirt!"

Vero understood, but he didn't care. He was sick of Danny. "He's the one that deserves it!" Vero said. "He beats me up at school!"

"We saw that. I'm the one who held your fist back so you couldn't hit him."

That explained why Vero couldn't punch Danny that day.

" 'Turn the other cheek' isn't some cute catch phrase. It's a way of life for an angel," Uriel said.

Vero leaned forward and put his head in his hands. Could he do this?

Uriel sighed heavily and sat down in the grass next to Vero. "Track is one of the few *good* things Danny has in his life," he said softly.

"Not quite," Vero muttered.

Uriel knew exactly who Vero was talking about.

"Vero, it can never be. You know what you are and what will happen when you complete your training."

It was a hard truth to swallow, but Vero nodded. As much as he loved the Ether, though, it didn't diminish his love for the earth and its people—especially certain people.

"Come on," Uriel told him. "Take my hand. It's a much faster way to travel."

Vero grabbed Uriel's hand, and the next thing he knew, his feet were landing on rocky soil. Vero and Uriel now stood before an ancient Greco-Roman style temple. But it wasn't exactly like the temples Vero had seen illustrated in history books because this one wasn't in ruins.

Vast rows of columns, brightly adorned in soft pastel colors, lined the rectangular structure. They held up a perfectly arched dome roof. The stark white dome matched the equally stark white walls. The temple's design was simple and elegant.

Vero felt small and inconsequential as he walked up the glossy marble steps. The massive stone doors swung open as if they were expecting Vero. The entrance hall did not disappoint. It was the size of several football fields. Vero spun around and saw that the temple was many floors high. Each level had massive balconies that overlooked where he stood. The inside walls of the temple appeared to be made of gold mixed with diamonds—a gold that sparkled with crystal clarity to its core. The dome ceiling was quite high, yet Vero's eye could make out the intricate colorful tile patterns laid into the top. Vero's mouth hung open in awe. Uriel smiled as he watched Vero's reaction.

"It's my favorite architectural style," Uriel said.

"Greco-Roman," Vero said.

"Ha! Hardly. The Greeks and Romans got all of their ideas from us."

"What do you mean?" Vero asked.

"This temple was here long before the Greek civilization existed. See, one of the jobs of an angel is to inspire humans. So when those future Greek architects were sitting around in mud huts, we thought we'd help them out a bit. I believe it was Raphael who gave them a vision of this place."

"How?"

"Mainly through dreams."

Vero was curious. He wanted to know everything there was to know about the angel's role. There was so much to learn, and he was growing impatient.

"Entering dreams is one of the toughest tasks for an angel, but you'll learn soon enough," Uriel said.

The soothing sound of wind chimes echoed through the temple.

"What's that?" Vero asked.

"First period bell."

"Much nicer than the bell at my school," Vero said.

Hordes of kids suddenly streamed out onto the balconies and down the steps. Some looked as young as six or seven; others were Vero's age and older. Though none of them had their wings extended, Vero suspected they were all angels.

"What is this? Angel school?" Vero asked.

"Yes, it's all part of your training. You are now standing

in the Cathedral of Angels for Novice Development, Learning and Edification. Or C.A.N.D.L.E. for short. You will be one of the fledglings."

Vero smiled. "I get it ... a fledgling is a young bird that's just gotten its wings."

"Correct."

"So all of these fledglings will be assigned a person to watch over, right?" Vero asked as he watched the angels walk across the marble floors to the different classrooms.

"Yes."

"Well then, who watches over that person until we're able to?"

"The Holders. They're an experienced group of guardian angels who fulfill your duties until you're ready ... unless, of course, the soul hasn't yet been born on earth."

As Vero took in the hustle and bustle of the temple, someone bumped into him hard, knocking him to the ground. He looked up to see a female angel about his age. She was tall and athletic with short brown hair shot through with blonde streaks. She had three small hoop earrings in each of her ears. And with her faded jeans, chunky boots, and forceful attitude, she looked every bit the way he imagined a fierce warrior angel would look. Vero reckoned she was not a person to be messed with. She walked away without so much as a 'Sorry.'

"I thought angels were supposed to be nice to each other," Vero said.

Uriel watched the retreating figure of the rude angel and shook his head. "Sure. But it doesn't always work out that way."

Vero and Uriel walked through the temple until they reached a small open courtyard under a bright sky. A few angels sat on benches surrounded by meticulously manicured shrubs. A fringe of mature, leafy trees ringed the courtyard.

"This is your classroom," Uriel said.

"Really?" Vero asked, turning in a slow circle and scanning his surroundings.

"Students learn faster in a natural, relaxing environment."

Recalling his stuffy, crowded classrooms on earth, where he'd been forced to sit in a straight-backed chair for hours, Vero said, "Can you give my principal a vision of this place?"

Uriel chuckled. "I'll see what I can do."

Vero recognized the other fledglings. Ada was sitting next to Pax on the bench, his glasses slightly askew. X was lying on a bench with his dark face turned up toward the sun. Kane sat on the ground, leaning comfortably against a small tree. Uriel waved his arm toward the others. "And these are your classmates, Vero, whom I think you already know."

The other angels looked over at Vero. He nodded, acknowledging them.

Suddenly an angel flew into the courtyard with the velocity of a comet breaking through the atmosphere. As the angel slowed to a stop, he relaxed his wings and shook his head, trying to regain his equilibrium after his rapid flight.

The angel wore a light blue iridescent cloak that went down to his ankles. He had an angular face with a distinctly bent nose and a white goatee, and his short white hair looked wild and untamed. This angel was much bigger than Uriel, and more muscular; yet they shared the same violet-colored eyes. When the mighty angel regained his bearings, he turned and looked at Uriel with an intense gaze. Vero could tell by their expressions that the two were conversing mentally about something serious. Vero wished he'd learned how to tap into his inner angelic ESP. And just as that thought crossed Vero's mind, the impressive angel's gaze landed squarely on Vero.

Were they talking about me?

Pax's head quickly turned in Vero's direction. Had Pax tapped into their conversation?

Uriel then bowed his head to the angel and turned to the class. "For those of you who don't know him, this is the archangel Raziel. He will be instructing you today."

Raziel nodded to the group.

"Before I leave, remember this—trust the voice inside each of you, for it is Truth itself. We call it *Vox Dei*. That's Latin for 'God's voice.'"

As Vero reflected on Uriel's words, Uriel unfurled his wings and disappeared in a blur.

"Gather 'round," Raziel said abruptly, motioning toward benches arranged near a podium sitting on the grass. "Come on, come on."

X sat up, and Kane took a seat on a bench. But Raziel's intense scrutiny had made Vero uneasy, so he hesitated a moment.

Raziel noticed Vero's reluctance. "Do you want a separate invitation?"

Vero felt his face burn. "Sorry, I was just, uh, looking for a seat." He quickly sat next to Ada. Here it was his first official day of lessons, and he was already on the teacher's bad side.

Raziel seems to be a bit more high-strung than Uriel. No sooner had Vero thought this then Raziel silenced his thoughts with a glare. Vero shrunk down in his seat.

Raziel peered at the fledglings. "I am Raziel. I will be your teacher in basic angelic knowledge and understanding.

I expect your full attention at all times because it is my job to provide you with a complete grasp of who you are and what is expected of you. Should I fail in my attempt to educate you, it would be a great loss not only to you, but also to the heavens."

"What do you mean?" Pax asked.

"Not all angels make the cut."

The fledglings exchanged worried looks.

"Should you fail in the training process, then you automatically forfeit becoming a guardian. It's over."

"But what happens if we fail?" Ada asked. "I thought we'd die on earth only when our training is completed."

"Yes, that is true. But your training is 'completed' in two ways … pass or fail. Should you fail your training, you will not be allowed back into your human body. To those on earth, you will appear to have died as per your most recent transition to the Ether, and your body will be buried. You will never become a guardian, and you will be assigned to the choir of angels."

"Is that a bad thing?" Kane asked.

"Of course not. Singing praises to the Almighty is a noble and joyous calling. But you'd better love to sing." Raziel paused a moment before continuing, "As you train, you will be judged according to your bravery, strength, character, combat skills, compassion, and, most importantly, your faith. Each of you has a crown waiting for you in heaven. Every time you do well, a jewel will be added to it."

"So the goal is to fill up the crown?" Ada asked.

"The goal is to get as many jewels as you can," Raziel answered.

"So are we in competition with each other?" X asked, a bit confused.

Raziel looked around at the group. "Don't think of it as competition, but rather as pushing each other to excel, to reach his or her full potential. Only the best can be guardians." For a moment, his expression seemed to soften. "This might be one of the hardest concepts for young angels to understand," he said. "I myself have struggled with this."

Vero mulled that over. He thought about the Navy flight school his father had attended. Since his childhood, Vero's dad had desperately wanted to become a Navy pilot. After college, he'd been accepted into Navy flight school, and he trained with a group of guys who all became close buddies. But even though they all trained together, only the best of the best would become pilots. So ultimately, the guys were competing with one another.

During flight school, for each maneuver mastered, his dad received an "attaboy" that went on his record. Though he received a decent number of attaboys, some of the other guys received more. His dad washed out of flight school, and the Navy assigned him to the job of supply clerk. His childhood dream to fly for the Navy went unfulfilled. After his father's tour with the Navy ended, he traded in that desk job for another desk job at the World Bank.

It had always bothered Vero that his father had been so close to getting his "wings" but had ended up sitting behind a desk.

"There are a lot of misconceptions about angels," Raziel continued. "First of all, we don't walk around with halos over our heads. Second, very few of us play the harp. Third, we don't lounge around on the clouds eating marshmallows all day. We are warriors — the fiercest of all warriors — because the enemy is always ready to strike, and the Fallen won't go easy on us. Your enemy prowls around like a roaring lion looking for someone to devour, so you will need to learn to defend yourself." Raziel's eyes rested on Vero. "Because we won't always be there to save you."

Vero's spirits dropped. Was Raziel angry with him because Uriel had to save him from the maltures on the roof? Does Raziel doubt he has what it takes to become a guardian?

"Vero, tell me some of the tasks that guardian angels perform," Raziel said.

"Uh, we protect humans ..." He thought of the prayer grid. "We answer prayers once God gives the okay. We're messengers. We try to influence humans ..."

"Mainly through ...?"

"Dreams," Ada jumped in. "We enter dreams to deliver messages."

"Good. Someone else?"

"We interpret visions," X offered. "We carry out God's commands, whether it be destroying entire cities or helping a person with a flat tire. We also assist humans at their death, helping them cross over."

An unfamiliar voice shouted from behind them, "We slay demons!"

Everyone turned to see that a new girl had entered the courtyard. It was the angel who'd rudely bumped into Vero inside the temple.

She sat under a tree.

"So nice of you to make it, Greer. Wouldn't you rather join us over here?" Raziel asked. The voice was polite, but the command was apparent.

"No. Not really."

Vero looked at Ada with raised eyebrows, awaiting

Raziel's response. Vero was sure that Raziel wouldn't let her get away with it. His eyes scanned the outdoor classroom, trying to figure out ways Raziel could punish her. But there was no corner to stand in or chalkboard to clean or even sheets of paper for writing essays.

Raziel silently stared at Greer for a moment, then said, "All right, let's continue."

Vero's forehead creased. *That's it?* Raziel had humiliated him in front of the whole class! He opened his mouth to protest, but Ada kicked Vero's leg and shook her head. Raziel's eyes flitted to Vero, then back to Greer. "Yes, you are correct. Slaying demons is another role of guardians. Our enemies' influence over humans can be strong. And often, slaying the demon is the only way to save them."

Kane raised his hand. "When do we learn that? When do we get our swords?"

"When you're deemed to be ready. And then Michael will instruct you," Raziel answered.

Vero's eyes lit up when he heard the name Michael. He knew about Michael from Sunday school — the archangel leader, a fierce warrior who cast Lucifer and his fallen angels out of heaven and banished them into darkness. From his studies at school, Vero knew about the Renaissance painter Raphael and his painting of Michael standing courageously with his mighty sword drawn, crushing the head of the fallen Satan.

In the Bible it was prophesied that Michael would slay the dragon and defeat Satan's army in the end times. Excitement rose in Vero's chest knowing that at some point in his training he would actually meet Michael. Would he be worthy to be in Michael's presence?

"And I'm not good enough for you?"

Vero snapped out of his thoughts to see Raziel standing over him, piercing him with a scornful look.

"Are you bored in my class?" Raziel asked.

Raziel can read my thoughts! Did Vero's admiration of Michael offend Raziel? Had Vero hurt his feelings? He suddenly felt totally exposed.

"I'm not worthy enough to hold your attention?"

What's Raziel's deal? Vero was beginning to realize he didn't like Raziel much, but then he immediately regretted the thought. The narrowing of Raziel's eyes confirmed it ... he was reading Vero's mind.

"I'm not bored," Vero quickly said. Then he deliberately thought, *I'm happy to be here.*

"Then it will do you good to keep your mind focused on the lesson," Raziel said.

Vero heard Greer snicker. He looked over at her, and she flashed him a smug smile. Vero turned his head back to the lesson, not wanting to incur any more of Raziel's wrath.

"All of the mentioned tasks of the angels are correct. But the one that you failed to bring up is probably the most important. The one which must be obeyed before all others."

The young angels leaned forward eagerly — except for Greer who idly plucked blades of grass from the ground.

"The most important task for all angels to master is learning to accept God's will over your own," Raziel said. "Accepting God's will above your own is the ultimate expression of faith and love. It is also one of the hardest of our tasks. And why is that?"

Raziel looked out over the class. No one raised a hand,

but Greer stopped pulling grass blades and focused her eyes on Raziel.

"Because it involves trials and tribulations, pain and suffering," Raziel said solemnly. "It will require you to deny yourself for the sake of others or for the greater good. It will not be easy. At times, your heart will shatter when you witness man's injustice and cruelty to one another—especially when all you can do is sit back and watch. You are powerless to stop it because you trust in the will of God."

Vero's mind drifted back to the track meet. He thought about how he'd failed to deny himself for the greater good, about how he'd humiliated Danny in order to impress Davina. He'd been cruel. Then Vero recalled the giant angels he'd seen guarding the skyscrapers in New York City. They stood with their swords drawn protectively around tall buildings. He could only imagine their grief when they had to step aside, lower their swords, and allow two airplanes to crash into the tallest high-rises in the city on that fateful day in September many years ago. Their hearts must have shattered into a million tiny pieces. The pain would have been unbearable. Yes, accepting God's will would not always be easy.

The group was silent for a few moments as Raziel's grave words and the enormity of what was expected of them sunk in. Before Greer dropped her head and resumed picking at the grass, Vero caught a look of trepidation on her face. He noticed her fingernails were bitten down to the skin. Perhaps she wasn't so tough after all.

"How can you tell if something is the will of God?" Kane asked. "I mean, how will we know?"

"First of all, you have to be open to it. Next, you free your mind of any hateful thoughts. It helps to put your right hand

over your heart and spread your fingers like this ... " Raziel
demonstrated the gesture for them. "And then ... just listen.
On earth the humans call it *intuition*. Here, it's *Vox Dei*—a
sixth sense, an inkling as to what you should be doing. It
is the voice of God working in your heart, directing you in
times of question. But you must be open to that direction.
You must be willing to listen."

Raziel's face grew even more sober.

"But not all messages come from God. The great deceiver
can gain access to your minds in moments of doubt and
weakness. If you give him any sort of opportunity, he'll seize
the moment and hold great influence over you. His maltures
will poison your minds." Raziel looked at each of them in
turn to drive home his point.

"So for your lesson today, you're going to put listening to
God's voice into practice, letting it guide you."

Raziel spread his wings. He flapped them in a graceful
manner and began to rise into the air.

"Follow close behind."

The fledglings rose and released their wings. It felt good
to stretch them. Vero admired the ease with which Raziel
ascended into the current, like sails on a sailboat, flapping in
unison with the wind. Vero was still awkward with his own
flying skills. He didn't want to give Raziel any new opportunity to criticize him, so he prayed he could keep pace. As
he fluttered his wings, Vero instantly felt lighter on his feet.
Up until this point, he'd needed a good jump off a cliff
to get airborne. He rose into the air, but only hovered. He
watched as Raziel and the others were getting farther away
from him. A feeling of dread overtook him because he was
going to flunk his first real lesson. Without warning, Vero

felt a forceful tug on his back. Someone was pulling him up by the back of his shirt collar! As he rose higher into the air, Vero cocked his head and saw Greer dragging him along.

"Humiliating, isn't it? Having a girl save you?" Greer snickered before she dropped him into the air.

It was, Vero thought, but he dared not admit it out loud. Then he felt his face turn bright red, betraying him.

❖

Raziel and the class flew over an area of the Ether that Vero had never seen before. It wasn't the plush, green landscape he'd come to love. Rather, it looked brown and devoid of any sort of life. From Vero's vantage point, the ground looked like desert—barren and rocky. Uriel had warned him that not all parts of the Ether were wonderful; looking below, he now believed him. Even the brilliant light that normally lit up the sky seemed to dim. Vero hoped they were just flying through this area because he really didn't want to sightsee down there. But then Raziel beat his wings a little less furiously, and Vero knew they weren't just passing through.

As he landed, Vero saw the area was much worse than what he'd glimpsed from above. The sandy ground teemed with jagged rocks so sharp that Vero could feel them through his shoes. He experienced pain with every step.

Suddenly, he was overcome with thirst. His mouth felt unbelievably dry. He'd do anything for a cool glass of water. But looking out over the barren land without even so much as a cactus in sight, the hope of finding refreshment seemed impossible. Vero glanced at the other fledglings and could tell they were equally miserable. X grabbed his stomach as dehydration overtook him. Ada stuck out her tongue, panting. All of them looked dazed and confused. All except for Greer. She seemed to be alert as she took in her surroundings. It was as if she was immune to the harsh world around her.

"Here's where I leave you," Raziel told the group. "This is your first official test."

"We can't survive out here!" Vero protested.

Vero knew he was showing weakness, but he was terrified of being left there. He was certain he'd quickly die of thirst—or worse.

Raziel placed his hands on Vero's shoulders. "Do what I told you," he said calmly. "Do not be afraid. Trust your heart. Erase doubt from your mind and let God guide you out of here."

Raziel stepped back, curled up inside his tremendous wings, and said to the group, "Do not follow me." Then he disappeared, flashing like a falling star across the darkening sky.

Vero looked around at the others. They were on their own in this forsaken land.

Uriel was standing in the green fields of the Ether when a sudden wind appeared, bringing Raziel with it. Uriel nodded to his fellow archangel, acknowledging him.

What do you think of him? Uriel asked through his thoughts.

I see nothing special about him, Raziel answered. *He can't even fly well.*

The Almighty hasn't given us any clear signs, but I suspect enough, Uriel said.

If he is the one, then we must keep his identity hidden from the Wicked One for as long as possible, Raziel said.

And even then, it may not be enough time, Uriel said with great sadness in his eyes.

16

◇

BEHEMOTH

I'm out of here," Kane said as he surveyed the vast desert.
"Raziel said not to follow him," Ada protested.

"I don't care."

Kane flapped his wings, determined to leave, but he couldn't get airborne. The more he flapped, all he managed to do was stir up sand and dust, creating a sandstorm. Particles of sand flew into the eyes and mouths of the others, making their already grim situation worse.

"Knock it off!" X shouted.

"Stop!" Vero said, covering his eyes with his arm.

But Kane grew more and more desperate, fanning his wings feverishly and making the sandstorm unbearable. Ada fell to the ground under the force of the gale winds and covered her head to protect herself. The others struggled to stay on their feet. Greer grabbed Kane's left wing and wouldn't let go.

Through his obscured vision, Vero watched as she pulled

Kane's other wing and tackled him to the stony ground. While holding him down, she rubbed his face into the dirt until he came to his senses. Vero marveled at Greer's incredible strength.

Kane's wings began to weaken and eventually stopped flapping. Greer released him and stood up.

"Way to stay cool under pressure," Greer said.

Kane sprang to his feet, spewing dirt from his mouth. Vero couldn't help smiling. Needing Greer to help him fly had made him feel inadequate. But now, seeing how easily she'd wrangled the well-muscled Kane to the ground, Vero felt a little better.

"Some force out there is clipping our wings," Greer announced. "Obviously, we can't fly out of here, as Kane just demonstrated."

Kane glared at Greer so intensely that it made Vero feel uncomfortable. Kane's look told Vero that Kane wasn't the type to let bygones be bygones, though Greer seemed oblivious to Kane's evil eye.

"So what are we going to do?" Pax asked.

"We're going to do what we were told to do. Close your eyes and listen for guidance," Greer said.

"It's kind of hard to concentrate when you're dying for a drink," Ada said.

"Whatever we're going to do, we'd better do it quick!" X shouted as he pointed to the sky.

All heads turned upward to see a flock of enormous condors circling above. They were massive! Three times the size of any birds that Vero had seen on earth.

And even from a distance, Vero could see they had a

ravenous look in their eyes. They began circling the fledglings, around and around, never breaking formation.

"Now we've got a ticking clock," Pax said.

"I can't do this!" Ada cried.

"Close your eyes and block out everything else," Greer said.

"It's not that easy!" Pax shouted.

"Of course not," Greer replied in a calm voice. "But it's your only shot at getting out of here."

Suddenly one of the massive birds nosedived right for them. X quickly picked up a rock, and with the skill of a quarterback, nailed the swooping bird right in the head.

"Eat that!" X shouted.

The bird flapped around in midair, briefly disoriented, and then rejoined the others, still circling above.

Greer turned to Ada and said, "Grab my arm."

The moment Ada latched onto Greer, Ada visibly relaxed.

Vero closed his eyes, which was rather unpleasant due to the sand particles that were now scratching his eyeballs. He desperately tried to ignore his fear and the strange, consuming thirst. He thought of his mother and wished she were with him, and then he decided to focus on her.

Vero pictured his mom sitting on the edge of his bed like she did when he was sick with a fever. She smoothed his hair, dipped a washcloth into a bowl of cold water on his nightstand, and dabbed his forehead. Thinking of its coolness and his mother's comforting presence eased Vero's discomfort momentarily. With his eyes tightly shut, Vero began walking as the image of his mother gently smiling at him guided him and reassured him that he'd be all right. He forged blindly ahead.

Again, his mother finished wringing out the washcloth and tenderly placed it back on Vero's forehead. This time he could actually feel the cold against his skin. Vero opened his eyes and discovered he was standing before a cold stone wall. He stepped back and saw an arched stone doorway. He did not see any of the other angels around. Desperate to flee the desolate scene behind him, Vero walked through the doorway.

Once inside, he instantly felt better. It was much cooler inside the lofty rock walls. Passageways greeted him in every direction. Vero counted three different paths to travel, but he had no idea which one to take. Vero felt a tap on his shoulder and quickly spun around to see X and Pax.

"Where are the others?" Vero asked.

"Don't know," X said. He was bent over with his hands on his waist.

Pax crazily shook his head like a wet dog to get the sand out of his hair.

"I feel like I can't breathe," X said between labored breaths. "I need water."

"Maybe we should go look for the others," Vero said.

"How?" X asked. "I can barely stand up. I need water first, and then maybe my head will stop spinning, and I can help find them."

"Shh ... " Vero held his finger to his mouth. Something was making his skin tingle. Vero placed his hands on Pax's shoulders to stop him from moving.

The three listened intently. The sound was difficult to make out at first, but after a few moments, it became crystal clear. Water! Faint droplets echoed throughout the cavern. The boys' spirits immediately rose.

"Let's go!" X rasped. "I hear it coming from this tunnel!"

X followed the sound into one of the tunnels, but suddenly stopped short. Pax and Vero ran into him.

"What?" Vero asked.

"I don't hear it anymore," X said, and the excitement drained from his face.

"Let's try this one," Pax said as he walked to the entrance of another tunnel. But once again, the sound of water droplets disappeared.

Vero stuck his head into the remaining tunnel. "Guys, it's definitely this one!"

Pax and X raced over to Vero. But when they stepped into the tunnel, only the sound of their labored breathing could be heard.

"I know I heard it!" Vero yelled in frustration.

"Maybe we're hallucinating," Pax began. "That's what happens when you get dehydrated."

"We're going crazy," X panicked. "It's all in our heads!"

"How can that be if all three of us heard it?" Vero asked.

"Then we're all going nuts," Pax said.

"No, I can feel it. There's water here somewhere." And Vero knew it was true. "Raziel said this lesson will teach us to hear God's voice. It's our only way out."

Vero put his hand over his heart and spread his fingers apart like Raziel had shown them. He closed his eyes tight and concentrated as hard as he could. The next thing he knew, something inside of him was nudging him forward. Vero stepped into the tunnel directly in front of him. X and Pax followed.

The tunnel grew darker, so Pax grabbed Vero's shirt. X

also reached for Vero's shirt. Vero pushed on through the passageway.

Vero felt like a mole. Moles were completely blind, yet they could successfully claw their way through their burrows to find food. Despite all the rocks on the ground, Vero was amazed he never stumbled. Pax and X held firmly onto Vero as he snaked his way through the winding tunnel. Gradually, slivers of light began to break up the blackness. Vero looked around for its source, but there wasn't any. The light just … was. Then Vero heard a voice.

"What took you guys so long?"

It wasn't God, but Greer. She was perched on the edge of a heavily eroded rock wall above a small pool. Next to Greer was a small stream that flowed into the pool below, where Ada was madly scooping water into her hands and drinking her fill.

Vero, Pax, and X ran to the pool and began gulping up the water at a frenzied pace. It dripped down their chins and soaked their clothes. X dunked his entire head into the pool.

When he'd finished drinking, Pax asked Greer, "Is Kane with you?"

"No, I thought he was with you," she answered.

"Then he's probably still out there in the dust," Pax said.

Vero looked at Ada nervously. He couldn't imagine being trapped in that awful desert. "He could die out there," Vero said.

"Then I guess he's gonna be singing tenor for all eternity," Greer said.

"We have to go back for him," Vero said.

"Have fun," Greer said.

"I don't get you," Vero said. "One minute you're acting all

nice and being helpful, and the next minute you're all rough and tough. So which is it?"

"First of all, I'm never all that nice. And second, when I save you, it's only because I have zero tolerance for stupidity. Going after Kane fits into the stupidity category."

"It's the right thing to do," said Vero. "Even if it *is* stupid."

Greer hopped down off the wall and got up in Vero's face, glaring at him, daring him to go against her word. But Vero held her gaze and refused to back down. He sensed that X, Ada, and Pax were waiting nervously to see which one would cave first.

It was Greer. She ran a hand through her spiky hair and pulled at the strands until the blonde streaks stood on end. Then she nodded at Vero with a smug, sideways smile. "You're not as wimpy as I thought," she said.

Vero stood strong, making sure he didn't crack a smile or relax his body in any way that might give an indication of weakness.

"You guys better drink up if we're going back out there," Greer said to the others.

Vero breathed a little easier. He was glad he hadn't backed down. But then he thought of the horrid desert and wondered what he'd gotten himself into. Going back into that oppressive air would be agony.

"All right, tough guy, let's go," Greer said.

Vero took one last drink of water. Ada doused her head like X had done earlier, flattening her wild red hair into tight, dark ringlets. Pax took off his glasses and opened his mouth under the running spring.

The group turned to leave but then stopped short.

The landscape had completely changed.

Where moments before there had been a tunnel, now there was a solid rock wall.

"Okay, Genius," Greer said to Vero, "what's Plan B?"

Vero ran his fingers along the wall. But no matter how much he explored or felt for that internal nudge, Vero felt nothing. And the wall remained an impenetrable mass of stone.

Vero beat his fists against the rock repeatedly. After one particularly hard punch, Vero screamed as he smashed his knuckles against the stone.

Greer crossed her arms as she stood back, observing. As Vero tried to shake off the pain, he became aware of the others watching him. "You done?" Greer asked.

Vero nodded, feeling the weight of their stares upon him. A moment ago he'd felt proud of himself for standing up to Greer and setting a good example to the other fledglings. Now he just looked like a fool.

"So since you're done and all," Greer said, "could you please move? You're standing on the exit."

Vero looked down and realized he was standing on top of a wooden door that was carved into the ground. Vero stepped aside as Greer kneeled down and pulled on a clasp that had been indented into the wood.

"Wait!" Vero said, grabbing her arm.

Greer looked up at him.

"If we go through that door, we're only gonna be that much farther away from Kane."

"Well, that little voice inside of me is saying the only way out is through this door," Greer shot back. "And my intuition is a lot more developed than any of yours."

"Oh really? And why is that?" Vero asked.

"Because I wasn't raised with some perfect loving family like the rest of you. When I was sent to earth, I got one lousy foster family after the other. Each one was worse than the last. You wanna know how I got to the Ether my first time? Do you?"

Everyone looked at her, waiting. Vero let go of her arm.

"Foster mother number seven lost her temper when she saw that I'd forgotten to make my bed, so she picked up an aluminum baseball bat and mistook my head for the ball."

Vero fell silent, not sure how to respond. No one spoke. But Greer wasn't the type to want their pity anyway.

"So the bottom line is—I had to tap into that intuition sooner than the sorry lot of you, or else I wouldn't have made it this far. And besides, do any of you see another way out of here?"

Vero studied their surroundings. Greer was right. Solid stone walls enclosed them on every side. The pool of water was still there, but now it was as if they were trapped in a big rock box.

Greer pulled open the door. There was nothing to see, only darkness.

"Later," Greer said, and she jumped feet first into the complete unknown, disappearing without a sound.

Ada peered into the open hole. "I can't see her. She's really gone."

Vero looked into the uneasy faces of his fellow angels. *What to do?* X walked to the edge of the hole and stood tall. His hair was still wet from the spring, and his T-shirt was soaked. X saluted the others and took a step into the darkness.

Now it was down to three.

Ada turned to Vero, "I really don't want to go down there," she said, nervously twirling a finger through her curls.

Vero sighed heavily and said, "Greer's right. There's no other way out."

"How about we hold your hand, Ada," Pax said. "So whatever happens, we'll be together."

Vero nodded, though he couldn't help thinking Ada was going to have to toughen up if she was going to make it as a guardian. No one would be there to hold her hand if the maltures came for her. Still, he stepped to the edge of the hole and smiled at her.

"Come on," Vero said. "Let's get this over with."

Ada and Pax stood next to him with Ada in the middle, and the three joined hands. Vero didn't know what they would find in the unnatural darkness, but he had to admit that he felt a little better knowing he wouldn't be facing it alone.

"On the count of three ... " Pax began, "One, two, three!"

Vero, Pax, and Ada jumped off the rim of the opening and blindly fell into the abyss.

Vero lost track of time as they plummeted through the darkness. It could have been two minutes or two hours. He was reminded of the time when he and Clover had made their way through a maze of mirrors at an amusement park. With strobe lights blasting and mirrors reflecting their distorted images, Vero had walked through it completely disoriented, as if in a dream.

This time, though, the feeling of Ada's fingernails digging into his palm kept him in reality.

Ha! Reality!

As they continued to fall, it suddenly occurred to Vero that if there would eventually be a bottom to this fall, then they could hit it at any moment.

"Open your wings!" he shouted. "Hurry!"

Vero willed his wings to open. But the space was tight, like they were falling down a narrow well. So his wings wouldn't fully extend. The others had trouble releasing their wings too. Flying was no longer an option.

"I can't fly!" Ada yelled.

"Just keep them open as far as you can! We have to slow our descent before we hit the bottom!"

As they continued to fall, Vero became aware of his outermost wing feathers as they scraped along the uneven crags of the rock walls. He shut his eyes, bracing for the inevitable impact. He hoped they wouldn't land on top of Greer and X.

Suddenly, his wings, even though they were still fairly close to his back, caught an updraft of wind. Finally his wings had some air to bite into, and he was no longer freefalling. The speed of his descent abruptly slowed to a leisurely glide, with his wings acting as a parachute. Vero had thought that his feathery appendages were only for flying distances, and he was never so glad to be wrong about something. Pax and Ada's wings had also caught the current.

As the three drifted down, a dull light began to illuminate their surroundings. It grew brighter and brighter until Vero had to blink repeatedly as his eyes adjusted to it. Suddenly, the stone walls disappeared, and their wings were able to fully extend. They all landed safely without so much as a sprained ankle.

But when Vero looked down, he understood why. They'd landed in mud up to their waists, and they were surrounded by tall, thick grass and reeds. Vero let Ada's hand drop.

"Thanks," Ada said to Vero.

"You're welcome," Vero said.

"Where are we?" Ada asked.

"Some kind of swamp," Pax answered.

"Gross!" Ada said. "The mud's on my wings, and it's so thick that I can't move them." She made a futile attempt to fly.

Vero parted the nearby reeds in the hopes of finding a way out. "Come on, let's get out of this muck," he said. But all he saw were more reeds and more marsh, no shore in sight, nothing to orient him. They couldn't just stand around in the waist-deep mud, so he began walking.

"Why that way?" Pax asked.

"We can't stay here," Vero answered. "We need to find the others."

"I feel like we should be going that way." Pax pointed behind them.

Vero wasn't going to fight Pax over the issue. The voice inside of him wasn't telling him anything except that he was thirsty again, so he turned and followed Pax, this time relying on Pax's intuition.

The mud was so dense that it felt like Vero had cinder blocks attached to his feet. *Please don't let this be quicksand.*

"I hope there aren't any leeches," Ada said. "I can't deal with leeches."

"It's the alligators that I'm worried about," Pax said.

"Now why'd you have to say that?" Vero asked.

"At least I didn't mention snakes," Pax said with a shrug.

This got to Vero. The thought of snakes swimming around made his chest tighten. "Let's just keep moving," Vero said.

"I'm glad we have daylight," Pax said, looking up at the bright sky above. "It's weird how the light in the Ether seems to appear out of nowhere."

"There's no sun in the Ether; only God's light. That's why the Ether doesn't follow the laws of day and night on earth," Ada said.

After a few minutes of trudging along, the group was exhausted. Pax stopped walking and tried to spread his wings to lift himself out of the muck, but the caked-on mud wouldn't allow it.

"My wings are pinned," Vero said.

"What if I climbed up on your shoulders? Then maybe I could see over the reeds," Ada said.

"It's worth a try," Vero said.

Ada faced Vero and placed her hands on his shoulders.

"Step on my knee and then try to climb up," Vero said.

Pax helped Ada balance as she attempted to hoist herself onto Vero's shoulders. She kneed Vero in the chest on the way up.

"Ouch!"

"Sorry ... " she said as Pax attempted to push her up from behind.

"Touch my butt again and you'll be missing some teeth," Ada snarled.

"I'm only trying to help!"

Pax moved behind Vero and tried to support him as Ada got situated. For just a moment, Vero imagined they looked like a really bad acrobatic act. And then Ada slipped. All her weight fell against Vero, and all three of them went down in the mud.

Great, Vero thought. *I've had sand in my eyeballs, and now I have mud everywhere!* He got to his feet first, grabbed Ada under her armpits, and pulled her up. Pax managed to stand on his own. They were completely covered in mud.

"Perfect!" Ada said with a look of disgust. "I think I'm gonna be picking mud out of places I never knew existed."

"Did you see anything before you fell?" Pax asked.

"There's land straight ahead of us," Ada said.

Vero spit sludge out of his mouth. He was beyond disgusted. "It's like we're swimming in a giant backed-up toilet!" Vero tried to wipe mud off his face.

Wait. What. Was. That? Vero frantically rubbed mud from his eyes so he could be sure of what he was seeing. It was a snake. But it was much bigger than any anaconda Vero had ever seen on the National Geographic channel. It made the snake that attacked Davina look like a night crawler! The enormous serpent was weaving through the reeds and gaining speed. It actually moved the mud with such force that it created a wake. The waves pushed Pax deeper into the reeds and out of sight.

"Pax!" Vero shouted.

With its head bobbing in and out of the sludge, the massive snake slithered over to Ada who was completely unaware of its presence.

"Ada!" Vero screamed. "Look out!"

Ada turned around, but it was too late. The snake was upon her. It began coiling.

"Vero!" Ada shouted just before the snake stole her breath.

The snake violently tossed Ada. Vero broke off a piece of

reed, intending to shove the end of it straight into the snake's eye. But as the horrific creature swam closer to Vero, he saw that it had no eyes!

The snake started to swim away with Ada firmly in its grasp. As its body swept past Vero, he grabbed Ada's legs. The snake shook both of them around as if they were rag dolls. It was like an amusement park ride neither one of them wanted to be on.

It took every ounce of Vero's strength to hang on while they were being viciously tossed from side to side. But Vero wouldn't let go of Ada's legs, hoping his weight alone would be enough to pull her free from the snake's grasp.

Suddenly, Vero and Ada were being lifted out of the swamp. They were still in the snake's embrace, but the height gave Vero a clearer view of their surroundings. And he realized the creature wasn't a snake at all, but some kind of dinosaur! They were in the clutches of its tail, and Vero wasn't sure if that was better or worse.

With one huge flick of its tail, the dinosaur uncurled its long extremity and flung Vero and Ada onto dry land. Ada heaved and coughed as the air came back into her lungs. Vero patted her on the back.

"What just happened?" Ada asked.

"I'm not sure, but I think that creature just helped us," Vero said. "But it swept Pax farther into the reeds."

"Maybe now we can clean off our wings and then fly out to find him," Ada said.

Vero didn't answer, but seconds later Ada tugged on his arm and pointed, speechless. Vero followed her gaze.

They were sitting on what seemed to be a bank along a mud river filled with patches of reeds and grasses. Farther inland Vero saw trees that looked like giant palms, and beyond the trees, a herd of sauropod dinosaurs peacefully grazed. Vero watched as their long necks stretched high into the air to eat leaves from the treetops. They moved gracefully, despite their massive bulk.

Months ago, Vero had gone on a field trip to a museum to see the dinosaur bones. He'd stood next to the display of reconstructed skeletons and reveled in their greatness. But that was nothing compared to seeing those bones with flesh over them ... and they were moving! The scene before Vero and Ada was nothing less than extraordinary.

"Unbelievable ... " Ada whispered.

"That must be what had us in its tail," Vero said.

Vero pointed to a dinosaur drinking from a pond. "That's a diplodocus. And over there is a brachiosaurus."

Ada stared at them and then quietly said, "Moves like a cedar ... "

"What?" Vero asked.

"It has a tail that moves like a cedar!" Ada said. "From the book of Job!"

"A cedar tree?"

"Yes, they're behemoths," Ada said. "Creatures of immense proportions."

"They still look like dinosaurs to me," Vero said.

"Maybe that's all the behemoths ever were," Ada said. "Giant herbivores. And if they only eat grasses, I don't think we need to be afraid of them."

"Unless a T. rex shows up!"

"We just need to keep a safe distance," Ada said.

"How about 200 million years?" Vero studied the sauropods in the distance, and he noticed there were enormous mounds of dirt all around the behemoths. "Do you think those are anthills?" he asked.

"I hope not," Ada said. "I can't deal with giant ants right now."

Off in the distance, a sauropod lifted its tail, and they both made the connection at the same time.

"Oh lovely," Ada said.

"Hey, at least they aren't giant anthills."

A nearby rustling sound caused them to quickly duck behind a clump of reeds. Visions of *Jurassic Park* flashed through Vero's mind, and he expected a T. rex or a velociraptor to appear at any moment.

Instead, a miserable-looking, mud-covered creature slowly trudged out of the swamp.

"Pax!" Ada cried.

Vero couldn't help but laugh.

"Laugh all you want, but you guys don't look any better than I do," Pax said before he collapsed onto the ground, exhausted. "Why would anyone ever want to take a mud bath? I can't believe people pay money for this … "

Suddenly, they heard a low rumbling, and the ground began to shake. Pax instantly bolted upright. "Earthquake!" he shouted.

"Worse!" Vero yelled. He grabbed Pax under his armpits and pulled him to his feet. "Behemoth stampede!"

Pax turned his head in the direction of the trembling ground. A herd of sauropods was charging straight at them. He did a double take.

"It's no dream!" Vero shouted.

The booming got louder.

"Run!" Ada screamed, but the heavy mud weighed them down.

"They're gaining on us!" Pax yelled. "An old person with a walker could move faster than us!"

Vero couldn't believe that something so big could move so fast! The herd of massive dinosaurs was nearly upon them. Vero tried moving his wings so he could fly to safety, but the hardened mud prevented them from flapping.

"Pax!" Ada yelled.

Vero turned and saw that Pax had fallen to the ground and was now struggling to get up under the weight of the mud. "Ada wait!" Vero cried, but she ran back to help Pax. They were sure to be crushed like little insects.

Then Vero recalled the day's lesson — allowing God's voice to guide him. So he did the only thing he could think of. He stood completely still and faced the charging creatures. Vero closed his eyes, placed his outstretched hand over his heart, and listened for the inner voice to lead him.

Once again, it was not easy to concentrate, but Vero focused and freed his mind of the impending danger. In seconds, Vero felt strength come over him and fill him with courage. He grabbed Pax by what little bit of his shirt collar he could find.

"Take his hand!" Vero shouted to Ada.

Ada grabbed Pax as the shadow cast from the charging dinosaurs overcame them, blocking out the daylight. The behemoths were massive at a distance, but up close ... images of giant redwood trees came to Vero's mind.

Following an inner pull, Vero dodged the gargantuan animals, guiding Pax and Ada between the legs of the beasts and through the stampede. They ducked, jumped, and skirted as the herd changed directions, and they were pelted by chunks of earth, rocks, and even dino muck kicked up by the herd.

Vero stumbled over a cluster of rocks. He was going down and he knew it. Pax and Ada fell with him onto the hard ground. An especially large behemoth charged. The beast's front leg lifted up and was poised to land on top of them! Vero refused to panic. He prayed hard and a way out presented itself to him — a ditch! Vero pulled Pax and Ada with him, and the three rolled into the safety of the trench. The beast's leg came down, narrowly missing them.

Finally, the last of the herd ran by. Safely hidden in the trench, the three angels eyed each other in a tense silence. Anger replaced the terror on Ada's face. And then she stood up and punched Vero squarely across his jaw.

17

THE BOOK OF RAZIEL

What was that for?" Vero asked, massaging his jaw.

"Because you made me jump into that hole!"

"I just saved your life!" Vero shot back.

"That's not the point!" yelled Ada.

Vero and Pax swapped looks, and then Pax shrugged his shoulders. Apparently Pax couldn't explain Ada's behavior either.

"Just *look* at us! Look what we're covered in!" Ada wailed.

A grin spread across Pax's face, and he began to laugh — shakily at first, but then his chuckles dissolved into all-out hysterical laughter until he was doubled over. Ada and Vero exchanged glances. Then Ada started laughing too. And finally Vero joined them.

"I don't know what's so funny," Greer said. "You guys stink! I can smell you all the way up here."

Vero looked up from the trench and saw Greer and X standing over them. They were perfectly clean — no mud or dino muck anywhere on them.

"If any of you swine would like our company," Greer said, holding her nose, "you'd better go wash yourselves in the river. Otherwise, it's been nice knowing you."

Vero, Pax, and Ada climbed out of the ditch and walked with X and Greer toward the river. The behemoths were no longer in sight.

"You guys didn't land in the swamp?" Vero asked.

"No, we glided to a smooth landing under a shade tree," X said.

"Maybe if you hadn't hesitated before jumping, you wouldn't have wound up in the swamp," Greer gloated.

Greer was right, and Vero knew it immediately. He hadn't listened to the inner voice when it told him to jump into the hole. As he washed himself off, Vero resolved to trust his instincts moving forward because he didn't want to pull dinosaur poop out of his ears ever again.

"Any sign of Kane?" Pax asked. They were now mud free, sitting by the river and eating wild berries with their wings retracted.

"He must be really lost," X said, shaking his head.

"That's *his* problem," Greer said.

"But aren't we all in this together?" Ada asked.

"No," Greer said. "Raziel made it very clear that this is a competition."

"No, he didn't. He said we were to push each other to our full potentials," Vero said.

"He also said we'd be judged based on our character and compassion," Pax added.

"Maybe, but you can't follow somebody down the wrong path," Greer explained. "I'm not gonna risk my chance to be a guardian for anyone."

"Did you ever think that maybe Kane's on the right path, and we're the lost ones?" Vero wondered aloud.

"I'm only doing what Raziel told us to do," Greer said. "And so far it's been working for me." She shot Vero a look, "And you're already on Raziel's bad side, so I'd recommend that you do what he says."

"Yeah, what's up with that?" Vero asked. "I just met him, and he hates me already."

"He doesn't hate you. Archangels do not hate," Ada said. "I think he's frustrated. He might feel like a failure. Did you ever learn about the Book of Raziel?"

Vero shook his head. He had no idea what she was talking about. The others were also listening closely.

"Raziel once stood close to God's throne. He was the Angel of Secrets. It was his job to write down everything he heard into a book made of blue sapphire. The book contained the entire history of mankind — past, present, and future. It included the secrets to the laws of the universe, the laws of creation, everything about the planets and stars, too. It named all of the angels and what they did, and it included information about how humans could summon angels and ward off demons."

Even Greer was giving Ada her undivided attention.

"After Adam was expelled from the garden, he was so

upset about what he'd done that God instructed Raziel to give Adam the book. It was partly to comfort Adam, but mainly it was to help him learn how to live outside the garden and show Adam and Eve how to find their way back to God.

Raziel did as God asked. Through the book, Adam gained great wisdom. He read about every single soul who was yet to be born for all the generations to come. Adam knew some things that many of the angels didn't know ... things they'd never been privy to."

"That's amazing," Greer said. "When the serpent told Eve that she and Adam would know all if they ate from the tree of knowledge, in a way he was right. Yeah, they got booted out of the garden, but the Book of Raziel really *did* give them the knowledge and wisdom of God."

They all considered her idea for a moment.

"Anyway," Ada continued. "Some of the angels got jealous that God had entrusted this book to man, his newest creation who'd already let God down. So they stole the book from Adam and threw it into the sea. But God ordered Rahab, the Angel of the Seas, to retrieve the book and give it back to Adam, who passed it down to his son Seth. It got passed on down through the generations until it eventually reached Enoch, and then it disappeared from man again. But Raziel gave the book to Noah who used it to figure out how to build the ark."

"How do you know all this?" X asked.

"I've been studying this for my Bat Mitzvah," she replied.

Vero knew a little bit about Bat Mitzvahs. He understood it was a ceremony that was done in the Jewish religion during which a kid becomes an adult. And then they have an amazing party afterward.

"Noah placed the book in a golden box, and it was the

first thing he brought with him onto the ark. Later, Abraham was given the book, and then his son Jacob, and then *his* son Joseph who used it to learn the secrets of dreams. The book was buried with Joseph after he died. But years later, when Moses led the Israelites out of Egypt, he removed the bones of Joseph from the Nile and found the book with them. And it was Raziel who made sure the book always got into the proper hands. Eventually King Solomon used it to build a temple for God in Jerusalem."

"So where's the book now?" Vero asked.

"No one knows," Ada shrugged. "Some think it was destroyed when the temple was burned down."

"Does Raziel know where it is?" Pax asked.

"I don't think so. He used to be the archangel closest to God's throne. Now he teaches at C.A.N.D.L.E. My guess is that it disappeared on his watch. Even though its disappearance must be a part of God's bigger plan, Raziel probably took the blame for its loss."

"But Raziel knew what was in the book. Can't he just write everything down in a new book?" X wondered aloud.

"No, supposedly his memories regarding most of the information was taken from him."

"Well, God has to know where the book is," Pax said. "Why can't he just let the angels know?"

"Sure, and while God is at it, why can't he just stop wars? Or for that matter, every single bad thing that happens?" Ada asked.

Vero reflected for a moment. "Because he won't interfere with free will."

"Exactly," Ada replied. "Just like people, angels make decisions, and their actions have consequences. It's prophesied that the book will be found again, but nobody knows by whom. And I'm sure Raziel is worried about it because if that book lands in the wrong hands—as in, the hands of the Fallen—then Lucifer's power will increase tenfold."

Vero hoped the book had been destroyed in the fire. That was far better than the alternative.

❖

The fledglings walked along the open plains. They had come a great distance from the swamp, but it felt as if they were walking to nowhere—almost like they were on a treadmill. The angels were searching for a way out, but to where?

"I think we passed that tree three times already," Pax informed the group.

"No, they're just all starting to look the same," X said.

"Does anyone know what we should be doing?" Ada asked. "Greer, what's your inner voice telling you?"

"Sorry, I got nothing," Greer answered.

"What about you, Vero?" Ada asked.

But Vero didn't answer her. While he was physically walking alongside the others, mentally he was somewhere else.

"I think Vero's got something," Greer said.

"Vero! Vero!" Greer smacked the back of his head to bring him out of his stupor.

Vero snapped out of it and turned to Greer. "Kane's in trouble."

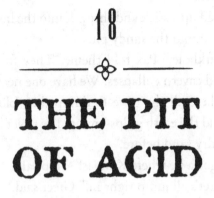

18

THE PIT
OF ACID

I could see him." Vero said. "He's scared. Really scared."

"Where is he?" X asked.

"I'm not sure, but it's dark. It looked like he's underground."

"That narrows it down," Greer said.

"I'm sorry, did *you* take a class in interpreting visions?" Vero asked sarcastically.

Greer looked away.

"Didn't think so," Vero said.

"Look over here!" Pax yelled.

Vero, Greer, Ada, and X turned their heads toward Pax. He was on his knees looking at a sandy indentation within an otherwise grassy field.

As they approached, Pax extended his arm like a school crossing guard, stopping them from coming any closer.

"Watch this."

Pax picked up a stick and threw it into the hole. Instantly it disappeared into the sandy pit.

"It's a sinkhole," Pax told them. "They form when an underground cavern collapses. We have one near our house. People go there all the time to dump their old appliances and stuff, and the earth gulps 'em up. I've never heard of one forming in dry sand before."

"That's gotta be where Kane is!" Vero said.

"Great! Let's all jump right in!" Greer said.

Vero looked at Greer for a moment. In spite of her sarcasm, Vero knew Greer had taught them an important lesson with that last jump — don't hesitate. So almost together, the others all leapt into the sinkhole.

"Wait!" Greer shouted. "I didn't mean it!"

But it was too late.

This jump was completely different than the last one. Vero felt perfectly relaxed, and when he opened his eyes, he found himself inside an illuminated underground cavern with Ada, Pax, and X. A moment later, a hole appeared in the ceiling of the cavern, Greer fell through, and then the hole closed up again. Greer landed on her feet and stumbled to one knee, but she quickly stood up again and brushed the sand out of her hair. The rings on her ears caught the strange light and made sparkling reflections along the cavern walls.

"Okay, hotshot, now what?" she asked.

"We find Kane," Vero said. "Is anyone feeling anything?" he asked the group.

"Nope. This one is all you," Greer answered.

"Fine. Then we'll go this way," Vero said.

"You mean right through that giant spiderweb you just walked into?" Greer asked.

"Ahh!" Vero swatted the air wildly. "Where's the spider? Is it on me? Help!"

As he continued to jump around like a crazy man, he noticed a playful smile on Greer's face.

"What?"

"There's no spiderweb," X said, chuckling.

Vero stopped hopping around. At this moment he had two choices. He could either get mad at them, or he could laugh at himself. He chose the latter. A smile formed at the corners of his mouth.

"Now can we go find Kane?" X asked.

The group walked along an underground trail. The dull light that surrounded them seemed to emanate from the floor, casting odd, eerie shadows on the walls. Greer's hand shot up, indicating that everyone should stop walking. She'd heard something. It was a rustling sound like the flutter of wings. She turned to look behind the group and screamed, "BATS!"

Hundreds, maybe even thousands of bats swarmed overhead, and they were headed their way. Greer took off running. And X, Pax, and Ada followed on her heels. Only Vero continued walking at his leisurely pace.

"Nice try, guys. I'm not falling for that again," he said.

Suddenly, a cluster of the black-winged mammals swooped down onto Vero's head. Vero screamed and ran, but he lost his footing on the slippery ground and slid a few feet on his back. The bats descended upon him, and Vero curled into a ball, covered his head with his arms, and closed his eyes.

Vero braced for an attack, but several seconds passed and nothing happened. When Vero dared to open one eye, the cluster of bats were hovering a few feet above him, swarming like a hive of angry bees. Something was preventing them from flying any closer to him. Vero opened his other eye. A jagged object that looked like an upside down-icicle had grown up out of the ground next to his foot. Vero jerked his foot back. The giant icicle was red and shiny like a crystal with razor-sharp edges.

Without any warning, thousands of the daggerlike icicles sprouted from the ground. And when Vero turned his gaze upward, he saw more growing down from the cavern's ceiling, hanging like jewel-covered sword blades. They weren't just red, either, but a vivid array of colors, bursting with light like the wildflowers of the Ether.

"Stalactites," X said, coming up behind Vero. He stared open-mouthed at the cave's roof. "I studied them in my science class. They usually take thousands of years to form. Here . . . " X looked at his watch, "it took about ten seconds."

Greer, Pax, and Ada stood among the massive formations.

"It's too bright in here with all of these colors, so the bats won't come any closer," X said. "The ones jutting up from the ground are stalagmites. They're usually made up of mineral deposits, though I'm not sure what these are made of."

The stalactites hung so far down from the ceiling that they nearly touched the stalagmites that shot up from the cavern floor. So it appeared as if they were in the mouth of some hideous beast with really nasty teeth. A pathway through the formations looked nearly impossible to navigate.

The walls also glistened with countless formations. Helictites had grown horizontally from the walls at all different angles, though none vertical. The formations seemed to defy gravity. They shot out from the walls in strange configurations resembling curly fries or clumps of worms. Yet the ends of the helictites were pointed like sharp needles. Brushing up against them, Vero knew, would not be wise.

"It doesn't look like we can go that way," Ada announced.

"Yes, but the bats are saying that's the only way," X said, his eyes fixed on the horde of nocturnal creatures who were madly teeming on the other side of the stalactites.

Pax thought he heard something. He held his index finger to his mouth to shush the others.

"What is it?" Ada whispered.

"I think I hear Kane."

The others strained their ears to listen as well. After a few seconds, a boy's voice drifted through the cavern.

"It *is* Kane!" Pax shouted.

"Shhh ... " Vero said. He craned his neck in the direction of the voice. He was able to make out the distant sound, and then the word *help* floated in the air. "He's in trouble!" Vero said.

Kane's pleas were coming from deeper inside the cavern.

"How can we get to him?" Ada asked.

"Fly," X said. "We can get airborne in here."

"But it's really narrow," Pax said. "Our wingspans are too wide."

"And besides, where are you gonna land? Right on some spiky stalagmite?" Greer asked.

"Maybe they're not as sharp as we think," X said. He tentatively ran his index finger over the tip of the nearest one, then quickly jerked it back. A bright red trickle of blood ran down his finger.

"Never mind."

"Somehow we have to navigate our way through this cave," Vero said.

No one looked too excited.

"You know what?" Vero said. "We slogged through the world's grossest swamp and outmaneuvered a herd of behemoths. So how much harder could this be?"

"I have a feeling those words are going to come back and bite you in the butt," Greer said.

❖

"Keep your head down so you don't trip," Vero said. Slowly they weaved their way, single file, through the maze of razor-sharp stalactites and stalagmites, with Vero in the lead.

Each step needed to be deliberate and cautious. As they wove their way deeper into the cavern, Kane's cries for help became progressively clearer, guiding them like a compass.

"We're getting closer," Vero said. "Stay focused."

Pax had a definite advantage, being smaller than the others. But it was a much more difficult journey for X who was nearly six feet tall and had to manipulate the formations while hunching over awkwardly.

"I can't take this much longer," X said. "My back's killing me."

"And it's cold," Ada complained. By now they could all see their breath.

"We're getting closer," Vero said. "Just keep going."

"You don't get it! I'm in agony!" X snapped, and then he abruptly stopped walking.

Greer plowed into him, causing both of them to lose their balance and fall.

Vero whipped around and saw X's face land just millimeters away from a stalagmite.

"Watch out! I almost got shish kebabbed!" Greer protested. Then she got back on her feet while being careful to keep her head tucked low.

"Sorry," X said. "My back is killing me."

"When someone's on your tail, you can't stop like that. We're all tired and hurting. But we can't stop now. Kane needs our help." She offered a hand to help X up, and her gesture seemed to be just enough to keep X moving forward.

As they continued through the cavern, Vero noticed it was becoming more difficult to breathe. He felt his thighs burn with each step. *The ground must be sloping upward.*

Finally they reached a break in the rock formations, a small clearing where no more sharp formations pushed out from the cave's walls, ceiling, or floor. But best of all, the ceiling in this small chamber was tall enough for them all to stand fully upright.

"Oh man, I never thought standing up straight would feel so good!" X stretched as tall as he could.

Pax laid flat on his back on the cold ground, trying to catch his breath. Vero and Greer stood next to X and stretched.

"I can't hear Kane anymore," Vero said.

Pax rolled onto his stomach and looked toward the back of the chamber. "Uh, guys," he said. "Better take a look at this."

"What now?" Ada asked.

As they walked over, they all saw what Pax was pointing to. Right where the back wall of the cave hit the floor was a dark hole ... a hole just big enough for a fledgling to crawl through. It reminded Vero of a mousehole, only bigger.

Still lying on his stomach, Pax stuck his head through the opening and began crawling through it.

"Hold on!" Vero called, but Pax had already disappeared into the darkness.

Vero dropped to his hands and knees to follow him, but at that moment Pax called back, "It's Kane! I can see him!"

The others crowded around the hole as Vero disappeared into it, quick as a mouse.

Once through the hole, Vero noticed immediately that the floor and the walls of the narrow passage were very smooth and tilted downward at a steep slant. He felt like he was crawling down the tunnel in a waterslide, and he had to push his hands and feet against the walls to avoid sliding all the way. He carefully crawled forward and wedged himself tightly next to Pax who was looking over a ledge.

Swirling below them was a steaming pit of bubbling water. A number of rocks and eddies were peppered throughout the pit, and the churning liquid sloshed against them, making a gurgling sound. And there was Kane, sitting forlornly on the largest rock right in the middle of the pit. Vero yelled to him, and Kane looked up, his eyes squinting.

"I'm stuck! I can't get out! There's nowhere to fly!" Kane shouted over the loud bubbling noises of the water. "No way out!"

Vero could see a smooth, solid rock wall surrounding the pit. So there was no way for Kane to get out that way.

"What's beneath me? I can't tell! What kind of wall is it?" Vero called to Kane.

"You're on top of a sheer wall! There's no footing beneath you at all!"

"Can't you fly up here?" Vero asked.

"No. That hole is how I got into this stinkin' angel trap in the first place! I slid through it and now I can't get back to it. The entrance is too close to the ceiling! I've already tried a hundred times to fly back up there ... but I can't get close enough while my wings are out, and there's no foothold on the wall for me to land on."

"Too bad there aren't any stalactites around here," Vero told Pax. Vero felt something tug on his legs, and then Greer yanked him back from the edge. She was lying on her belly in the narrow tunnel.

"Move it, angel. I'll handle this," Greer said, and then she combat crawled right over Vero and landed on top of Pax who grimaced under her weight. She stuck her head out over the ledge and saw Kane sitting on the rock. "Kane, this is Greer! You need to just suck it up and swim over to us!"

"Can't!" Kane shouted.

"Don't tell me you can't swim!"

"No ... that's not it," Kane said.

"Look," Pax said, "the walls and rocks in here are lime-stone. That means that liquid in the pit is highly acidic. Watch ... " Pax reached around to his back and winced as he pulled out a small feather without extending his wings.

"Impressive trick," Greer said.

"Inch out a little more," Pax instructed.

Greer army crawled a little farther while bracing herself against the walls with both hands. She looked at the water below.

"Now watch." Pax held the feather over the slogging

liquid and let go. Greer watched as it floated gently down-ward. The lone feather hit the surface — and disintegrated into a puff of smoke upon impact.

"Okay, so swimming is out," Greer said. "I officially have no plan."

"Everyone, get out of the passage, now!" X boomed from behind them.

Vero, Greer, and then Pax all had to inch out of the tun-nel backward and single file, using their hands to push them back up the narrow tunnel and into the chamber.

"We need a plan here!" X said, as he paced the small cavern. "What are we going to do?"

"The only way to get Kane out of there is to drag him back through that claustrophobic tunnel," Vero said.

"And he's going to have to fly up to the tunnel," Greer agreed. "Swimming is definitely out."

"But he can't get close enough to the entrance with his wings extended," Pax said.

"And if he tries to retract his wings, the pit of acid is right there, and he'll fall into it. He needs time to be able to pull in his wings," Ada said.

"I've got it!" shouted X. "We'll form a human chain through the tunnel. Whoever's at the front will have to dan-gle out over the edge and grab hold of him. That'll buy him the time he needs to withdraw his wings, and then we can all pull him back through the hole."

"That's a great plan," Ada said excitedly.

"Yeah, if you're looking for a one-way ticket to choir prac-tice," Greer said. "We'll be burnt to a crisp in that drink!"

"X is right, though," Vero said. "It's the only way."

They looked at each other, silently weighing their options. Kane's faint cry for help drifted through the mouse hole.

X sighed heavily. "Okay, I have the best upper body strength from spending my life in a wheelchair, so I'll be the one to catch Kane."

"No," Vero said. "We need your strength to anchor the chain. I'll grab Kane."

"No arguments from me," Greer said.

The others solemnly nodded. Vero laid down on his belly and squirmed his way back down the steep tunnel. Pax went next and grabbed Vero's ankles. The others completed the remainder of the human chain with X holding Greer's feet as they stuck out through the mousehole.

When Vero's head reappeared over the edge, he shouted instructions to Kane. "You're going to have to fly over to me and grab my hands. Then — and do this as quick as you can — retract your wings, and we'll all pull you back through the tunnel!"

Kane looked uncertain. It was definitely a risky plan, but Kane stood on the tiny rock island and nodded.

"Wait 'til I give you the sign!" Vero shouted.

The others remained in position, with X serving as the anchor back in the chamber, then Greer, then Ada, and then Pax held Vero's ankles as Vero extended his entire body over the ledge. Using his left hand to brace himself against the ceiling, Vero extended his right hand as far as possible so he could grab and hold on to Kane. It would be close, but he knew they could do it.

"Ready?" Vero called down to Kane. When Kane nodded, Vero shouted, "Now!"

Kane opened his wings and lifted off the rock. He hovered in the air for a moment and then flew over to Vero.

As Kane approached, Vero held out both hands to grab Kane, but at the last moment, Kane hesitated.

He shook his head. "It won't work!" he said.

"Yes it will!" Vero yelled. "Come on, hurry! We're losing strength!"

Kane continued to waver. And every second of waiting depleted Vero's energy. He felt Pax's grip weakening too.

"Come on, Pax! I've seen you move SUVs with your bare hands!" Vero shouted. "Hold tight!"

"But I was answering a prayer at the time!" Pax yelled back.

"Yeah? Then hear MY prayer and ... DON'T LET GO!"

Pax tightened his grip on Vero.

"Kane, grab a hold of Vero's hands now or rot on that rock forever!" Greer shouted from the mouth of the tunnel.

A huge bubble burst in the acid below, and the spray reached Vero's face and singed off his right eyebrow. "NOW, Kane, or we're leaving you!" Vero shouted.

Kane flew up to Vero and clasped hands with him. His weight pulled Vero farther out over the ledge as he quickly retracted his wings.

"Got him!" Vero yelled to the others. "Now pull!"

The chain of angels tugged hard, but Kane was still suspended over the edge. And Vero's grip was loosening.

"Hurry!" Vero shouted.

X pulled Greer's ankles tight as she backed out of the tunnel and reentered the chamber. When she was clear of the mousehole, she told X to come grab Ada's other ankle. But as X let go of Greer, the whole line started sliding forward.

"Don't let go!" Pax shrieked. "Please!"

"I can't hold on any longer!" Ada yelled, feeling her fingers slipping away from Pax's ankles.

Suddenly, Ada felt a mighty force around her left ankle. The strength of the grip told her that X was now pulling her back toward the chamber. His power was incredible. Ada breathed a sigh of relief. But then X lost his footing. He pushed back on his heels, but he couldn't find any traction. They all started sliding back toward the acidic water.

"Your wings! Open your wings!" Ada shouted back to X. "They'll anchor you!"

X willed his wings to protrude, and they shot open with the force of an umbrella battling a windstorm. His wings wedged against the chamber walls, arresting his slide toward the hole. He was finally able to pull Ada safely inside the chamber, then Pax, Vero, and finally Kane.

As everyone caught their breath, Kane looked at his rescuers and muttered faintly, "Thanks, guys."

Thank you doesn't even begin to cover it, Vero thought, as he touched his missing eyebrow.

19

THE NARROW PATH

How did you wind up on that rock?" Pax asked Kane.

"I'm not sure. I was standing out in that desert. It was burning hot, and the sand was whipping against my face, so I closed my eyes and tried to listen to the voice of truth like Raziel said. Next thing I know, I'm in here—in this room."

"There were only two ways out ... through those stalagmite things or through that hole. I figured only an idiot would try to go through those, I mean, did you see how sharp they are? So, I decided to see what was on the other side of that hole. I didn't realize it was a trap 'til I was sliding downhill into that cavern. I spread my wings and caught my fall—thank you, God—and I managed to land on that rock. But then I was stuck there."

Vero and the others stared at Kane as he finished his story. Greer appeared as annoyed as Vero felt.

"What?" Kane asked.

"We were the big enough *idiots* to crawl through those stalagmites to rescue you," X said, still massaging his lower back.

"Oops. I'm sorry, guys," Kane said guiltily. "Here, let me just pull my foot out of my mouth."

"Good idea. That way, I can shove my fist in there instead," Greer said.

Vero thought for a moment. How was it that he and the others had wound up in the cool room with the pool of refreshing water, but not Kane? Why had the voice led Kane to a trap and not the stream? Why was Kane led to danger?

"Do you want to know why you ended up alone on that rock with no way out?" Greer asked Kane. "It's because you were being a total jerk. You were mad."

"Yeah, but if he was listening to his inner voice, and Raziel said that voice is God, then why was God punishing Kane?" Vero asked.

"No. It wasn't God's voice. It wasn't his *Vox Dei*. Didn't you hear what Raziel told us?" Greer asked.

Vero flashed her a puzzled look. He tried to recall Raziel's lesson, but he was on sensory overload.

"When you doubt or get angry with God, Lucifer seizes that opportunity. He sends his minions, and they slip in and cloud your thoughts, totally messing with you. That's what happened to Kane."

Vero silently pondered what Greer said. The thought of being under the devil's influence, especially here in the Ether, was terrifying. He was determined it wouldn't happen to him — no matter what.

Ada stood and looked up at the ceiling of the cave. "I'm

feeling really claustrophobic and kind of cold," she said. "I'd like to get out of here."

"Me too," Pax agreed.

Vero closed his eyes and focused his mind on doing the right thing. He tried to block out everything and concentrate. But thoughts raced in and out of his mind. Kane on the rock ... Ada in the tunnel ... Clover at dinner ... Danny and Davina at the movies. *No! I need to focus!*

He thought about the track meet and how good it felt to pass Danny. Then he recalled how he felt unexplainably guilty. He thought of Blake and Duff and how they seemed glad that Vero had won the race. He thought about the raven with the long tail, about the constant battle between good and evil—whether it was physical, like with the maltures, or mental, like how he constantly battled his innate nature.

No, he had to accept the goodness. God's goodness. He remembered the feeling of peace that overcame him on the night he made his snow angel, and he let that feeling fill him once again. *Please God, know my heart.*

Suddenly, Vero felt true goodness wash over him, and after a few moments, the path became clear to him. He opened his eyes.

"We need to keep moving forward through the stalactites," Vero said.

"I don't know how much more I can take in there," Ada said.

The angels surveyed the area that lay ahead of them, and then the area that lay behind them. Their options were limited. Either way looked pretty much the same—the roof, walls, and ground were decorated with stalactites, stalagmites, and helictites.

"I say we listen to Vero and move on," X said.

"You're only saying that because you don't want to walk hunched over," Pax said.

X nodded and said, "Maybe. But the truth is, it doesn't look much different either way."

X looked to Kane for his opinion.

"Don't look at me. You saw which way I picked," Kane said. "This time I'm keeping my mouth shut."

Pax turned to Greer, "I say we go back."

"I say we go ahead," Greer nodded to Vero. Then she turned to Pax and said, "But we could always split up if you feel strongly about it." She looked at each angel in turn. "If I had to go on my own, I would. I could do this alone."

Pax shook his head. "We stay together."

❖

The angels snaked their way through a seemingly endless maze of stalactites and stalagmites. At times, the way was so narrow that Vero sucked in his breath and tried to make himself thinner. Vero sensed their reflexes dulling.

Suddenly Pax screamed out in pain. Vero carefully turned his head and saw the right side of Pax's face covered in what looked like dozens of cactus needles, from his forehead to his chin.

"He brushed up against some helictites!" Ada called to the others.

Pax cried out, "Get them out! Please! They burn!" Tears ran down his face.

Vero looked around. The space was way too tight for anyone to be able to stand next to Pax and pull them out.

"Pax, I'm sorry," Vero said. "But you're gonna have to keep walking until we find a place big enough where we can help you pull them out."

"Try not to think about them," Kane said, as they slowly made their way through the deadly obstacle course.

"I can't," Pax whimpered. "It hurts too much."

"We need to distract him," Ada told the others.

"Ninety-nine bottles of beer on the wall, ninety-nine bottles of beer ... " Greer began to sing. "Take one down, pass it around, ninety-eight bottles of beer ... "

"That'll really push him over the edge," X said to Greer, cutting her off.

"I'm only trying to help." Greer shrugged.

"Pax, what's your favorite color?" Vero asked, hoping to distract him from the pain.

"Blue."

"You like pizza?"

"Yeah."

"Good at sports?"

"No."

"Then I bet you get good grades?"

"I don't go to school."

"Really?" Vero said, surprised. "Why not?"

"I'm severely autistic on earth," Pax said. "I don't have any language. I wear a helmet all day to keep from hurting myself."

Vero stopped walking and carefully turned around to look at Pax. Vero's eyes were full of emotion as he said, "I'm sorry."

"Maybe that's why you're the only one of us who can hear thoughts," X said. "Maybe because you can't speak on earth, you've learned to communicate in other ways. My life on earth is tough too, but being in a wheelchair has made me stronger—and not just my arms, but mentally too. I think it's all part of our training."

Vero thought about that as the group walked on in silence. Compared to X, Pax, and Greer, Vero's life was pretty good. Was it sheer luck or was his family life preparing him for something? He didn't know.

Mercifully, the cavern's landscape began to change. Rocks and boulders gradually replaced the stalactites and stalagmites. Finally, the cavern widened, and the angels could stand and stretch.

"Hold still," X said to Pax. X gripped one of the needles and gently pulled it out.

"Thank you," Pax said softly. "It feels better already."

One by one, X pulled out the rest of them and let them drop to the ground.

"You okay?" Vero asked. Pax's face looked a bit swollen, but otherwise he seemed all right.

"Yeah," Pax replied. "But I have a headache."

"So do I," Kane said.

"Well suck it up, boys," Greer said. "We have a climb ahead of us."

The fledglings looked and saw their next adventure involved scaling a steep mountain of rocks and large stones.

X sighed heavily. "Well, at least we can stand up straight."

"I say we fly to the top," Pax suggested.

"Me too," Greer said. She began flapping her wings, but nothing happened. Then each of the other angels tried, but no one rose into the air.

"This makes no sense," Kane said.

"We must be at high altitude," Vero reasoned.

"How do you know?" Pax asked.

"My dad trained to be a pilot for the Navy. He used to explain to me that everything that uses air for flight propulsion—jets, helicopters, or even birds, has an altitude ceiling. Above that height, the air is just too thin for flight."

"Altitude sickness would explain the headaches," X said.

"And why I feel out of breath," Kane added.

"Okay, science class is now over," Greer said irritably. "Let's scale this baby."

As the angels climbed, X led the way, carefully placing each foot on the treacherous mountain of crumbled brown rock and shale. With each step, the unstable rubble would shift and sometimes roll downhill, causing other rocks and debris to slide.

Besides falling and cutting themselves on jagged rocks, Vero feared that upsetting the wrong rock could trigger an avalanche and bury them all.

"X, how much farther is it?" Pax asked, his face streaked with sweat.

"I can't tell," X answered. "I can't see the top."

As Ada grabbed onto a rock to pull herself up, the rock slipped out from under her and rolled straight toward Greer who was climbing behind her.

"Greer!" Ada yelled. "Look out!"

Greer looked up, saw the rock, and jerked her face out of its path just in time. The rock barely missed her head, but it smashed her left leg, shattering the bone.

Greer screamed in agony and grabbed her leg. Vero and the others watched helplessly as Greer lost her balance and plunged to the ground.

"Greer!" Ada shouted.

Greer didn't answer. X quickly maneuvered his way through a cluster of boulders and reached her side. Greer was sitting on the craggy ground, leaning against a smooth rock.

"Look," Greer said. She lifted her injured leg with her hands and let it drop back to the ground. It was completely useless.

"I guess walking is out," X thought aloud.

The others climbed back down to Greer.

Ada's normally olive skin was white as a sheet. "I'm so sorry … "

"Does it hurt?" Pax asked, bending down close to her.

"At first, but now it's just numb."

"I'm really sorry," Ada said again. "I didn't mean to … "

"Well you did," Greer said.

"It was an accident," Pax said. "It wouldn't have happened if we hadn't come this way."

Greer locked eyes with Vero, "Maybe it was the wrong way to come."

"I'm sorry you got hurt," Vero said. "But I really feel like we need to keep going."

"How?" Pax asked. "Do you think Greer's gonna be able to climb up there?"

"Yes," Vero said. "We'll help her."

"No. I'm taking her back the way we came, whether any of you come with us or not," Ada said.

"You think getting her through those stalactites will be any easier?" Vero asked.

"At least that way I know what we're dealing with."

Vero looked to the others for support, but he didn't find

any. Greer looked dazed and pale, Pax was shaking, Kane looked frustrated, and X ... "Where's X?"

"He was just here," Kane said.

Vero looked around and found X crouched behind several large boulders with a rock in his hand.

"What are you doing?" Vero asked.

"Watch," X said.

X chucked the rock as hard as he could, and it disappeared into the darkness.

Vero wasn't impressed. "Are you losing it?"

"You didn't hear it land, did you?"

X was right. Vero never heard the rock hit the ground. "I ... I don't know ... "

As X picked up another rock, Ada, Pax, and Kane helped a limping Greer hobble over to the boulder.

X gently threw the rock directly in front of them. It disappeared without a sound.

"It just vanished into thin air," Kane said.

"I say we do the same," X announced.

"Are you crazy?" Pax said.

"Are you willing to carry Greer back through the stalactite cave or up that hill of boulders?" X asked. Everyone was silent.

But something didn't feel right to Vero. "I don't know about this," he said.

"I say we take a chance," said X.

Vero once again looked to the others, and the fact that no one would look him in the eye gave Vero his answer. Kane stood and put one of Greer's arms around his neck, while X did the same with her other arm. They hoisted her to her feet.

"I'm sorry," Greer whispered.

Kane and X did a double take. "What?"

"As much as it kills me to say it," Greer said, "I really do need you guys."

Vero and Ada exchanged glances. Vero knew it was hard for Greer to admit that.

Pax smiled at Greer, and Ada gave her an awkward hug.

"Whatever," Greer said, feeling awkward with all of that positive attention.

Vero watched as Kane and X assisted Greer. Without looking back, the three of them walked toward the spot where the rock had vanished, and then they simply disappeared into thin air. Ada glanced at Vero and shrugged. Then she took Pax's hand in her own and followed the other three until they also vanished before Vero's eyes.

Everything inside of Vero was telling him not to move forward. He wanted to scream, *"Don't go!"* But then the fear of being left alone overshadowed his instincts, and so ignoring his own instincts, Vero ran after the others.

20

◆

GOLEMS

Vero found himself being pulled at an alarming rate, by an overpowering force, as if he were a tiny scrap of metal being yanked forward by a gigantic magnet. The rapid motion turned his stomach, and faster and faster he went until ... *Bam!* He found himself flat on his back in the middle of another cavern. Only this one was fairly large and filled with light from the torches that lined the walls. Above him was a high domed ceiling carved out of stone.

As soon as he was able to sit up and take in his surroundings, Vero saw the other angels sprawled around the room. Greer was sitting against the cavern wall with her busted leg out straight in front of her, biting her fingernails. Vero thought she looked smaller and worn out due to the pain. She leaned her head back against the wall and closed her eyes. "I hate this. I hate not being able to walk on my own."

"Where are we?" Pax asked.

"Wherever we are, at least it's warmer in here," Ada said as she walked over to Vero.

"I'm starting to wonder if we'll ever see the green grass of the Ether again," said Kane.

"Don't blame me," Vero said, looking around nervously. "I didn't want to come this way. It doesn't feel right."

"When was the last time anyone heard their inner voice?" X asked.

"All I hear right now is a bunch of whining," Ada said.

"I have a good reason to whine," Greer moaned, massaging her leg.

"I'm starving and tired," X said, as he sat down on a large rock jutting out from the wall.

"Instead of worrying about how tired we are, I think we should be more worried about who lit these torches," Kane said.

The group fell silent.

Vero looked at X. Then he did a double take. "I think I'm seeing things. That rock you're sitting on looked like it just moved."

"I thought I felt something," X said. He looked down at the exposed rock between his legs.

They heard a muffled grunt. They all stood and looked around—all except Greer who could only scoot away from the wall—and everyone was on full alert.

Suddenly, the rock under X divided, and X fell between the moving ledges onto hard, stone ground! Massive chunks of stone began to break away from the cavern walls. The fledglings circled protectively around Greer, standing back-to-back, and they watched in horror as the gigantic rocks formed into the shape of an enormous creature. The rocks that X had been sitting on were actually monstrous feet!

Those feet were attached to legs, the legs were attached to a torso that had boulders for arms and fingers, and above them all—a massive head!

"Wh- ... wha- ... what ...?" X stammered.

The creature was made out of stone and hard clay, and it stood more than thirty feet tall.

The fledglings staggered backward and gathered even closer to Greer who grabbed ahold of Kane's shoulder and pulled herself to her feet. Her low groans revealed how much pain she was in with every move.

Her groans were echoed by the others—only ten times louder—when another hard-clay creature broke away from the opposite wall. Now two oversized, craggy ogres towered over the angels!

"Maybe they're friendly?" Greer said, though she sounded less than confident.

"Any ideas?" Pax asked, his face tense with fear.

No one had any.

The first creature blocked the way they'd come in. The other creature blocked what appeared to be a doorway carved in the stone. The fledglings were trapped.

"Fly!" X shouted.

"Where?" Vero yelled back.

"Up!"

Kane and X steadied Greer as she opened her wings and rose unsteadily into the air. Then they followed her, keeping close. Ada and Pax flew to the top of the domed ceiling. Vero now stood alone, trapped between the two creatures as they closed in on him. He looked for an escape route, but saw none.

"Vero! Up here!" Kane yelled. "What are you waiting for?"

"I can't just take off! I need a running start!"

"If I can do it with a broken leg, you definitely can!" Greer shouted.

The giant creature's hand swatted downward, and Vero jumped to the side, his hair ruffled by the giant's hand as it smashed into the ground where Vero had been standing just seconds before.

"Definitely not friendly!" Greer said.

Vero closed his eyes. *Fly ... fly ... fly!* he repeated in his head.

Nothing happened.

The creature's hand smashed down a second time with even greater force. Vero danced around it. Now the golem cupped its hands, intending to wrap them around Vero and crush him into dust.

He glimpsed Ada turning her head away, too afraid to see what would happen to him. Just as he felt the stiff clay brushing up against his body, a steely resolve came over Vero. In his mind he pictured himself as a strong, fierce angel with glorious wings. His eyes narrowed, and then he shot up into the air like a missile. He flew right past the creature's shoulder, and he didn't stop until he hit his head on the domed ceiling. Vero rubbed his head.

"Yeah, I guess there's no altitude problem in here!" X said to Vero.

The loud grunts coming from the stone creatures bounced off the chamber's walls. It was painful to their ears, and they had to shout to be heard.

"Now what do we do?" Ada asked as she dodged one of the creature's hands. They all hovered up by the ceiling, but they were still barely above the reach of the rock monsters.

"What are they?" Vero asked.

"I think they're golems," Ada said. "They're mentioned in the Talmud ... "

"The what?" Vero asked.

"The Talmud. It's one of the sacred Jewish books, a companion to the Torah," Ada said. "In it, golems are described as being crude and unthinking beings made of clay who could be brought to life by the high priests in times of great need. But I thought they were just Jewish folklore."

"Obviously they're not folklore," Kane said. He flew back against a wall to avoid a golem's fist that was coming straight toward him.

"Spit it out. What do you know about them?" Greer asked, her voice thick with pain.

"Golems were created by rabbis, or holy men, to be their servants or protectors. Only religious people who were close to God could create them, although they're inferior to any of God's creations. That's why they have no soul."

One of the golems jumped into the air and took a swipe at X, but it missed and landed heavily, causing the entire cavern to rumble and shake like an earthquake.

"Do they have any weaknesses?" X asked.

"They're not very smart," Ada shouted over the golems' bellows. "They don't have brains."

"I can tell," Pax said. "I'm trying to read their minds, and there's nothing there."

"Just tell us how to kill them!" Greer shouted.

"The only way is to destroy them," Ada answered. "But it's pretty dangerous."

"What? What is it?" Vero asked.

"In one version of the ancient texts, a golem comes to life when its maker inscribes a sacred word on its forehead, like the Jewish word for *life*. Another version claims the word is written on parchment and put into its mouth to bring it to life. A golem is brought to life by the power of that specific word."

"So if that's true, then it must be in their mouths," Vero reasoned, "because there's nothing written on their foreheads."

"I guess so," Ada said.

"So we need to get the parchment out of their mouths?" Kane asked.

"Yes, but in order to kill the creature, you have to read the word back to them."

"It sounds as simple as taking candy from a baby," Greer said matter-of-factly. "Except these big babies could bite your arm off."

"Maybe we use the Heimlich maneuver and make them spit it out," Pax suggested.

Greer flashed him an annoyed look, "I think I see a word written on your forehead ... it says *Idiot*."

Vero swallowed hard. This was not going to be an easy task. But why should he be the one to step forward? He'd volunteered when he grabbed Kane over the acidic pit. Why couldn't one of the other ones do it this time? But then he thought of his crown waiting for him in heaven — the crown Raziel spoke about. He wanted to fill it up with jewels. So he bravely faced the others.

"I'll give it a try," he said. "But I have no idea how to do it."

"We need to distract them," Greer said, "get them to open their mouths so somehow you can sneak attack and stick your hand in there."

"It's a well thought-out plan ... except for that *get them to open their mouths so somehow you can sneak attack* part," Vero said, rolling his eyes.

They hovered in the air, silently. Vero had no ideas, and he could see Greer was in a lot of pain, even though she was still acting all tough. If they didn't come up with something, and soon, they were going to start dropping.

Kane spoke up. "Ada, you and Pax fly around that one," he said, pointing to the smaller of the two golems, "and keep him busy. The rest of us can buzz around the other big guy so maybe he'll open his mouth and Vero can reach in. Everyone think like mosquitos!"

Ada and Pax flew circles around the smaller golem, while Kane and X glided around the other one. Greer started out with them, but then she pulled back, gasping. "I'm ... I'm sorry," she said. "It just hurts so bad."

"It's okay, Greer," Vero said. "Just stay as far back as possible."

The golems struck at them like King Kong swatting at fighter planes. The fledglings dodged the golems' wild grasps, but the creatures did not tire.

"Time for a little action!" Kane yelled. He swept down to the ground and picked up a large rock.

"Over here!" Kane shouted, as he hovered in the air once more.

When the ugly golem turned around, Kane threw the rock at its head. It was a perfect shot, hitting it right between the eyes. The golem opened its mouth and howled loudly. Vero flew to its mouth, but he was too late.

"Kane, throw another one!" Vero shouted.

Kane swooped to the ground, grabbed another rock, and dive-bombed the golem. He made another direct hit — this time hitting the back of the golem's head. The golem roared and focused his black, lifeless eyes on Kane, who flew within the golem's reach.

"Watch out!" Greer screamed.

But it was too late. The creature punched Kane with its full strength, slamming him against the rock wall. He fell to the ground, unconscious.

"Kane!" X yelled.

But Kane didn't move. Now the golem was moving toward Kane, ready to stomp the life from him, when Vero, looking for a distraction, shoved his arm deep inside the golem's nose.

Vero locked eyes with the creature but continued poking around, reaching through the nasal cavity.

"What are you doing?" Greer shouted.

"I'm going through its nose to get into its mouth!" Vero shouted back.

The creature tried to swipe at Vero but hit itself on the cheek. Then it roared in frustration, and Vero thought his eardrums would explode. But with its mouth open during that deafening roar, Vero got the chance he needed. He pulled his hand out of its nose and put it into the monster's ferocious mouth. He pulled out a piece of parchment and then flew out of reach again.

"Read it!" Greer shouted. She sounded desperate. "Quick!"

Vero's hands were shaking violently, so he couldn't open the parchment.

Vero could hear Pax and Ada trying to distract the other golem. But it must have realized that Vero's golem was in need because it started toward Vero with a thunderous roar.

Behind him, Ada screamed, "Hurry!"

Vero turned and saw that Ada and X had flown circles around the approaching golem's head and caused it to lose its balance. Vero saw the golem slowly tip sideways until it fell and bashed its head against the wall. The blow shook the entire chamber. Rocks broke free in an avalanche, and Vero watched in horror as the golem fell facedown and narrowly missed Kane who still lay unconscious on the ground.

The golem landed hard. It let out a tremendous *Oof!* as the wind was knocked out of it, and the parchment shot out of its mouth.

"Get it!" Ada shouted.

With lightning speed, X dove and grabbed the parchment while the golem struggled to regain its balance. A moment later, the golem was upright again, swatting furiously at Ada and Pax.

"Hurry up! Read it before one of 'em steps on Kane!" Ada yelled.

X and Vero feverishly opened the parchments while flying haphazardly through the air and trying to stay aloft. Vero got his open, only to be overcome with dread. "It's blank!"

"Mine too!" X said.

"It can't be!" Ada said, and she flew to Vero's side. Her curls flew wildly around her face as she attempted to see the piece of paper. "There has to be something on it ... "

Both golems lumbered over to Kane.

"Kane! Wake up!" Greer screamed.

The golems were now upon Kane. Ada turned the parchment over desperately hoping she could see some writing, but it was blank on both sides. Just as the golem raised its mammoth foot above Kane's body to crush him, Vero stared intently at the parchment in his hands.

Please, God, let me read it, Vero prayed. Then suddenly, symbols began to appear before his eyes. And they formed a word.

Behind him, Ada screamed, "Hurry!"

"Emeth!" Vero shouted as loud as he could.

The golem turned toward Vero. Greer and Pax seized the moment, and in a well-orchestrated move, they grabbed Kane. They lifted him into the safety of the air—and not a moment too soon because the golem began to crumble before their very eyes. Piece by piece, the hard clay that formed the largest golem broke off into rock chunks.

"Read this one!" X shouted as he handed his parchment to Vero.

Vero had an easier time reading the second parchment. The symbols quickly formed before his eyes. "Shamad!" he yelled.

The second golem also began to crumble, creating a massive rockslide in the chamber. The rumbling noise jostled Kane, who woke up just in time to see the last one collapse.

"Awesome," Kane muttered.

They swooped down and landed on the crumbled rocks, exhausted. Greer flew to the ground with a rough landing and sat down hard. Her leg was bent at an awkward angle in front of her.

Vero clutched the parchments tightly, but they began to

wither until all that remained was a tiny lump of dust in the palm of his hand.

As they caught their breath, Ada asked Vero, "Did you ever study Hebrew?"

"Me? No."

"You shouted the word *emeth* to the golem. It means 'truth.' And *shamad* means 'destroy.'"

Vero shrugged.

"When I looked at that parchment, there was nothing there," Ada said.

"I didn't see anything at first either," Vero said. "But then it was like lines appeared and then the symbols, and I could read them."

"But I didn't see it," Ada said.

Vero couldn't explain how the symbols hadn't been on the paper at first, and then suddenly they were. Looking around, he felt the intense scrutiny of the other angels. He couldn't read their thoughts, but he knew what they were thinking. *Freak.*

21

THE BLACK MIST

After the destruction of the golems, the young angels surveyed the damage. Unfortunately, the golems had collapsed right in front of one of the exits, so they had only one possible choice for making their escape—another small, dark, claustrophobic tunnel.

"It's not *too* small," Vero said, holding a torch near the opening. "And it seems like there's enough room that one person can help Greer. But there's definitely not enough room to fly."

"I'll help her," Kane said.

"Ha," Greer said.

"What?" Kane's perplexed look made Vero chuckle.

"I think what Greer is trying to say is that you're not in much better shape than she is," Vero said.

Kane's normally dark hair was plastered flat with red and

gray dust from the rocks. He had dried blood on his cheek from the cut on his nose, and his upper lip was split. All of their faces were covered with dust, and their lips were cracked and chapped.

"Let's see where this tunnel leads us," X said, pulling another torch off the wall. "Hopefully to a hot shower."

Vero and X took the lead, holding their torches out in front of them. The others followed close behind, and Greer leaned on Kane for support. Worn out, they all walked in silence. Vero glanced over his shoulder. Greer was grimacing with every step.

"Everything we've gone through so far was supposed to be one huge training exercise," Ada said, breaking the silence. "What lesson do you think we're supposed to learn from the golems?"

"That we're resourceful," X said.

"And pretty smart," Pax added.

"We outsmarted two brainless creatures," Greer pointed out. "Think about it: How smart does that really make us?"

Kane chuckled, "Good point."

Vero noticed they were now walking through a low-lying mist, about shin deep. "Hold up," he said, raising his arm to signal that the others should stop. He shuffled forward while fully expecting to hit something. But after taking a dozen steps without bumping into anything, Vero relaxed. "I guess it's okay," he said. The group continued on ahead.

Soon, the fog grew denser, and it was now up to their waists. Within two more steps, it swirled all around them, thickening and getting darker. They breathed it in, but it had no scent. It filled their ears, but it was silent. It filled their mouths when they spoke, but it had no taste.

"You know what? Maybe we weren't supposed to learn anything from the golems except that we shouldn't have been in that cavern in the first place," Vero said. "It never felt right going that way. I went against my inner voice. And now that I think about it, I feel like ever since we rescued Kane, we've been getting farther and farther away from God."

"What?" Kane asked sharply. "So this is all *my* fault?"

"Yeah," Vero answered. "Pretty much."

"Why don't you do me a favor and not talk to me anymore!" Kane yelled.

"With pleasure!" Vero yelled back.

"Shut up, Vero. I think we've all heard enough out of you and your *special* voice and your *special* ideas!" X's raised voice echoed through the tunnel.

Pax tripped and bumped into Ada.

"You're such a stupid klutz," Ada said.

"Why don't you whine about it a little more!" Pax shot back. "That's all you do!"

How could Vero have been so thankful for these other *fledglings* just a short time ago? X said it himself: Vero *was* special! He didn't need them. He didn't care about them. Why should he?

From behind, Vero heard Kane sigh in frustration. "I'm tired of you leaning against me. You're nothing but dead weight! We should have left you behind!"

"Go ahead and leave me!" Greer shouted. "It sure beats hanging out with you losers. I don't need you guys to help me!"

"Cool," Kane replied.

With that, he let go of Greer, and she collapsed to the ground. Luckily, her hands helped break her fall.

"You heartless jerk!" she shouted up at Kane.

"How do *you* like it?" X yelled, as he marched over and shoved Kane to the ground.

Furious, Kane sprung to his feet and pulled his arm back in one smooth motion. Then he swung his fist hard across X's mouth.

"Get him good!" Now seemingly oblivious to her injured leg, Greer sat up and cheered, though Vero didn't know which one she was cheering for. And he didn't care either.

Ada grabbed Vero's arm. "Stop them!"

But Vero just smirked and yelled, "Deck him!"

"We have to get out of here!" Ada cried. "This isn't right!"

Suddenly, the fog grew thicker. It was so heavy that it extinguished the torches, plunging the fledglings into darkness. A wet clamminess wrapped around Vero. He called to the other angels, but they were no longer there. Silhouettes began to emerge out of the heavy mist. Vero tried to make sense of them, but they were only shapes without any tangible form. The hairs on his neck bristled.

Suddenly he heard a strange noise, like the clanging of chains. It was still totally black in the tunnel no matter which direction he looked. Without warning, ear-piercing shrieks emanated from the shadows, like the war cries of men charging into battle. The dark shadows began to swarm, and then the horrifying wails changed to creepy clicking sounds, causing Vero to envision first a locust and then a swarm of locusts devouring a farmer's field full of crops. A chill rose from the depths of his soul, and he knew he'd stumbled into the presence of pure evil.

"Ada! Kane!" he yelled, as panic seized him.

Nothing. The other angels were all gone. No one would

be coming to his rescue. And how could he blame them after the things he'd said? Why did he say those awful things after everything they'd been through together? Shame enveloped Vero followed by a feeling of being utterly alone.

And then, a horrific creature broke through the black void. It had the head of a man with long black hair and a hideous mouth filled with sharp teeth that looked like they belonged to a lion.

The man's body resembled that of a locust, but with scales like iron breastplates and a scorpion's tail full of venom. His fluttering wings sounded like chariots and hundreds of thundering horses running into battle.

An immense fear gripped Vero—a fear so deep it took his breath away. He gasped for air.

The creature glared at him with a ravenous look as it came closer, closer. Its mouth full of lion teeth opened, clicked, and then hissed, "Vero ... "

Vero's legs buckled, and he collapsed under the weight of his own terror. He registered a sudden flash of white—and then nothing.

22

❖

THE KING
OF THE
BOTTOMLESS
PIT

Ve-ro! Ve-ro!" Chanting voices.

Vero opened his eyes. He was back on earth! In fact, he was in the middle of jumping a track hurdle, leaping in midair as the crowd cheered him on.

Tack's shot put throw was still on target for his head. But with lightning-fast reflexes, Vero jerked his head back just in time. The maneuver ultimately saved his life but cost him his balance. He crashed down hard onto the hurdle, which knocked the wind out of him. He was still lying on the ground and holding his side when Coach Randy raced over to him.

"Vero, are you okay?"

Vero attempted to sit up.

"Take it easy," Coach Randy said.

Then Tack appeared. "Dude, I'm so sorry!"

"I'm okay," Vero managed to say.

"Thank God," Coach Randy said.

"It was so weird. That shot put just slipped out of my hands," Tack said.

"Do you think you can run the next race?" Coach Randy asked with a hopeful look.

"No," Vero shook his head. "I think my days on the track team are over."

Tack extended his hand, and Vero grabbed hold of it. Coach Randy pulled Vero's opposite hand, and the two of them helped Vero to his feet.

Coach sighed heavily. "I'm glad you're okay, Vero, really. It's just, I had such hopes ... such high hopes ... "

With his free hand, Coach pulled a sweat rag from his belt and let loose with a loud bellow as he blew his nose into it. "Yes, well ... let's get you checked out."

"Hey, don't cry, Coach! You've still got me on the team," Tack said.

"Uh, yeah," Coach said. Then he blew his nose into the rag again.

Nervously watching from the stands, Nora breathed a huge sigh of relief when Tack lifted Vero to his feet. Vero was all right.

Nora saw Dennis drop his big foam hand as a runner

from Lexington Junior High crossed the finish line first, and Danny took second. Seeing her husband's disappointment, Nora linked arms with Dennis, and together they made their way through the crowd to Vero's side.

Clover watched as Blake and Duff stomped their feet, pointed at Vero, and laughed obnoxiously.

"What a loser!" Blake yelled as Vero limped off the track. "Hey, Danny! You whipped him good!"

But Danny didn't acknowledge Blake. He was bent over at the waist with his hands on his hips, still trying to catch his breath.

"And there goes mommy to kiss his boo-boos!" Duff mocked, as Nora felt Vero's ribs for any injury.

What is up *with those guys?* Clover thought. She had a mind to go over there and let them have it. But they seriously creeped her out. Still, she didn't take well to people giving her brother a hard time — even though she'd been doing that a lot herself lately.

Clover thought that if she distanced herself from Vero, then maybe her problems would go away — the problems with Vero and her "overactive imagination," as her parents liked to call it whenever they dismissed her concerns.

For her whole life, Clover had had a special awareness, an ability to look at Vero and know what he was thinking. And she could always tell when something was bothering him. For instance, that when he was in third grade and he fell off the stage during a musical number in the school's production of *Beauty and the Beast*. He'd laughed along with the audience, but Clover knew her brother was totally embarrassed.

But she could also see things that she knew couldn't

really be there, like a man in a tree on a wintery afternoon eight years ago, or a raven with red eyes and a rat tail.

So over the years, Clover had tried to ignore her feelings and these visions. She'd watched endless reruns and reality shows on television. She'd played online games with anonymous gaming partners for hours, or wasted time texting her friends. Anything to distract herself.

And she'd been downright nasty to Vero just to try and get him to stay away from her, since most of her imaginings revolved around him. But it only made her miss her brother more. And lately, she'd been finding it harder and harder to ignore her visions or feelings. Whatever you wanted to call it, Clover was seeing things.

And seeing Vero lying hurt on the track made her think about what could have happened if the shot put had actually hit him in the head. What if Vero had died and she'd never gotten a chance to make things right with him?

Clover stood up and flashed her nastiest look at Blake and Duff. Blake glanced in her direction with eyes that were so icy blue, she was convinced they had to be contact lenses. A strand of dark, oily hair flopped down and covered half his face as he opened his mouth in a nasty, crooked grin. Clover turned and walked away, feeling a chill along her neck despite the heat.

❖

Uriel bent down and picked up a handful of tiny stones, then let them sift through his fingers. He turned his gaze to Raziel, who solemnly looked back at him.

It's been centuries since anyone's gotten past the golems, Uriel directed his thoughts to Raziel.

The two archangels were now standing in the very spot where Vero and the other fledglings had beaten the golems. Raziel looked around the chamber, which resembled the aftermath of an earthquake.

It's the sign we've been waiting for. This confirms he's the one, Uriel wordlessly conveyed to Raziel.

Raziel nodded in agreement and turned his gaze upward. *It has begun.*

❖

As Vero lay on his bed, he kept replaying the events leading up to his departure from the Ether, hoping to reach some kind of understanding about what exactly had happened. What was that scorpion creature whose image now haunted his memories? And what happened to the other angels? Had they made it back to safety, or was he the only one who'd escaped to earth? Would Greer's leg still be broken when she returned home? What happened between all of them at the end? Why had Vero been so *hateful* toward everyone? But most importantly, Vero wanted to know why he no longer felt safe in his own home.

In that dark tunnel, Vero had felt such evil, he wasn't sure he'd ever be able to shake it.

An abrupt knock on the door startled him, and Clover walked in without waiting for his response.

"Mom said dinner's in five minutes."

"Okay," he said softly, as his blood pressure slowly returned to normal.

Clover turned to leave, but she paused at the last moment, looking at Vero with a strange expression on her face. Vero tried to sit up but then grabbed his ribs in pain.

"Sorry about the meet," Clover said. "You should have won that last race."

"I'm done with track. The doctor said I have to let my ribs heal for a few weeks."

"I'm glad they're only bruised. But it's probably smart that you quit. It's become too much of a high-risk sport with Tack out there." She smiled at him.

And there it was. Clover had finally cracked open the door, inviting Vero back into her life. Vero knew this was an apology of sorts. He'd waited such a long time for his sister to come back, he'd wanted it so badly. But now as he looked at her sloppy, sideways smile and those green, green eyes, Vero knew he couldn't tell her the truth. She was better off not knowing all the things he'd seen and learned in the Ether.

"Tell Mom I'm not hungry," he said, rolling over to face the wall. "And please close the door on your way out."

❖

Creatures formed a circle around Vero. There were three of them, and Vero saw they all looked the same. Each had hollow, black eyes that were sunk deep into their skulls. Their partially decomposed faces were streaked with dried blood, and a few pale hairs sprouted from the tops of their heads. Vero's white outfit was a stark contrast to their dark figures.

The creatures threw something black and furry to one another as Vero tried to snatch it away from them. He wasn't sure what the object was, but he knew he desperately wanted it. They hurled insults at him, but Vero didn't care because behind them, Vero glimpsed Davina. She looked beautiful in a simple white dress that clasped over her left shoulder like a Roman toga. She was also visibly upset. Her eyes darted around, searching—searching for what? Vero didn't know. But her worry became his worry. He desperately wanted to help her, but he had to get past these creatures first ...

Vero woke up drenched in sweat. It had all been a dream.

But he knew this dream had meaning. The Ether, or someone from the Ether, was trying to reveal something to him.

❖

The dream played over and over in Vero's mind as he made his way through the school parking lot after school. He needed answers. What had the dream meant? Did it have to do with the evil presence he'd stumbled upon back in the dark tunnel?

The unmistakable sound of brakes skidding against the pavement made Vero's heart skip a beat. His whipped around and found himself staring down the grill of a yellow school bus.

"Watch where you're going!" the bus driver yelled out the window.

It was Mr. Harmon.

"Do you want me to file another report on you?" he asked.

Vero ignored him.

Tack, having seen the encounter, briskly walked over to Vero.

"Hey, Wayne!" Tack shouted. "Chill!"

"That's 'Mr. Harmon' to you."

"Well, I'm not on the bus right now, *Wayne*," Tack said.

Mr. Harmon laid on the horn, which startled Vero and Tack, and then they rapidly stepped out of the bus's way as it drove past them.

Tack turned to Vero and said, "There goes our ride home."

"I was planning to go to the library to study anyway," Vero said.

"Oh, c'mon! You're already the smartest kid in class! You don't need to study any more. Take your mom's advice and dumb yourself down a little."

Vero walked away without replying.

Tack chased after him, grabbed him by the arm and spun him around. "What's your problem? Are you mad at me about the shot put?"

"No!" Vero said. "I know that was an accident."

"Then why don't you want to hang out with me?" Tack asked. He looked hurt.

Vero's face softened. "I'm not mad at you."

Vero *was* feeling angry, but not at Tack. He was mad at Uriel and the other archangels. How could they expect him to keep his two worlds separate? It's impossible! Oh, how he wished he could tell Tack the truth.

"You act like you don't even want to be friends anymore," Tack said. "Are you hanging out with new people?"

Vero put both hands on Tack's shoulders and flashed him a heartfelt smile, "You're always gonna be my best friend." Then Vero dropped his hands and walked away. He hoped his words would be enough to reassure Tack, because they'd have to be. Right now he needed to get to the library and try to figure out what he'd encountered in the Ether.

But as he raced up the library steps two at a time, Vero got the feeling that someone was following him. He glanced over his shoulder and saw Tack quickly duck behind a maple tree. Somehow he had the sneaking suspicion that Tack would have to see for himself whether or not Vero was hanging with a new crowd.

Vero knew Tack had never felt comfortable inside a library. It was too quiet for him. So as Vero entered through the main doors, he hoped Tack wouldn't follow him inside but just go on home.

The library was two stories tall with stairs that led to the second floor. Upstairs, row upon row of dark wooden bookshelves formed a circle overlooking the main floor. Vero walked to the second story and immediately pulled several books from the shelves.

"Can I *help* you?" a woman's voice asked rather loudly on the main floor.

Vero leaned over the balcony and saw Tack spin around to face a thin older woman with her hair pulled back in a tight bun. She was one of the librarians, and she looked just like what Vero would expect a librarian to look like. The woman had a very serious demeanor. She probably hadn't cracked a smile in decades.

"You must be looking for the comic book section," she said.

Offended, Tack's eyes narrowed. "Actually, I was looking for something—"

"Shhhhh!!" the librarian cut him off and whispered, "We whisper in here."

Tack rolled his eyes.

"I'm not looking for comics. I'm looking for something in today's news, for a report," he whispered loudly.

"That's called a *periodical*," the librarian whispered back. "The newspaper and magazine section is upstairs."

"Thanks," he said in a normal voice, forgetting all about the whisper rule.

The librarian shot him a nasty look before she turned around to restack some books.

Vero watched as Tack made his way up the stairs and over to the periodicals, passing men and women sitting at worktables engrossed in their books, papers, and laptops, while little kids sat quietly on tiny chairs, flipping through picture books.

Vero sat at a table with a stack of books scattered in front of him. He carefully combed through each one, intently studying them. He no longer cared that Tack was spying on him from just a few feet away, hiding his face behind a copy of *The Wall Street Journal*.

Vero had already looked through copies of *Connect with Your Angel*, *Angels and the Bible*, and *Celestial Beings*. But when he turned a page in a book titled *Heavenly Warriors*, Vero felt the blood drain from his face. He sat back in his chair and looked across the room, feeling dazed. His eyes met Tack's. Tack immediately put down the newspaper and walked over to Vero.

"Dude, what's wrong?" Tack asked.

Vero didn't answer.

Tack's eyes dropped down to the open book. He saw a hand-drawn illustration of a frightening creature. It had a face like a man but with fangs. His body resembled a cricket with arms wearing armor, and it had claws for hands. His tail had spikes on the end of it.

Tack read the caption beneath the sketch. "Abaddon, the Angel of the Bottomless Pit."

Vero felt his face flush as a shiver traveled up his spine.

"What are you so upset about?" Tack asked. "It's not like he's real."

Vero's face bunched up. "Is that what you think? Do you think angels and demons and everything are just made-up stuff? That the Bible is nothing but a bunch of fairy tales?" Vero asked angrily.

With a guilty expression on his face, Tack said, "I don't really think about it much." He shrugged.

"Well, you'd better!" Vero shouted, then he slammed the chair back under the table and stormed out of the library.

❖

Vero now knew he'd encountered Abaddon in that black tunnel. According to Revelation 9:11, Abaddon was the king of the locust-like creatures who guarded the bottomless pit—or the lake of fire. Abaddon was given the task of the Destroyer. He'd set the Great Flood upon the earth, sparing only Noah and his ark. He'd demolished the cities of Sodom and Gomorrah.

God created Abaddon to be different from the other angels. Their nature was goodness and kindness, while Abaddon's nature was destruction. And because of that nature, Abaddon does God's will but doesn't live in the presence of God.

He's a very complicated guy, Vero thought.

It was written that Abaddon would open the bottomless pit and release the locust creatures upon the earth when God said it was time. And he was also the one who would seize Satan and throw him into the pit.

So basically, Vero figured, Abaddon wasn't really on anyone's side—he just wanted souls for his pit. He didn't care if they were good or bad, human or angel. Body count was what mattered to him.

Vero couldn't understand how he'd come face-to-face with this creature and yet managed to escape. An angel in training was no match for Abaddon. What had happened down there? Vero was desperate to find out.

Then a new thought occurred to him—Ada. The other fledglings lived all over the world, but Ada said she lived in a large city on the East Coast. That's all he knew. She'd never told him which city, and he'd never asked. If Vero could reach her, maybe Ada could shed some light on all of this. That is, if she wasn't already singing with the choir of angels.

As soon as he got home, Vero used his family's computer to search the Internet and try to locate Ada. He knew her last name was Brickner, so he searched through online phone books starting with Boston and working his way down to New York City. He called every Brickner he could find, but there were no matches to Ada.

"I need to use the computer," Clover said as she walked into the office. "You've been hogging it ever since you got home. And no one can get on the phone because you're using that too."

"You have a cell phone," Vero said, not taking his eyes off the computer screen.

"I don't want to use up my minutes."

"Vero, I need you to take out the garbage!" Nora called from the kitchen.

Vero finally looked up at Clover. "Five minutes."

Clover gave him a look as he clicked the mouse and then left the room. Once he was gone, she sat at the computer and watched as the screen saver flashed photos of the Leland family. A wistful look came over Clover's face. There was a photo of a young Vero and Clover body surfing in the ocean, another one of little Vero and Clover wearing matching cowboy hats and riding a pony, and one of Vero flashing the victory sign after winning his first track race.

Feeling curious, she clicked on the "History" icon to see what Vero had been researching. Her brow furrowed when the name "Ada Brickner" came up on the screen multiple times. She wondered who that could be.

Vero came back into the office. "Time's up," he said.

"Who's Ada Brickner?" Clover asked in a half-teasing voice.

"None of your business."

"I think it's a girl you like."

"Fine," Vero sighed. "I do like her."

"Where'd you meet her?"

Vero hesitated. "Um ... well ... uh ... " he stammered.

Clover scrutinized him.

"At the last track meet!" he quickly covered. "But she doesn't go to our school, and I didn't get her address."

Clover eyeballed Vero. She knew he wasn't telling her the whole truth; he was hiding something.

"Clover, come set the table for dinner!" Nora called.

Clover gave Vero one last suspicious look and then walked out of the office.

Over the next two days, Vero spent every spare moment making phone calls. He was driving his family crazy because no one else could use the phone. Clover squealed to her parents that he was trying to find his "crush." Nora thought it was cute. Dennis was just grateful their long distance plan had unlimited minutes.

By the time Vero got to the Philadelphia phone book, he was becoming discouraged. At least there were only seven Brickners listed in Philly — wait a minute! One listing was actually for an Ada Brickner! Vero couldn't believe it! His fingers trembled as he dialed the number. He waited for the phone to connect, and as soon as someone answered, Vero said excitedly, "Ada, it's me! Vero!"

"Speak up!" an old woman's voice came through the receiver. "My hearing aid ran out of batteries!"

"Oh, I'm sorry. I was looking for a younger Ada," Vero said.

"Well, I look a lot better than I sound," the old lady replied. "But maybe you're looking for my granddaughter, Ada."

"Yes, I am!"

"Get a pen, and I'll give you her number," the lady instructed. "And hurry before I forget what it is."

Ada was alive! Vero hoped that meant the others were all right as well. He dialed her number and felt his heart pounding. Were the guardian angels allowed to have contact with one another outside of the Ether? He reasoned they must be, or else Uriel would have intervened by now.

The phone rang a few times, and then a voice picked up on the other end.

"Hello?"

It was a voice Vero recognized.

"Ada, it's Vero!" he said.

There was a moment of silence. Not the response he was hoping for.

"Excuse me while I go to my room where it's a bit more quiet. My brothers have the TV on too loud."

Vero heard a door shut and then Ada came back on the line. "Thank God, you're alive!"

It was definitely Ada. Vero was thrilled.

"How did you find me?" Ada asked.

"The Internet. I really need to talk to you."

"We thought they got you," Ada said in a rush.

"No, I'm alive. But what happened to you and the others?"

Vero could hear Ada's brother banging on her bedroom door and yelling, "I need the phone!" Then another brother picked up the kitchen phone and sang, "Ada's got a boyfriend! Ada's got a boyfriend!"

"Get off the phone!" Ada yelled.

He made kissing sounds into the phone before he hung up.

"Could you come to my bat mitzvah this weekend? It's here in Philly. We can talk there. I'll just say you're a friend from summer camp."

Ada gave Vero all of the necessary information just before a third brother picked the lock and opened her bedroom door. She quickly hung up the phone.

And Vero realized he was going to his first-ever bat mitzvah.

❖

"No way!" Tack shouted as they shot hoops in Tack's

backyard. "You expect me to cover for you, and you're not even gonna tell me why?"

"It's important," Vero said. "I told my parents I'm spending the weekend at your house."

"Well I might just have to call and tell them otherwise. And here I thought you actually came over to hang out," Tack caught the ball and headed inside the house with Pork Chop at his heels.

Vero needed to come up with something quick.

"Okay! The truth is ... I met this girl. She invited me to her bat mitzvah this weekend. She's really cute, so I want to go. I've got enough allowance money for the train ticket, and I can go up for the day and come back without anyone knowing about it. They're gonna have a live band and everything."

Tack spun around and a smile erupted across his face.

"A bat mitzvah?" Tack pulled off his Attleboro Middle baseball cap and ran his fingers through his sweaty hair so it stuck straight up. "That means there will be lots of thirteen-year-old girls there. Older women. I'm coming with you."

Vero shook his head and chuckled. "Fine," he said. "But you definitely need to get a haircut first."

Then a thought occurred to Vero. "Since you're coming along, can you get Martha to go too?"

"My sister? What? Why? She's no fun."

"Um, she's seventeen and she drives ... " Vero explained. "It would solve how we're going to get to and from the train station. And no one will question us if she's with us."

"It's risky, but I know something that could help," Tack said, as he held the back door open for Vero and Pork Chop.

"What do you two want?" Martha asked suspiciously, as Vero and Tack walked into her bedroom. Vero was holding a tray full of food, and Tack was holding Pork Chop.

"Nothing more than your happiness," Tack smiled. "Right, Vero?"

Vero nodded eagerly.

Tack put Pork Chop in bed with Martha. "Here's your favorite puppy."

Hugging the dog, Martha sat up on her bed and stared the boys down. She was waiting for one of them to crack. Vero noted her eyes were the same deep blue as Tack's. And with her messy strawberry-blonde hair, there was no denying the two were brother and sister.

"We made your favorite: a potato chip omelet," Vero said, placing the tray on her bed.

Martha's eyes narrowed.

"How would you like an all-expense-paid day trip to The City of Brotherly Love in exchange for giving us a ride ... this Saturday?" Tack asked.

Martha bolted out of bed. Vero took a step back, suddenly feeling a bit afraid for his life. Pork Chop scooted under the bed with a whimper.

But then Martha did something completely unexpected. She ran over and gave Tack a big bear hug. He was totally caught off guard by her display of affection.

"I've always wanted to see the Liberty Bell!" Martha exclaimed. "Mom and Dad never took us there!"

Over Martha's shoulder, Tack winked at Vero. "Who knew?" he asked.

23

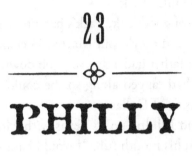

PHILLY

The train ride from DC to Philadelphia took less than two hours, and Tack ate the entire time — mostly mini microwave pizzas that were being served in the café car. As the three of them sat at a table, Vero watched the landscape go by, feeling very much as though his life was moving as fast as the trees, houses, and cars that whipped past the train window.

"Ouch!" Tack said.

Vero turned and saw that Tack was holding his hand across his mouth. "I burned my tongue," he explained.

As Vero watched Tack pant to get some cool air on his tongue, a wave of sadness hit him. Vero knew that eventually these ordinary moments would be a thing of the past. In just a few years, he'd be gone from the earth for good.

Tack took a huge bite of pizza that left a string of melted cheese dangling from his chin. Tack pulled the cheese off and shoved it into his mouth.

Vero would miss Tack.

In a stroke of good luck, Tack's parents were out of town that weekend, and they'd put Martha in charge of her little brother. Their father had a dowsing job down in Texas, and their mother had tagged along so she could visit her sister who lived outside of Dallas.

"I'm so glad I didn't go to Texas with Mom and Dad," Tack said with his mouth full. "I would have missed out on these pizzas."

Martha looked up from her tourism book on Philadelphia.

"You didn't go because they didn't invite you," she said. "Dad knows you're totally worthless on dowsing jobs."

Vero saw Tack's face drop. He knew this was a sore subject for Tack.

"Don't worry, Tack," Vero said, trying to encourage him. "Didn't you tell me that your mom is always saying she knows the dowsing gene is in you because no matter where she hides the Ding Dongs, you always find them?"

Rolling her eyes, Martha stood and walked down the aisle. "I need to use the ladies' room."

Tack had apparently lost his appetite. He dropped his slice of pizza on the plate.

Vero looked at him, not sure if he should say anything more.

But then Tack said, "You remember the other day, when you asked me about God? The reason I don't think much about him is because I know he doesn't listen to me."

Vero gave him a curious look.

"Every night I prayed that he would let me be a dowser, but it's never happened."

"Not yet," Vero said.

"But what if it *never* happens?" Tack asked miserably.

"Then it means he wants you to do something else with your life."

As Tack contemplated Vero's words, an announcement came over the PA system: "Next stop. Thirtieth Street Station, Philadelphia."

"Tack, you have your cell phone, right?"

The boys looked up to see Martha standing over them. Tack nodded.

"We'll meet back here at the train station at four o'clock sharp. We're on the four-thirty train to DC. Don't make me sorry I trusted you, or you'll regret the day you were born!"

"Are you sure you don't want to come with us?" Vero asked. Tack kicked him under the table.

"No, thanks. I'm spending the day sightseeing — the Liberty Bell, Ben Franklin's printing press, the Schuylkill boathouses, the Philadelphia Museum of Art ... "

Tack rolled his eyes. "Boring."

"And then I'll top it off with my very first authentic Philly cheesesteak sandwich."

Tack did a double take, "Hey! Bring me one, too!"

"Shalom," said a middle-aged man, as he held out his hand to the boys.

Vero shook the man's hand, "Um ... shalom."

"Yeah, shalom right back at ya," Tack said.

Vero and Tack had just arrived at the synagogue. As soon as they'd stepped outside the train station, Martha put them in a cab while she went in search of the Liberty Bell.

"I'm Ada's father," the man said. "But I'm sorry, I don't believe I know either of you."

"Oh, we're friends of Ada's. We met her at summer camp," Vero told him. "I'm Vero, and this is Tac—um, this is Thaddeus."

"Yeah, we went to camp together. I remember when I first met Ada. The counselors were teaching us how to surf," Tack said.

"In upstate New York?" Ada's father asked.

Tack froze. Luckily, Vero was quick on his feet.

"Um ... he means surf the Internet."

"Ah, yes, of course." Ada's father handed both of them a small cap and said, "Please go in and find a seat. We're about to begin."

Vero and Tack placed the caps on their heads.

"What is this?" Tack whispered. "A beret?"

"It's a yarmulke," Vero whispered back. "It's worn in the synagogue as a sign of respect to God."

Tack raised his eyebrows as Vero. "How do you know that?"

Vero felt his face flush. "Uh, I learned it in school."

"They don't reach religion in school."

"I meant Sunday school," Vero said quickly.

"Oh," Tack said.

How could Vero explain that Old Testament and Jewish traditions are things he's learned about at C.A.N.D.L.E.? Once again, Vero felt shame in having to lie to his best friend.

The synagogue didn't seem all that different from his church at home. Light streamed in through stained-glass windows. The rows of pews faced a large, raised platform with an altar like the one at Vero's church. And behind the altar, beautiful embroidered curtains in shades of deep purple and royal blue were pulled back to reveal the ark, the cabinet where the Torah scrolls are kept. But today, the scrolls were laid out on a table.

Ada stood in front of them, looking nervous. Her olive skin looked flushed, as though she'd just run a mile. But she looked really pretty in her simple white dress.

A woman primped Ada's hair, kissed her, and then sat down in the front row. Vero thought she had to be Ada's mother. Sitting on her mother's right were two older boys—probably high school age, or maybe even college—and next to them were two younger boys, maybe six and seven years old. Vero knew these younger two were probably the ones who'd tormented Ada when he'd called her.

An elderly woman slowly walked down the aisle on the arm of Ada's father and then sat with the family. Vero heard one of the brothers call her *Bubbe*, which somehow he knew meant "Grandma." And he noticed that she *did* look as old as her voice had sounded on the phone.

The ceremony began. Everyone grew quiet.

As Ada read in Hebrew from the Torah, the congregation replied with the appropriate prayers. Without realizing it, Vero answered in perfect Hebrew right along with the rest of the congregation.

Tack looked at Vero with a strange, almost scared expression on his face. "When did you learn Hebrew?" Tack whispered.

"What do you mean?" Vero asked.

"You're speaking perfect Hebrew."

This came as a surprise to Vero. He'd never spoken a

single word of Hebrew in his life, save for that incident back in the Ether with the golems. He was as confused as Tack was, but he couldn't show it.

"Um, I've been studying it," he said matter-of-factly.

"Wow, you must have it *bad* for this girl," Tack said.

❖

Loud music filled the hotel ballroom as two DJs whipped up the bat mitzvah crowd. Guests of all ages showed off their best moves on the multicolored dance floor. Bussing dirty dessert plates and silverware, the serving staff skirted around the dancers as they headed back to the kitchen with their arms full. Vero killed time by dipping strawberries on long toothpicks into the chocolate fountain.

He was growing worried. He still hadn't had a moment alone with Ada because it seemed like every single one of her friends and relatives had come up to congratulate her. And now Vero was running out of time. He and Tack needed to catch the train back to DC; and from the look of things, it was going to be hard to drag Tack off the dance floor.

Ada glanced across the room at Vero. He locked eyes with her and then motioned with his head for her to follow him. Ada finally excused herself and walked over. She led him down a hallway away from the noise of the party, and they sat beside each other on a bench.

"Mazel tov," Vero said.

"Thanks. I'm guessing you didn't know you speak perfect Hebrew?"

"Yeah . . ."

"It happens when you enter the synagogue. "It's one of those hidden guardian angel talents."

Vero glanced at his watch. "Ada, I need some information, and I'm almost out of time. What happened down in that tunnel?"

"Well, as you'll recall, after we got past the golems, everyone was fighting with each other. It was really bad—and really strange. Then all of a sudden, you just disappeared. And a moment later, Uriel and Raziel appeared and took us back to the Ether—the nice part of the Ether."

"Did Uriel or Raziel say anything?"

Ada shook her head. "They wouldn't tell us anything. But Pax picked up some of their thoughts. They were really worried about you, and they couldn't go after you."

"So how did I get back to earth?"

Ada shrugged, "I don't know. But here's another thing Pax heard: No one has been able to read those parchments for centuries."

Vero tried to make sense of it all, but it was hard to put the pieces together when he didn't even know what the pieces were.

Ada locked eyes with him. "Vero, where did you go?"

Vero looked away, not wanting to answer.

"What did you see down there?" she persisted.

Finally, Vero looked into her eyes. He wanted so badly to tell her. He needed someone else to know the truth about what had happened to him. "Abaddon," he said.

Ada gasped and started nervously twirling a finger in her hair. "How do you know?"

"Because I researched it," Vero told her. "Pure evil, face-to-face."

Ada leaned back with a troubled expression on her face. "That explains why we were at each other's throats. The presence of Abaddon was seeping into us."

She flicked at a spot on her white dress, lost in thought. Vero wished he knew what she was thinking. Once he learned how to silently communicate in the Ether, would he be able to communicate with angels while here on earth?

"How did you get away from him?" she asked.

Vero shook his head and stood. "I don't know. I was so scared that I couldn't breathe. He literally stole my breath from me. It actually hurt. I remember falling to the ground, a flash of white light, and then I was back on earth."

Ada looked intense as she sat there thinking. Her eyes held a ferocity Vero hadn't seen in her before.

Suddenly the music from the party got louder, and then a conga line burst through the doors and down the hallway—with Tack right in the mix.

Vero knew time was short, so he grabbed Tack out of the conga line.

"Hey!" Tack protested.

"We have to go," Vero said. "Or else we're going to miss the train." Vero turned back to Ada. "Thanks for inviting us. I'll call you."

Ada flashed Vero a smile, "Too bad you can't just fly back to DC."

"No way!" Tack said. "Then we'd miss out on the awesome microwave pizza."

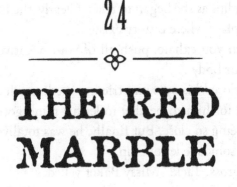

24

THE RED MARBLE

"Okay, everyone open your yoga mats," Coach Randy told the class.

Vero sat on the gym floor next to Davina. "Since when do we do yoga in gym class?" Vero asked.

"Since Tack joined the track team," she chucked. "I think Coach Randy is looking for ways to lower his stress level."

"Come on, now get on your mats . . ." Coach said.

"Hey, thanks for saving me a spot," Danny said to Davina. He squeezed in between Vero and Davina and "accidentally" pushed Vero over as he unrolled his mat. Danny snickered as Vero righted himself. Vero knew Danny wasn't about to let him have any alone time with Davina.

"Now, close your eyes and slowly inhale . . ."

The gym full of students had become silent. Vero snuck a peek at Davina with her eyes closed. She looked so beautiful.

Vero especially loved the little smile that formed at the corner of her lips as she began to relax. Clearly, the Ether wasn't the only place where beauty existed.

"When you exhale, push all of your negative emotions out of your body ... "

Vero closed his eyes and tried to meditate. It took a few moments for him to be able to let his mind go, what with Davina being so close. But finally, he was totally relaxed — and then someone let one rip.

"Oh, gross, Tack!" Missy Baker yelled.

"What? Why do you think it was me?" Tack asked, laughing.

"It smells like a stinking Ding Dong!"

"I was just doing what Coach said — pushing all of the bad stuff out of my body."

"Shhh! Let's try again," Coach Randy said. "And Tack, this time please don't push so hard."

The class was silent once again. Vero stole another glance at Davina and then closed his eyes. This wasn't too unlike the exercise that Raziel had been trying to teach the fledglings when he'd urged them to clear their minds and listen for God's voice. Angels weren't the only ones who needed to master it; humans did too.

Vero relaxed and as he retreated into his mind, his surroundings gradually began to disappear. He became completely unaware of the gym and the other kids around him. It was as if he were seeing a movie playing right before his eyes.

Vero saw himself running through thick woods. It was dark outside, but the moon was bright. He was scared. His face stung where tree branches had scratched him while he ran. Vero could feel burrs from the underbrush clinging to his clothes and piercing his skin. When he finally came to a clearing, he saw a new house under construction sitting on a patch of earth where no grass grew. An ominous feeling of dread plagued him. Hesitantly he approached the house. As Vero got closer, his eyes could just make out a form lying on the front porch.

Vero knew that whatever he found lying there would bring him great pain, but something urged him on. He reached the top stair of the porch and realized it was a person, lying lifeless on the cold floor. Agony filled his heart when Vero recognized the person's outfit. It was a toga. He bent down on one knee, placed his hand beneath the person's shoulder, and rolled the body over. It was an exercise in futility because Vero already knew who was lying there. Even so, he was struck with a feeling of horror when Davina's face came into focus. She lay there motionless with blood trickling from her left temple. And he noticed a single red marble lying next to her.

Grief paralyzed him, but it wasn't just his grief alone. Someone else was there. He could feel it. Vero looked up and saw Danny's tear-streaked face looking down at him. Vero knew Danny was the one who had done this to Davina.

Danny dropped his slingshot onto the porch and began weeping. "I'm sorry! I didn't know she was there!" he confessed between sobs. "It was an accident ... "

"Yoga is not supposed to move you to violence!" Coach Randy yelled, snapping Vero out of his daydream.

Vero's eyes quickly scanned his surroundings. He was back in the school gym. But now his hands were clenching the front of Danny's shirt, and Vero was violently shaking him. When Vero realized what he was doing, he let go of Danny and stood up. Everyone was looking at him, and no one dared move. Even Davina inched away from him.

Danny glared at Vero. "You're dead meat," he growled.

❖

Vero faked a migraine so Nurse Kunkel would send him home early. This way he figured he'd avoid getting another after-school beating from Danny and his thugs. As Vero walked down the hallway to meet his mother, he saw a boy stealing a kiss from a girl as they pretended to look inside his locker. Two jocks high-fived each other and reminisced about winning some basketball game. Three girls were sitting beneath a huge banner and selling tickets for the upcoming dance. A display case showed off various trophies and ribbons won by the school's students. Everything Vero saw defined an ordinary day in the life of a middle school — a life that Vero no longer felt connected to. Sadly, he walked through the front doors and got into his mother's car.

"How's your head?" Nora asked.

Vero didn't answer. Instead, he reached over and pulled the key out of the ignition so she couldn't drive away. Vero locked eyes with his mother. "Tell me about the night you found me."

"What?"

"I need to know every detail."

Nora had known this day would eventually come. She'd had twelve years to come up with a story, to carefully prepare her answers. But when Nora saw the conviction in her son's eyes, she decided to tell him the truth. A tear ran down her cheek, and she quickly brushed it away.

"There had been a terrible storm that night," she began. "I was working the night shift in the ER. An elderly man came in. His head was bleeding pretty bad. There was something about him, some connection. I don't know what it was, but I felt really upset when he died. As I went to close his eyes to give him some peace, he grabbed my arm and said, "Name the baby Vero. Raise him as your own.""

Vero gave her a look of complete surprise.

"I guess the doctors had called his death too early. He died moments later. I went out to the nurses' station and there you were. Just lying on a chair. I've replayed that night over and over in my mind, and the best I can come up with is that the old man either brought you in to the ER or somehow knew you. Or ... Vero, I've watched a lot of people die in the ER. And sometimes they see or know things that go beyond our normal perceptions. I think it's because they have one foot in this world and one in the next. I truly believe God sent that elderly man to me. Or maybe he was an angel."

"They're real, Mom," Vero said as his eyes drifted up to the patch of sky gleaming through the sunroof.

"Who?"

"Angels. They love us and they want to help us," Vero said with conviction.

Nora looked at her son, not sure where this was coming from. "I believe that's true," Nora said.

"So was that it?" Vero asked. "Was that all that happened that night?"

Nora hesitated. She knew she could bail out at this point,

and Vero would accept what she'd told him as being the whole truth. She could get away with it. Since the day she'd brought Vero home, Nora had tried to keep his world as normal as possible. She'd never wanted to scare him. She'd even tried to convince herself that Vero was just a typical little boy.

However, deep in her heart she'd known differently. Sheltering him from the truth had done no good. Strange things still occurred. In that moment, Nora realized that if she really loved Vero, she owed him the truth.

"On the way home after my shift ended, I took you into the grocery store so I could buy some diapers and formula. A man wearing a long black coat began to follow me. I was terrified of him. He was wearing a hood, so I never did see his face. But something told me he was pure evil."

"What did he want?" Vero asked.

Nora looked at him with the utmost seriousness, "You."

Vero dropped his head. It was overwhelming to hear.

Nora held his face between her hands and locked eyes with him. "I'm sorry, Vero, but you needed to know the truth."

Vero nodded. He understood. Just then Uriel's words came to mind, "everything in its own time."

Nora put her hands back on the steering wheel and continued, "The man chased me into the storeroom and we were trapped. I thought it was the end for both of us. But then that huge steel gate—you know, the one that lifts up by the loading docks so the truck drivers can deliver their goods? Well, that gate flew up and this light—"

"What kind of light?" Vero was giving Nora his undivided attention by this point.

"It was brighter than any light I'd ever seen before—or since. I couldn't even look at it for fear of being blinded. Yet at the same time, the light was comforting and I no longer felt afraid. When the light faded, the man in black had vanished. Run off, I guess. I never saw him again. Thank God that produce deliveryman showed up right then."

Nora began to sob. She unlatched her seatbelt, reached over, and hugged her son tight. She never wanted to let him go. But by telling Vero his story, she'd unknowingly taken the first step toward doing so.

❖

A few days passed and Vero somehow managed to avoid Danny and Blake and Duff. He'd stayed close to Tack at all times and made sure he was always the first one on the bus. He knew that if he were to miss it, he'd be easy pickings if he walked home alone. It really ticked Vero off that while he could defeat golems and dodge behemoths, he still ran scared of a thirteen-year-old bully and his pals. He felt helpless on earth—especially when it came to Davina.

His vision of Davina lying lifeless on that porch continued to plague him. He feared for her, but he didn't know how to help her. Sometimes when he was home alone, he'd call on Uriel and Raphael for guidance—screaming their names at the top of his lungs. But he never received a response. It was as if everyone from the Ether had forgotten him.

Whenever he felt utterly abandoned, he'd pick up the phone and call Ada. Just hearing her voice confirmed that his life in the Ether was real, that he hadn't imagined it after all.

Neither Ada nor Vero had returned to the Ether since their last training exercise.

"They'll call us back when we're needed," she reassured him.

But Vero wasn't so sure. He sensed that Davina's life was in trouble, and he couldn't just sit around twiddling his thumbs. So Vero kept a close eye on her both during school and after. Davina's house was near enough to Vero's that he could ride his bike to it. So he pedaled past it as often as he could. He'd ditch his bike in a nearby field and climb a tree across the street to keep watch. Sometimes he'd keep watch for hours until he had to go home for dinner.

One late afternoon as Vero kept watch in the tree, Danny and Davina walked out of her house together. They were laughing and obviously enjoying one another's company. Surprised to see Danny there, Vero lost his footing and had to grab onto a lower branch to keep himself from falling to the pavement below. He held his breath as Danny and Davina crossed the street and sat on the curb directly beneath the tree's wide branches. He prayed they wouldn't notice him up there. He'd never be able to live it down if they did. He could hear the gossip now: "I heard Vero Leland was spying on Davina Acker from up in a *tree*. Can you believe it? What'll he do next?" Even Tack wouldn't understand it.

"I think my mom really liked you," Davina said to Danny.

"Where's your dad?" Danny asked.

"He's on a business trip until next week. Maybe when he gets back, your parents could go out with mine?"

Danny's face flushed. He looked down at the street and kicked some pebbles with his foot.

"What? What's wrong?" Davina asked.

"My mom left us a few months ago. She moved to Arizona with her boyfriend."

"I'm so sorry, Danny. I didn't know. Do you visit her?"

Vero hadn't known either. He felt bad for Danny.

Danny shook his head. "Every time I ask if I can, she always says she's too busy or it's not a good time. Me and my older brother live with my dad. But Dad drives a tractor trailer and has to haul loads to Colorado three times a month. So I don't see much of him either. It's so quiet in my house that sometimes I turn on the TV just to hear people's voices."

Davina held Danny's hand, "I'm sorry."

Danny looked over at her. "Why do you hang out with me?"

"'Cause you're nice."

Danny hung his head, "I don't always do nice things."

"Well, that's true about everybody."

"No, I ... I ... " Danny stuttered.

"Is it true what the kids are saying at school?" Davina asked. "Did you shatter the windows on that new house?"

Davina looked straight into his eyes, and Danny didn't look away. He nodded.

"Why?"

"I don't know. I just get so mad at my parents ... I know I shouldn't do it, but it makes me feel better."

"Promise me you won't do it anymore," Davina said. "The next time you feel mad at your parents, call me instead of going out to that house. Okay?"

Danny's lips formed a tight smile. He nodded.

Davina stood and turned to head home. Danny quickly got to his feet.

"Do you want to go to the dance with me?" Danny asked shyly, with his eyes cast down, and his hands shoved deep in his pockets.

"Sure," Davina said with a smile. Then she turned and crossed the street.

For the first time ever, Vero saw a genuine look of happiness on Danny's face.

❖

"Elvis, baby!" Tack yelled, waving a white sequined jumpsuit in Vero's face.

"What?" Vero asked, truly confused.

"It's for the dance. We're gonna be the Elvis brothers!"

Oh, that. Vero had let Tack talk him into going to the school dance—their very first one. The thought of dancing with girls was more frightening to Vero than facing craggy golems. He had no idea how to dance, but Tack had convinced him it wouldn't be a huge deal because everybody had to wear a costume. If they made complete fools of themselves, no one would ever know who they were.

"Here's an Elvis wig and a pair of sunglasses," Tack said, shoving them into Vero's hands. "Try 'em on."

Vero put on the oversized rhinestone sunglasses, which covered most of his face. The wig made his head itch, but he could deal with that.

"Are you going to ask someone to go with you? Maybe that girl from the bat mitzvah?" Tack asked.

"No," Vero said.

"Good answer. You're smart to keep your options open," Tack said. "I don't want to be tied down to just one girl either."

Vero laughed. He knew they'd be lucky if Nurse Kunkel agreed to dance with them.

The real reason Vero was going to the dance was to keep an eye on Davina. And it wasn't just because she was going with Danny. Sure, he was jealous. Sure, it hurt. Why did she like Danny more than him? But regardless of his personal feelings, Vero's dream still haunted him. He was determined to be near Davina any chance he could.

❖

On the night of the dance, Vero and Tack walked into the Lelands' living room wearing their Elvis outfits. Nora snapped a photo.

"My baby's first dance," she said, pretending to be misty-eyed.

Next, Clover walked in wearing a hippie outfit from the sixties. After Nora snapped photos of the three of them together, Clover laughed and pointed at Vero. "You look like the young Elvis," she said, "and Tack looks like the old fat Elvis."

"Oh yeah, cupcake? That kind of talk won't get you a slow dance with me," Tack warned her.

"Be nice, Clover," Dennis said as he walked into the room. "Besides, nasty comments like that really clash with your outfit. You dig?"

Clover instantly began to rethink her costume choice. Maybe a peace-loving flower child from the sixties wasn't a good fit for her personality. But she sure loved the white go-go boots.

As Dennis drove them to the dance, Vero peered out the car window when they passed Davina's house. Vero couldn't see her, but all appeared calm.

"There's Danny!" Tack said.

Sure enough, Danny was walking in the opposite direction and headed toward Davina's house. He was dressed in an old-fashioned convict's uniform—a pair of baggy black-and-white striped pants and a matching shirt. Vero couldn't help but feel a pang of jealousy when he noticed Danny was carrying a corsage in a clear plastic box.

Tack rolled down the car window and yelled, "Hey, Konrad! Didn't you hear? It's supposed to be a *costume* party!"

"Shut up!" Vero hissed and elbowed Tack in the ribs—hard.

Clover rolled her eyes. "Tack, you seriously need to get a life," she said.

"No, don't you get it? He's headed for prison one day," Tack explained matter-of-factly.

"Get down! He's gonna see us!" Vero hissed again.

"Relax. We're in disguise, buddy," Tack reassured him.

With that, Dennis steered the car closer to the curb and pulled up alongside Danny.

Danny stopped walking and stared at Tack and Vero sitting in the backseat.

"Tack, you should apologize," Dennis said.

Tack's eyes went wide and he turned beet red. "Um, sorry, Danny," Tack stammered through the open car window.

Danny didn't say a word. He just kept staring at Tack.

"Okay, well ... enjoy the dance!" Dennis said, giving Danny a little wave before he drove off.

Vero shot daggers at Tack while Tack rolled up the window.

"Don't worry about Konrad," Tack said under his breath. "There's only one of him and two of us."

"Don't forget his goon friends. That makes *three* of them and only *two* of us," Vero whispered.

"What friends? The guy's got no friends," Tack said.

"What do you mean? What about Blake and Duff?"

"You're dreaming, dude," Tack said. "No one would be friends with that guy."

Using the mirror on the passenger side sun visor, Clover looked at her brother in the backseat. From the expression on his face, she could tell he was totally confused by what Tack had just said. She opened her mouth to argue with Tack but thought better of it.

25

THE DANCE

A disco ball hung from the center of the gym ceiling. Multicolored twisted streamers stretched from the ball to each corner of the gym. Strobe lights flashed, and a professional disc jockey played dance music through an elaborate sound system.

Cupcakes, cookies, potato chips, pretzels, and all kinds of other snacks filled a huge table, and there were two punch bowls—one at each end. Nurse Kunkel was watching over the food, and Vero had seen her sneak at least two cupcakes so far.

Parent chaperones and teachers circled the gym, and they had the focus of a hawk. Albert Atwood walked around with a field hockey stick in his hands, poking kids who were dancing too closely.

"There will be no dirty dancing on my watch!" he said, poking Missy Baker and her date as they slow danced to a rap song.

Vero stood off to the side, watching Tack dance. He was out there in the middle of the floor, not dancing with anyone in particular, and he displayed no grace whatsoever. He just jerked his body around as if someone had poured a jar of spiders down his shirt. And he was having a total blast.

Clover walked up behind Vero. "Is Tack okay? I mean, is that voluntary, or should we call 9–1–1?"

"And those are his best moves," Vero said. He continued scanning the room, looking everywhere for Danny and Davina. *They should have been here by now,* he thought.

Vero was so preoccupied by his search that he barely appreciated the fact that Clover was talking to him ... in public ... at a school function.

Clover followed Vero's gaze to the gym doors. She knew something was going on. "Are you worried that Danny and his buddies are coming to get you? Because Tack was pretty stupid to egg him on like that."

Danny was exactly who Vero wanted to see right now, because if Danny walked through those doors, then Davina would be with him, and that would mean she's safe. Before he could answer his sister, a guy dressed in a Batman costume grabbed Clover.

"Let's dance," Batman said.

Clover went along with Batman but gave Vero a little wave and a shrug as she was being pulled onto the dance floor. Something was going on, and she had a bad feeling about it.

"Hey, it's Elvis," someone said.

Vero turned around. Three big kids wearing identical masks circled Vero. The rubber masks were made to look as if the facial features had been partially decomposed. They were streaked with blood. Vero had a hard time seeing their eyes as the mask made the sockets appear hollow. They looked like zombies. One of them grabbed Vero's black wig off his head and threw it to one of the other guys.

"Monkey in the middle!"

Vero lunged for his wig, but they quickly chucked it from one to another before Vero could snatch it back.

"Seriously?" Vero asked. "Are we in first grade again?"

I don't have time for this, Vero thought, and he was just about to walk away and forget the wig when he noticed some stray hairs sprouting from the tops of their masks. Those hairs triggered a memory. He'd seen these masks before in his daydream during gym class. But in his daydream, he'd assumed he was surrounded by demons. Now he realized they were only middle school boys wearing masks.

Whatever the Ether had been trying to show him that night was happening now! Vero looked over the guys' shoulders and knew exactly who he'd see—Davina, wearing a toga and scanning the room with panic in her eyes. And there she was!

Vero's heart leapt into his throat, and he pushed his way past the trio of tormentors. In his race to reach Davina, he bumped into some kids on the dance floor.

Clover watched her brother hurry past and saw Vero tap Davina's shoulder. When Davina spun around, Clover saw the worried expression on her face.

"Have you seen Danny?" Davina asked Vero. "Did he come in here?"

"He's not here," Vero said.

"I have to find him!" Davina shouted over the music.

"I saw him walking to your house earlier," Vero said.

"He came to my house, but then he got really upset and

stormed off," Davina said. She was visibly upset. "I really need to find him!"

She turned to leave, but Vero stepped in front of Davina and blocked her exit.

From Clover's vantage point, it looked like Davina was trying to get around him. *Something is seriously up*, she thought.

"Please, Davina, don't go out there!" Vero pleaded. He grabbed her hand and tried to hold her back.

"I have to go, Vero," Davina said, trying to pull free.

The next thing Vero knew, Mr. Atwood's field hockey stick jabbed him hard in the back.

"Let's keep our hands to ourselves, eh, Vero?" Mr. Atwood said.

Seizing the moment, Davina escaped and scurried across the crowded dance floor.

Vero chased after her. "Davina, wait!"

Clover watched as Mr. Atwood dropped his field hockey stick and grabbed Vero from behind, locking his arm across Vero's chest. Vero struggled to get free as a group of onlookers formed.

Angus walked over to help his dad restrain Vero, but Mr. Atwood waved him off. Vero heard Angus say to one of the onlookers, "We live next door to him. He pulls this kind of stuff all the time."

"Let go of me, Mr. Atwood!" Vero yelled.

"You're going home! Now!"

"Davina!" Vero fought to free himself, but he gave up as soon as Davina had disappeared from view.

As soon as Vero stopped fighting him, Mr. Atwood let him go. "We're calling your parents, Vero," he said. "This party is over for you."

Vero's mind raced frantically. *He had to stop Davina!* He'd seen what would happen if he didn't.

Clover sensed her brother's panic. She had no idea why he was so desperate to stop Davina from leaving the dance, but she instinctively knew he would never hurt the girl. He must have a good reason. The next thing Clover knew, she was pulling the fire alarm. With the same conditioning as Pavlov's dogs, kids ran to the exits in droves. And in all of the chaos, Vero disappeared into the crowd and escaped through a side door.

Vero searched the school grounds for Davina, but she was long gone. He closed his eyes and calmed his mind. Then he recalled the events in his daydream: the shattered window, the house under construction, Danny with his slingshot, and Davina dead on the porch.

Vero's eyes shot open. He knew where to go! And he had to get there before Davina did. Vero looked around for some sort of transportation and saw the bike rack by the school's front doors. He ran over and frantically started checking the bikes. Luckily, he found a red mountain bike that had been left unlocked. Vero pulled the bike out of the rack.

"Taking that bike would be *stealing*," Blake hissed.

The sound of his voice sent a wave of chills down Vero's spine. Vero whipped his head around and saw Blake and Duff perched on the bench near the front door. "Mind your own business!" Vero said sharply. His strong voice disguised the fear he felt rising in his gut.

"But this *is* our business," Duff replied. He stood and walked toward Vero with a maniacal smirk.

Vero froze, mesmerized by Duff's unnaturally blue eyes. Duff peered down at him before grabbing Vero's wrist and squeezing it. Vero screamed as an excruciating pain shot through his body.

Behind Duff, Blake pulled a black iron chain from under the bench.

"You're going to leave Danny alone, once and for all," Blake sneered. "He's ours."

"You're coming with us," said Duff.

Duff held Vero's wrist in an agonizing grip, while Blake bent down and tried to wrap the chains around Vero's feet.

Vero had his hands on the bike's handlebars, but he remained frozen, hypnotized by Duff's eyes. He felt helpless as Blake approached him with the chain.

"Soon, you'll be ours as well," Duff said, and his eyes flashed from brilliant blue to red.

Vero blinked. Duff's hold on him was momentarily broken, and as he looked straight into the depths of Duff's eyes, Vero understood that Blake and Duff were maltures! They'd been plaguing Danny this whole time. No wonder Tack couldn't see them!

Duff leaped on top of Vero and attempted to pin him down, but Vero thrashed wildly. Then seemingly out of nowhere, Blake pulled out a metal wrist cuff to use with the chains and attempted to fasten it around Vero's arm.

Vero fought with all his might, but the maltures were stronger than Vero.

"Uriel! Help!" he screamed.

But Uriel did not come.

Vero then realized that as long as he was on earth, he would remain a powerless guardian angel. Somehow he had to get to the Ether and fight them there — that was the only

way to defeat the maltures and make them release their hold
on Danny.

Suddenly, a girl's voice cut through the darkness. "Get
off my brother!"

Vero turned his head and saw Clover charging toward
them, swinging Mr. Atwood's field hockey stick like a
sword. Her outfit might have said peace and love, but her
face said warrior.

Wait. Clover could see them? Surprised, Blake and Duff
hesitated, and that was all Vero needed. He rolled out from
under Duff's grasp and scrambled to his feet.

Clover continued to charge, more fearsome than Vero
had ever seen her.

"You're dead meat!" she shouted.

Suddenly, sirens wailed, and the flashing lights of a fire
truck appeared from around the corner of the building. Vero
paused for a moment and looked at Clover. He wanted to
explain, but there was no time. Grabbing Duff and Blake by
the backs of their shirts, he stepped right into the path of the
speeding fire truck.

Clover's screams penetrated the night air.

❖

Completely hysterical, Clover searched under the fire truck
for her brother as a fireman shined a flashlight underneath.

"He's under there!" she cried.

The fireman turned off the flashlight and stood up, pulling Clover up with him.

"There's no one under the truck," he said.

"No ... my brother," Clover insisted.

Spotting another fireman talking to the crowd that had gathered, Clover ran over to him. "Fireman Bob! You remember Vero. Please, did you see him step in front of the fire truck?"

"No, I didn't see him," he said. "And I know Vero well. Why don't I call your parents and ask them to come take you home?"

Something shiny on the ground near the fire truck's wheels caught her attention. Clover bent and picked up the sunglasses from Vero's Elvis costume.

"Are those yours?" Fireman Bob asked.

Clover didn't answer. As she held the glasses in her hand, Clover could no longer brush off all of the instances she knew to be true. Yes, she'd seen the man who twisted Vero's ankle when they were little. Yes, she'd seen Vero grow a pair of massive wings when he was making a snow angel. Yes, she'd been having vivid dreams about angels and demons that seemed completely real. She knew Vero was different, and she could no longer deny the fact that she saw things beyond her earthly eyes.

Since Blake and Duff had disappeared into thin air with her brother, Clover now understood that they were more than just a couple of school bullies. And she knew Vero was in grave danger. Wherever the three of them had gone to, Clover wouldn't be able to help her brother. She knelt on the ground and closed her eyes. "Please God. Please help my brother."

❖

Unbeknownst to Clover, five young hands shot up and caught streaking bursts of light in their palms. She had been heard.

26

◈

FIVE ANSWERS
TO A PRAYER

Vero landed in what appeared to be the Arctic. Everywhere he looked, he saw snow and ice. And mammoth glaciers surrounded him. He was standing on a frozen ocean. Blake and Duff were gone. Vero was alone and shivering violently. His sequined Elvis jumpsuit was definitely not the proper attire for Arctic conditions. Vero needed to get out of there, or he'd surely freeze to death.

As the winds whipped across the tundra and pelted him with icy snow, Vero regretted falling into the fire truck's path — but especially now that Blake and Duff were nowhere to be seen. Tiny icicles formed on his eyelashes. He tried to walk, but there was nowhere to go — the floating icebergs seemed infinite against the horizon. He was a mere blemish in the white vastness. Even if Vero had tried to cry, he couldn't — his tear ducts were frozen.

To think that he'd come this far and then failed completely! He'd allowed himself to die in front of Clover; he'd allowed Blake and Duff to get away. And after all that, Davina was still about to die.

Vero lifted his head and screamed at the frozen sky. He felt so angry that he needed the release. But then, in the midst of his rage, Vero remembered Uriel's promise to him — that he would never be alone. Even in this barren, icy wasteland, someone was keeping watch over him. Vero forced himself to practice what he'd learned during his training in the Ether. He calmed his mind, closed his eyes, and placed his hand over his heart. Then he listened for God's voice, his *Vox Dei*. Gradually, Vero became impervious to the harsh elements around him.

The voice directed him to dig away at the snow beneath his feet. Vero dropped to his knees and, despite his numb fingers, furiously swept the snow out from under him. Within moments, he reached a sheet of clear ice. And through that thick ice, he clearly saw X, Kane, Pax, Ada, and Greer about fifteen feet below him. It felt like he was peering down at them through a glass-bottom boat. Vero saw his fellow fledglings standing in a passageway, looking up at him in astonishment.

Suddenly, the ice began to crack. The cracks quickly grew, and then the ice shattered like a mirror. Vero fell through and landed on top of the other angels.

"Ouch! Get off!" Greer yelled.

It took Vero a few moments to realize that he was no longer *on* the iceberg, but *underneath* it — sprawled on the floor of an icy hallway, a channel that ran through the glacier. The first thing that registered was that it was surprisingly warm and bright in there. And then he became aware of Greer's elbow poking him in the chest.

"There's nothing like dropping in on your friends," Ada said, smiling warmly.

Suddenly, they heard thunder overhead, and the hole in the ice began shaking violently. They looked up to see the hole shrinking until it had completely closed over. The fledglings were now trapped under sheets of ice.

"I guess flying out of that hole is no longer an option," X said. His brown skin glowed golden in the strange light of the tunnel.

"Trust me, you wouldn't want to," Vero said. "Boy, am I glad to see you guys!"

"Likewise," Kane said. "We thought we'd lost you."

For the first time in a long time, Vero got a good look at his new friends. Ada slipped on the icy floor and grabbed onto X to steady herself. Pax adjusted his glasses. Kane stood with his arms crossed, smiling at Vero. And Greer gave him her customary smirk. Vero noticed that her leg was better. He pointed at it, and she said, "Uriel took care of it."

Only a short time ago, Vero had felt like an outsider with this group, and yet now they all stood here, a true team. A fierce loyalty and love for these friends filled Vero's chest.

"Ada filled us in on the whole Abaddon thing," Pax said.

"It's amazing that any of us survived after being so close to him like that," Kane said.

Vero swallowed hard. "Yeah, well, I need to go back there."

The group fell silent as the seriousness of his words sank in.

"Are you insane?" Greer asked.

"Some maltures have a hold over a kid at my school," Vero said. "And if we don't break it ... Davina will die tonight."

"Davina?" Kane asked.

"She's a friend of mine," Vero said, but the emotion in his voice betrayed him.

"Sounds like she's more than just a friend," Kane said.

Vero looked down, embarrassed.

"I get it," Kane said sadly. "I've been in love with a girl since kindergarten. She's even come up with names for our kids. There's a part of me that doesn't want to complete my training so I won't have to leave her."

Vero looked at him. It was nice to know someone understood how he felt.

"But we don't have our swords yet," Ada said. "We have nothing to fight with."

"You're wrong," Vero said. "We have something stronger than swords."

"Me," Greer said, stepping forward.

"I was thinking more along the lines of faith," Vero said. But he couldn't help smiling.

"Well, yeah, that too." Greer flashed him a big smile.

"But you guys need to understand what you're getting yourselves into," Vero said. "To find the maltures, we need to go to the entrance of the bottomless pit ... "

"Where Abaddon reigns," Ada said somberly.

The fledglings exchanged glances, and Vero felt their concern. "That's right," Vero said.

"That was bad down there," Kane said, running his fingers nervously through his dark hair.

"It's where we need to go," Vero said.

Vero saw the fear in their eyes.

"I know all of you vowed to help me; but I can't lie to you, it's a dangerous mission. If any of you want to bail, I'll understand. No hard feelings."

The angels considered for a few moments.

"Forget you," Greer said. "You just want to hog all the glory." She sounded different, and Vero realized she didn't have that subtle sneer in her voice anymore. Vero studied her and finally figured out that her I-got-someplace-better-to-be stance and her this-had-better-be-good look were both gone. Yet she was still every bit the fierce warrior who'd bumped into him on his first day at C.A.N.D.L.E. She looked ready for battle. "I say bring it."

Ada had a determined look on her face, but she began twirling her curls. She nodded at Vero.

"I'm also with you," X said. He looked like he was already formulating tactics and evasive maneuvers in his mind. "After all, we are answering a prayer, so we should get extra strength to carry it out."

Kane walked up to Vero. "Aren't you wondering how we found you here in the middle of nowhere?"

"Well, yeah, now that you mention it … "

"We all got a hit from the prayer grid," Kane said. "All of us got the exact same prayer. We were told to help you, so here we are. If you need to battle a couple of maltures, then I won't let you down." Kane stood up straight and strong.

Vero looked over at Pax with his oversized glasses; the familiar worry shone in his eyes.

"Do you believe you're better than us?" Pax asked Vero.

"No, I don't."

"Sometimes I can hear angels' thoughts, and I've heard

some things I wasn't supposed to hear. For instance, Uriel said you're special."

Vero collected his thoughts for a moment.

"I'm Vero Leland. I get beat up by bullies on earth. I have trouble flying in the Ether. I can't even carry out a simple little prayer like flagging down a cab on my own. I *know* I'm not better than anyone else."

Pax mulled Vero's response. "That's too bad. If we're going over to malture territory, then I was really hoping you had something good up your sleeve."

"Sorry, I don't."

"Are you in or not?" Greer asked impatiently.

"A prayer is a prayer," Pax said, "and I'm an angel of God. I'm in." Pax knuckle-bumped Vero.

Greer turned to Vero, "When you were giving your little speech about not being better than anyone else, you forgot to add that you have the worst taste in clothes. What the heck are you wearing?"

Vero looked down at his outfit. He'd forgotten about the Elvis jumpsuit.

"Yeah, the maltures might not take you very seriously in that getup," X added.

"Long story," Vero said.

He took off the jumpsuit, revealing a red T-shirt and jeans underneath. Vero dropped the jumpsuit to the icy floor. The temperature was comfortable inside the ice tunnel, so he was relieved he wouldn't need it for extra warmth.

"So where to now?" Kane asked, looking to Vero.

Vero's eyes took in their surroundings. There were two options—travel ahead in the tunnel or turn around and go in the opposite direction. Vero placed his hand over his heart, took a deep breath, and closed his eyes. After a moment, his eyes opened.

"My *Vox Dei* is telling me we should go straight ahead. Trust me. I know I can find it."

Moving unsteadily on the slippery ground, Ada tugged at X until they both fell flat on the ice.

"I hope we're gonna fly there," Ada said as Vero helped her and then X stand up. "I was never great at ice skating."

❖

The angels flew at breakneck speed underneath the ice as Vero guided them. They followed his *Vox Dei* like it was an internal radar system. When he was a little kid, Vero had watched a news story about a dog that got separated from his family while they were on vacation. The family searched for the dog for days until they'd finally had to go back home without him, heartbroken. Miraculously, three months later the dog showed up at their doorstep. He'd traveled over three hundred miles to find his way home. Vero had been amazed by the story, but now he understood.

Vero led the others in a V shape. Just like geese, their bodies naturally formed the pattern. By having each fledgling fly slightly higher than the one in front, the formation caused a decrease in the wind resistance, which helped them conserve energy and keep track of one another.

The snowy white ice above their heads began to grow darker. The bright light, which had shone through it, now dimmed while the temperature warmed even more. Vero noticed the walls and floors of ice were progressively transforming into walls and floors of stone.

They flew faster, and gradually the tunnel walls widened. And as the walls grew farther apart, the tunnel's height also grew taller and taller. Eventually, Vero saw twilight above them, and he knew they were no longer inside the tunnel. The sky was dark and filled with black clouds that obscured the tops of the stone walls.

The next thing Vero became aware of was a strong smell of salt. Then humidity. Droplets of water hit his face. And there before them, the angels saw a vast ocean framed by massive rock cliffs.

This ocean wasn't the beautiful crystal blue of the Caribbean Sea. Rather, it was dark, completely black, and it matched the clouds overhead. The water appeared to be thick and move slowly, like bubbly mud. *Was it an illusion?* Vero wasn't sure, but he wasn't going to let this unsightly body of water slow their progress as the angels continued to fly well over the sea.

"Don't think I'll be swimming down there," Ada said.

"It looks like sewage plant runoff gone way wrong," Kane said.

The black clouds cast shadows on the angels' lily-white wings, making them appear gray and gloomy. Their V formation broke as each flew in closer to one another, afraid of the sinister water below.

From behind them they heard an ear-splitting scream, which stopped them mid-flight. Vero saw Greer and Pax fall into the water. And his eye glimpsed something long and scaly disappearing quickly into the water.

"What was that?" X shouted.

Whatever it was, it rose up out of the murky water again and slashed at them, throwing them into the sea along with

Pax and Greer. Vero tried opening his eyes under the water to see what they were up against, but it was too dark to make out anything. He accidentally swallowed some water, noting that this was probably what motor oil tasted like. When he resurfaced, Vero saw the others bobbing up and down as they treaded water to stay afloat.

A gurgled "Help!" caught Vero's attention. He swam in the direction of the plea and saw Pax's arms thrashing about as he desperately tried to keep his head above water. Dense waves of water rushed into Pax's mouth, and then he went under.

"Pax!" Vero shouted.

Vero swam to Pax, grabbed him around the chest, and pulled his head up out of the water. Pax wasn't responsive. Vero looked in all directions until he spotted a small cluster of rocks. He tried swimming toward the rocks while dragging Pax behind him. Pax sputtered and coughed, but at least he was alive!

Pax began to slip out of Vero's grip. Vero struggled to hold on to him, but Pax was like dead weight. He pulled Vero under.

"Hold on!" Kane shouted, and he swam over and pulled Pax away from Vero.

"Over there!" Vero told Kane.

Kane hooked his arm over Pax's chest and swam with him to the rocks while Vero followed. Kane pushed Pax up to safety. Greer, Ada, and X were already there. Pax was unconscious.

"I don't know how long that thing had Pax under the water," Vero said, panting, "but I saw him take a mouthful of that noxious water."

"Let me try," Greer said. She turned Pax onto his stomach

and pushed on his back as hard as she could. Pax's wings were gone. Everyone's wings had disappeared when they hit the water.

"Come on, Pax!" Greer cried, and she gave another mighty heave.

"Please, Pax," Ada said. Her long auburn curls appeared black from the seawater. She struggled to regain her breath as she watched Greer work on Pax.

Finally, Pax coughed out great bursts of dark, slushy water. Greer helped him turn onto his side, away from the waves that crashed along their tiny outcrop of rocks. Vero sent up a silent prayer of thanks.

"What *was* that thing?" X asked, wiping the water from his eyes.

"Is it gone?" Pax whispered hoarsely.

"I don't know," Vero said. "But we need to keep going. Can everyone fly?"

"I don't think my lungs can take it," Pax said between coughs.

"That thing might have gotten us just by pure luck," Vero said.

"Twice?" Kane asked.

"I'll try flying past, and then you can follow."

Vero concentrated and his wings appeared. He rose into the air and flew straight over the water. Five yards, twenty, fifty—the farther he went, the more sure he was of his escape.

Vero looked back and flashed the others the thumbs-up sign. "Come on, we're clear!" he called to them.

"Vero!" X shouted.

Vero turned in time to see an enormous sheet of scales rising from the sea—right before he was smacked back down into the water like a fly getting hit by a fly swatter. Momentarily stunned, he swam back to the rocks.

"Got any other brilliant ideas?" Greer asked.

"As a matter of fact, I do. I'll just have to fly higher."

Vero stood on the rocks, opened his wings and shot high into the air. Vero was rising faster than he'd ever flown and gaining altitude quickly — until he was slapped back down into the water again.

The others winced. Whatever they were dealing with, it was apparently massive. It smacked Vero like a volleyball getting stuffed at the net.

"It won't let him go higher," X said.

"Very observant," Greer said.

But Vero would not be deterred. He swam back to the rocks, got himself airborne for a third time, only to be smacked back into the water.

Finally, Greer had enough. "Hey, moron! Do you know what Albert Einstein said the definition of *insanity* is?"

Vero didn't answer her.

"It's doing the same thing over and over again and expecting different results. That thing will *not* let us pass!"

Greer was right. Vero needed to come up with a new tactic. He swam back to the rock cluster and Kane pulled him up. He sat down and gazed out over the black ocean. "If we only knew what that thing was, we could figure out how to get around it," Vero said.

Without warning, the water all around them began to bubble like a tarpit. As a few specks landed on his arm, Vero yelled, "It's boiling!"

"Oh, no ... " X stuttered.

"What?"

"Now I know what we're up against."

Before X could say more, a gigantic creature resembling a dragon lifted its ugly head out of the water. Its eyes shone like a lighthouse beacon. The beast was covered in scales that were as thick as iron. Its mouth was lined with rows of sharp teeth. The teeth alone were easily two stories tall. Smoke billowed from its nostrils. As the rest of its body rose, the angels could see sharp fins running the length of its back. Now they knew what had been knocking them into the water—it was the creature's tail.

"And I thought the behemoth was big," Pax said. "This thing is the size of a roller coaster!"

"X, what is it?" Vero asked.

"It's the Leviathan from Job 41!" X said. "An invincible, fire-breathing sea monster. Nothing on earth is its equal."

Vero's heart sank. He looked at X for anything more that might help them. Some glimmer of hope.

"Job was pretty specific in his description. I won't go into all of it; but basically, we have no chance here."

"Then what do we do?" Ada asked.

"Turn back," Kane answered.

That was the last thing Vero wanted to do because the voice inside of him had only grown stronger. And it was urging him to continue in the direction they'd been headed.

"We're already in the middle of his ocean," Vero said. "I don't think he'd let us go back even if we wanted to."

Everyone was at a loss. The sky turned darker as a storm began to brew. Then Vero noticed that Greer had her eyes closed in concentration, praying for direction. Her fingers were stretched over her heart.

"Wait ... Greer might have something," Vero said.

Her eyes fluttered open as she came back to them. "Seriously? For real?" Greer said, questioning whatever directions she'd received.

"What is it?" X asked. "What did you hear?"

"Well, it's not for the faint of heart," she began. "But I know how to get around this overgrown crocodile."

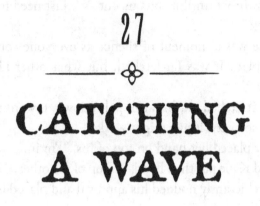

27

CATCHING
A WAVE

F ly *into* its mouth?" Pax exclaimed. "Are you crazy?"
  "It's like Jonah and the big fish. He was able to live
in the fish's belly for three days and three nights until the
whale finally spit Jonah onto dry land," Greer said.

"But a whale doesn't have fangs that are two stories tall!"
Ada said.

"We'll have to get the Leviathan to swallow us whole in
one gulp," Greer said.

"Do you know what the *real* definition of *insanity* is?"
Pax asked. "Your plan!"

"Greer, we don't have three days and three nights to
spare," Vero said.

"We won't need that long. Once we get in there, we'll
wait until its head is pointed beyond here, you know, to
the land on the other side. And then we'll use our wings to

tickle its throat until it spits us out. We just need to hit his gag reflex."

There was a moment of silence as everyone considered Greer's plan. It was far-fetched, but what other ideas did they have?

Vero stretched out his arm, palm down, toward the others. "It's so crazy, it just might work."

Greer placed her hand on top of his. "I'm in."

X and Kane put their hands on top of the others. "Us too."

Pax reluctantly nodded his approval and placed his hand on the pile.

Only Ada was left. She shrugged and said, "Okay, fine. But I just want to state for the record that I'm totally against this whole thing."

"Noted." Vero smiled.

"Okay, so we'll need to hold on to each other. When a huge wave comes along, we'll all jump on top of it and ride the wave straight into its mouth," Greer said.

"That's a fine idea, except the water is boiling," Pax said.

Kane stuck his finger in the water to test it.

"It's not boiling anymore. I think the water must only heat up when the thing breathes fire."

"Oh, yes. Now it's perfectly safe," Pax said, pushing his glasses higher up on his nose with his index finger.

The storm was now beginning to churn the water. The winds whipped the waves higher and higher, smashing them against the rocks. Vero knew the angels' strength was waning.

"I can't hold on much longer!" X yelled, as if he'd read Vero's mind.

"Wait for it ... wait," Greer said. "Just a few seconds more until it opens its mouth ... "

As the waves tormented the Leviathan, the creature grew angry. It raised its head. And when it opened its mouth to howl, Greer saw their opportunity.

"Now!" she cried.

Clinging to each other, the angels jumped off the rocks into the water below. Then a huge wave came up from behind them.

"Hold tight!" Vero shouted.

When the sea monster wailed at an ear-splitting level, the angels all body-surfed straight into the Leviathan's mouth and landed safely on the other side of those two-story fangs. Its mouth closed, and the creature began to gag when it felt the intruders inside.

"Oh no, it's going to spit us out! But it's too soon!" Greer yelled. "We're in too deep! We're too close to its throat! Quick, run back toward the front of its mouth!"

The angels quickly ran forward, and the gagging motions stopped.

"I thought the idea was for it to barf us out?" Pax said.

"Only after it turns around so it shoots us in the other direction," Greer explained.

Ada looked around. Being in the Leviathan's mouth was like being inside a cavern—a cavern with a squishy, fleshy ceiling and floor.

"It reeks like rotten fish in here," Ada said pinching her nose.

No one contradicted her.

X cupped his mouth and said, "I might puke before the Leviathan does."

"So now what do we do?" Kane asked.

"We wait," Greer said. "We wait until we feel it turn around."

❖

So they waited and waited, but the Leviathan never turned its body around. Vero grew impatient with each passing moment. Plus, it was no thrill sitting in the dark inside a creature's disgusting mouth. The only relief came when the Leviathan opened its mouth and a wave of fresh air and light came through.

"I can't wait any longer. I've already wasted too much time," Vero told the others. "I have to get out of here."

"It'll just spit us back onto the rocks, and then we're back to square one," Greer said.

Everyone took a moment to consider their predicament. Pax then broke the silence. "I'm gonna hate myself for saying this, but there is another way out to the other side."

"How?" Vero asked.

"We could follow his stomach down through his digestive system and then ... "

A look of horror crossed Ada's face. "And then it passes us out ... you mean, *that* end?" she demanded.

Pax nodded.

"No way!" Ada yelled. "I've done enough for you guys, but I have to draw the line somewhere! Some prayers go too far!"

Greer winced. X and Kane had similar looks on their faces.

"We're already inside its mouth, so how much worse could it be?" Vero offered.

"You know, I should be home right now relaxing on the sofa and watching TV. Instead, I'm here trying to help you! And now I'm about to be pooped out into a black ocean by some sea monster?" Ada punched Vero hard in his gut. He fell backward. The release made Ada feel better.

"Thanks, I needed that," Ada said. "Okay, let's go."

Vero and the others flew past the Leviathan's throat and into its massive stomach. They landed in the knee-deep, rancid, disgustingness. What little light they'd had within the Leviathan's open mouth was extinguished once they entered its gut.

"I hate you!" Ada yelled to Vero as the darkness set in.

"Angels aren't allowed to hate, Ada," Vero shot back.

"It's creepy in here," Ada said. "I can't see."

"I don't like this," Pax said, echoing her sentiment.

Vero could hear the panic in their voices. "It's okay," he said. "Let's move together." But then a huge rush of gastric juices knocked him down and completely submerged him. He came up sputtering and gagging.

"Oh this is just perfect," Vero said. "I can feel fish guts in my wings."

"And I can smell 'em," X said.

"Wait!" Kane shouted. "I just remembered something." Kane clicked on a small LED flashlight attached to a keychain, and the beast's belly lit up.

"That's so much better!" Ada said.

"Yeah, now we can actually see the chewed fish guts and bloody fish carcasses," Greer said.

"That's pretty powerful for such a small flashlight," Vero remarked.

"My mom worries about me coming home in the dark," Kane admitted a bit sheepishly.

Occasionally, a huge rush of water would knock them all down. The water carried them farther along as if they were on a slide at a water park. They could make more ground riding the waves than by flying.

"Does this thing ever end?!" Kane yelled.

"Do you think we're getting any closer?" X asked.

"Who knows?" Pax said.

Something brushed against X's leg. He looked down and his eyes went wide. X tried to scream, but no words came out. All he could do was point. Kane shined his light in X's direction. A crocodile's headless body floated past them.

"A crocodile?" Kane yelled. "Man, that is just wrong."

"Do you know why Leviathan lives alone?" Pax asked, as they waded through the massive beast. "Because he ate his chum."

"Real funny, Pax. Remind me to throw up on you," Ada said.

"C'mon, Ada, sometimes being an angel is more than just a job, it's a doody," Greer smirked. "Get it? Doody?"

"Not funny," Ada said.

"I agree. We really need to get to the bottom of this," X chimed in.

"Not you too, X!" Ada groaned.

"Yeah, well, I can't wait to finish this program so we can *log out*," Kane added.

Ada looked like she was going to be sick.

Greer laughed, "C'mon, Ada. Would it hurt you to tell a joke just once?"

"Get me out of this beast, and I'll be the first one to tell a joke," Ada retorted.

Just then, an enormous wave rushed toward them. It was so high that it reached the top of the stomach roof. It was like a tsunami, taking everything in its path.

"Hold your breath!" Vero yelled.

The wave swept them farther down the stomach before it finally dropped them over a waterfall into a pool below. One by one, the angels poked their heads up through all the liquid muck. The water slowly receded and they were finally able to stand. Kane shined the flashlight at them while Vero took a head count.

"We're all here," Vero announced.

"Talk about catching a wave," X said.

"The good thing is, it pushed us a lot farther," Pax noted, looking around.

"The bad news is ... " Ada said as she pulled something blue and squishy out of her hair, "now I have whale blubber in my hair."

"You mean the Leviathan just snacked on a whale?" X asked.

"That explains the huge wave," Pax said.

The angels continued on. The more they walked, the more the walls began to narrow.

"Hopefully, we'll be out soon," Vero said as he sniffed the air with a wrinkled nose. "You guys smell that?"

Ada looked at Vero, disgusted. "Eww, Vero!"

"It's not me! It's the Leviathan. We're in its bowels now!"

The foul stench wafted through the whole place.

"I need to get out of here!" Ada yelled. "I can't take it any longer!" Ada grabbed the flashlight from Kane and plowed ahead.

"Ada, come back!" Greer yelled.

She wasn't stopping, so the others ran after her. The odor grew more and more putrid the farther they went. As Vero covered his mouth and nose, he kept telling himself that the offending odor was a good thing. It meant that soon they would be out. Vero slipped in something, which he quickly tried to convince himself was only mud.

Before he could get back up, some unseen force shot him out into the sea. He swam to the surface and saw land just a few feet away. Pax, Greer, Ada, Kane, and X popped up like fishing bobbers next to him.

"Land ho!" Greer shouted.

The angels swam to shore and plopped down on the beach, exhausted. They were covered with sea sludge, but at least the seawater had washed off the monster's waste.

True to her word, Ada raised her head and looked at the other angels. "Thank God that's over," she said. "I'm just happy everything came out okay in the end."

"I guess the girl has a sense of humor after all," Greer smiled.

28

CHASING MALTURES

Vero was the first to stand up on the rocky shore. A feeling of dread formed in the pit of his stomach as his eyes took in the sight before him.

A forest — trees everywhere he looked. But they weren't green, leafy trees ... these trees were grotesque, gnarled. They were naked with no leaves to cover their branches. Twisted trunks. Branches contorted like distorted limbs. And thick sheets of moss hung off the sickly trees like decayed flesh.

"Out of the belly of the Leviathan and straight into hell," Greer said, as she took in the landscape.

"Stay together," Vero said.

Silvery moonlight provided enough light for the fledglings to navigate their way through the dead forest. Vero noticed it was eerily silent. There were only the sounds of their feet crashing through the underbrush. Vero's eyes darted between the nearest diseased trees. He had the feeling they were being watched.

Kane's foot caught on a fallen branch. "Aahh!" he cried out as he face-planted. "This whole thing is a bad idea!" Kane sat up and tugged on his foot, wrenching it free from the branch.

"Yeah, Vero, why do we have to do everything *your* way? You think you're so much better than us!" Ada snarled.

"We're starting to fight. That means we're close to the maltures' territory," Pax said. "Resist their influence! We need to be strong. We need to do this together."

"If we turn on one another," Vero said, "we're all doomed."

"It's not easy," Ada said. "I feel angry and scared. Everything is hopeless and so dark."

"No, it's not. It just feels that way here. We're approaching their side of the Ether, and it's a world filled with hatred, deceit, and hopelessness. For demons and maltures, these feelings are the air they breathe. It's their essence. But it's not ours," Vero said.

Vero stood in front of Ada and grabbed her shoulders. He locked eyes with her and said, "Ada Brickner, you are an angel of light, full of love and goodness. That is your essence. Remember that, and nothing can harm you."

Vero looked over at the others. "That goes for all of us."

"Send forth your light and truth, let them guide me," X recited.

"Psalm 43," said Ada.

X nodded.

The verse helped fortify them. Vero removed his hands from Ada's shoulders and walked ahead of the others. As they journeyed deeper into the putrid forest, it became darker as the trees grew thicker. The wind howled as if it were the cries of a horrible beast.

All kinds of crazy thoughts swirled around in Vero's mind. He, too, felt the harmful influences surrounding them. Confusion and feelings of despair tormented him. Vero pressed his temples and repeated over and over, "Your Light. Your Truth, let them guide me."

Suddenly, Vero was attacked from behind. Someone—or something—jumped on his back and pounded his face into the ground over and over again. His nose smashed against a rock, and blood flowed down his face. Vero heard Ada shrieking. *A malture!*

Vero craned his head and saw not a malture, but Kane! His eyes were wild with fury.

"You think you're so special! Well, you're not!" Kane shouted.

"Kane! Get off of him!" X yelled.

But Kane couldn't hear him. When Vero looked into his eyes, he knew Kane had checked out. Greer and X pulled Kane off of Vero, only to have Kane turn around and punch Greer in the mouth. He was like a caged animal who'd finally been set free. He shoved Greer up against a thick tree trunk and pinned her.

"Do you think I've forgotten how you rubbed my face in that dirt? Do you think it's over?"

Greer looked terrified.

"Well, now it's payback time!" Kane shouted.

Kane slammed Greer against a tree trunk. Vero, Pax, and X pulled him off of her.

"Kane! Remember, his Light. His Truth. Let them guide you!" Vero shouted in his face.

As X and Vero restrained him, Vero's words seemed to have some positive effect. Kane calmed slightly as he noticed Vero's bleeding nose. It looked as if he was coming back. Then, from out of the dark shadows, a thick black chain sailed through the air and lassoed Kane around his torso. The chain coiled itself the same way a snake snares its prey. Then it squeezed Kane until he could no longer move. The chain didn't stop coiling until it had bound Kane up to and around his mouth. Kane lost the ability to speak. But what his mouth couldn't say, his eyes conveyed clearly.

His previous rage was replaced with raw fear. Vero and X were trying to free him from the shackle when Vero heard a stirring in the trees overhead. His heart thundering, Vero lifted his head toward the treetops. The blackened clawlike branches swayed ominously as the wind picked up. Goose bumps spread across his body. He could feel the hair on his arms stand on end. Yet no one was there.

Greer screamed.

Vero whirled around to see two sets of red eyes glowing through the thick moss that drooped from a knotty branch toward the ground. He stretched out his arms and pushed the others behind him as Blake and Duff walked through the moss. They looked exactly as they had appeared on earth—two teenage thugs with pimply faces and greasy hair.

"We'll be taking this guy as a souvenir," Blake said, picking up the end of the chain and holding it like a leash. "He was such an easy target."

"No!" Vero shouted.

With lecherous grins, Blake and Duff looked at the other angels and eagerly sized them up.

"The rest of them should be easy to take down, too," Duff said with a cruel laugh.

"Don't give in to them!" Vero cried.

X cried out, "We are light!"

Duff walked over to X.

"Oh, we've got a tough guy here. Let me ask you something, X," Duff said in a mocking tone. "The Light, the Light, where is your precious Light when you're sitting in that wheelchair? Huh? When you can't even raise your arms to give mommy a hug?"

X's face lost all color.

"Why would you feel any loyalty toward someone who did that to you?" Duff asked as he bent down and picked up a rock. "Perhaps it's because you have rocks in your head?" Duff slammed the rock against X's skull, and X went down. He was out cold.

"Leave him alone!" Greer shouted. She raced over to help X.

In the blink of an eye, Duff rushed her and caught her in his grip. She winced and couldn't escape his hold. He began stroking her face.

"Oh, you may talk tough, sister. But how about you … how was that tenth birthday, Greer? If memory serves me correctly, you spent it locked in the closet of what? Foster family number five?"

Greer began shaking.

"Two whole days in a closet without any light. You thought darkness was your only companion. But we were there with you. We kept you company in that closet while your precious Light turned his back on you — just like he's doing again today."

Duff punched Greer in the stomach. With the wind knocked out of her, she doubled over and sank to her knees.

"Greer!" Vero yelled as he ran to her and put his hand on her back. She slumped the rest of the way to the ground, fighting for a breath.

Ada began crying. Pax gripped her hand.

"Oh, look how touching," Blake said to Duff. Then he turned to Pax and said, "Is that bogus little gesture of support supposed to comfort your crybaby girlfriend?"

"It's not bogus. There is only Truth and Light here," Pax said calmly.

"It *is* bogus," Blake said. "Because when I wrap you up in my chains—trust me, you're gonna let go of her hand real fast."

Blake snapped off a twig and threw it at Ada and Pax. In midair the twig spun several times end over end, and then it transformed into a heavy, black chain.

"Run!" Vero shouted.

But the chain was too fast. With lightning speed, it coiled itself around Ada and Pax, tightly tying them together.

Blake laughed as he looked at their hands, still clasped. "Guess I was wrong."

Vero had seen enough. He left Greer and charged at Blake. But when Vero angrily shoved him, Blake barely flinched.

"You have unfinished business with me, *not* them!" Vero shouted.

Blake got right up in Vero's face and snarled, "And what unfinished business are you talking about?"

"Release your hold on Danny," Vero said, wiping a trickle of blood from his nose.

"Danny Konrad? A kid nobody cares about? His own mother and father don't even care," Blake smirked. "Isn't he the same kid who loves beating the crap out of you? Who stole pretty little Davina away from you?"

Vero grew enraged. The blood pumped to his face.

"And how are you going to make us do that anyway?" Blake asked. "Are your friends really here to help you?" He laughed.

Blake motioned to X who was still out cold on the ground. Blood trickled down his forehead from where the rock smashed his head. Greer was lying in the fetal position clutching her stomach. Kane, Ada, and Pax all struggled to break free of their chains.

"Pathetic," Duff scoffed.

"If I were you, I'd get revenge on a guy like Danny," Blake said. "It's so much more satisfying."

Vero grabbed Blake by the shoulders and shook him. Blake laughed maniacally, unfazed and unthreatened. Next, Duff jumped in Vero's face.

"Your angelic efforts have all been in vain anyway, Vero," Duff said. "You're too late!"

"That's a lie!"

"Think so? Then why don't we all take a look, shall we?"

In a dramatic gesture, Duff swept his hands apart, revealing a festering black light. The blackness grew wider the farther apart he spread his hands. Eventually, the dark mist clouded all of their vision. Then, in the cloudy darkness, Vero heard someone walking. Slowly, the darkness cleared. Although they were all standing in the same positions, their surroundings had changed. They were now on earth, standing in front of the abandoned house from Vero's daydream.

Only this wasn't a dream. Danny was now walking toward them headed up the driveway. His face was consumed with anger, and he had a slingshot firmly in hand. He gave no indication that he could see any of them.

Vero lunged toward Danny, but Blake and Duff grabbed Vero and held him down.

"Easy there, hotshot. This is for viewing pleasure only," Blake snarled. "We thought it would be fun for everyone to watch your little girlfriend die."

Vero tried to escape, but their hold on him was too strong.

"It's a trick, Vero!" Pax shouted, while still trying to free himself and Ada from the black chain. "Remember, this hasn't happened yet! Time on earth stops when we're called to the Ether!"

"Is that what you learned in class? Well, what if Vero wasn't exactly called back to the Ether?" Duff said with an evil smile. "There wasn't any class scheduled for today, was there, Fledgling? If I recall, you jumped in front of that fire truck and took us with you. And that was what? A good hour ago?"

Vero's heart sank. It was true. He'd returned to the Ether of his own accord.

"Because of that, what you're seeing is happening right now—live," Blake told Vero.

"Or didn't they teach you that in angel school?" Duff snickered.

Vero looked toward the woods behind the house. If what Blake said was true and if Vero was now watching his daydream happening in real life, then Davina should come running through those woods any minute now, and Danny's red marble should strike her in the temple, killing her instantly.

Vero knew he had to stop it from happening. But how? Vero closed his eyes and tried listening for his *Vox Dei*. But he heard nothing. A look of disappointment crossed his face when he opened his eyes again.

"I guess just like your teachers at C.A.N.D.L.E., that voice in your heart deceived you again," Duff taunted him.

X began stirring. "X, wake up," Ada whispered.

Pax shushed her, and then Vero sent this thought to Pax: *Try to get into X's mind! Try to reach his consciousness.* Vero prayed that Pax could read his thoughts. *Please, God . . .*

Pax's head whipped around. He'd heard Vero!

"Poor Danny finally thought someone cared about him. He even bought Davina a corsage," Duff said.

Danny stopped walking and was sizing up the windows on the house.

"What a loser," Duff scoffed.

Duff and Blake laughed, and Vero experienced an overwhelming feeling of compassion for Danny.

"Davina never cared about you," Blake said.

"Davina's not like that!" Vero yelled.

"Nobody on earth cares about anyone but himself," Blake said. "Do they?"

"Danny, please!" Vero shouted.

Vero's desire to save both Danny and Davina became overpowering, and suddenly he was just as consumed as he'd been on the day when that corn snake had attacked Davina during science class. With a deafening roar, he threw off

Blake and Duff with newfound strength. His wings shot out, and he flew to Danny's side.

"Davina cares about you!" Vero yelled in Danny's ear. "She's on her way! Don't do this!"

Stunned by Vero's sudden surge of power, Blake and Duff appeared even more shocked when Danny hesitated. So with renewed force, they sprang into action.

"You're gonna pay dearly for that," Duff hissed, and he tackled Vero to the ground.

"Hold on, Vero!" Greer shouted as her breathing finally returned to normal. She got to her feet and began unraveling the chains that were constricting Kane.

Blake ran at Danny and began whispering in his ear again. "No one cares about you, Danny. Davina was just toying with you. She sure made a big fool out of you tonight."

Danny furrowed his brow and started walking toward the house again, completely unaware that the hateful thoughts in his mind were being planted there.

As Vero saw Blake yelling in Danny's ear, he had an epiphany. He remembered how Blake had yelled in Danny's ear in that exact same way on that day when Danny had beat up Vero. Danny had apparently never even been aware of Blake and Duff's presence. Even though they'd always been with him, they'd been invisible to him!

Duff smashed Vero hard into the ground, and then he quickly rejoined Blake, whispering negative encouragement in Danny's other ear. As he did this, Vero noticed something different about Blake and Duff ... *was it panic?*

"You have every right to be angry, Danny. You're not loved," Duff whispered. "You never have been."

Blake whispered in the other ear, and their words dripped like poison.

Vero flew at Duff and tried to pull him away from Danny, but Duff was too strong.

Vero shouted to his fellow angels, "Guys, I need your help *now!*"

X sat up quickly, feeling confused and rubbing his head. As he took in the scene, he didn't recognize the environment, but he saw that Vero needed help.

"I'll be back," Greer said to Kane, and she sprang to her feet, leaving him still partially chained.

Greer and X released their wings. Then they swooped down on top of Duff and attacked. They pulled him away from Danny, giving Vero a clear shot at Danny's ear instead.

Vero desperately yelled into it, "Don't listen to their hateful thoughts, Danny!" Vero shouted. "It's all lies!"

Danny looked down at the driveway for a moment, his concentration on the house now clearly interrupted. Vero's words were getting through!

Blake and Duff grew enraged. With astonishing strength, Duff grabbed Greer and X simultaneously and threw them onto Pax and Ada who were still bound together by the black chains. They landed in a bone-bruising heap.

Blake tackled Vero, pinned him down by his arms, and sat on him. "That's enough out of you, angel boy!"

"Your own mother doesn't care about you, so why would Davina?" Duff shouted in Danny's ear.

Danny's momentary hesitation quickly passed as Duff's words sank in. The anger returned to Danny's face, and he stormed over to the house.

"No!" Vero cried.

Blake gritted his teeth as he screamed angrily in Vero's face. "He's *ours*! We'll never let him go!"

A feeling of dire urgency came over Vero as he saw Duff whispering in Danny's ear, "Smash some more of those windows. It'll feel good ... "

Danny reached into his pocket and pulled out a red marble. He loaded it into the elastic band of the slingshot. Vero watched in horror as he saw Davina running through the woods. She was about to burst through those trees and run straight for the house, right on time.

"No! Danny! No!" Vero yelled.

Suddenly, a black chain struck Blake hard across the face, knocking him backward and off of Vero. He was momentarily stunned. Surprised, Duff looked up to see Kane holding the chain. He'd freed himself!

"The next one's for you!" Kane growled in fury.

Kane swung the chain around his head lasso-style, readying to strike Duff.

"You guys aren't so scary after all," Kane taunted as he swung the chain at Duff. But in a peevish rage, Duff grabbed the chain with his hand and jerked hard, flinging Kane high into the air.

Kane managed to grab a tree branch as he sailed through the air. And then right before the fledglings' eyes, Duff began to morph. His boyish appearance turned monstrous, with burn marks stretching from ear to ear. His flesh boiled into a slimy hide. His hands became claws, and his feet were now talons. And that single eye that had haunted Vero ever since his first run-in with maltures went all the way through his head and burned with pure hatred. "Am I scary now?" Duff grinned, showing rotted, sharp fangs.

Blake also mutated into his hideous self. Turns out they were the same maltures that had attacked him in the bathroom at Dr. Weiss's office! It was clear they intended to finish the job this time.

"Oh man ... " X said with his mouth hanging open. He freed Pax and Ada, letting the chain drop to the ground.

The angels watched in total fear as Blake lifted his arm toward the sky. His claw grew into a scythe, and the long curved blade became an extension of his arm.

"It's perfect for a beheading," Greer said, mesmerized by the terrifying blade.

Vero heard a swish of air as Blake swung the scythe at Vero's head. He quickly ducked and narrowly missed the lethal blow.

Roaring in frustration, Blake turned to Pax and Ada who recoiled. "How about if I behead one of your friends instead? Who will you save?"

"No!" Vero cried racing over to them.

As Blake swiped at them, Greer and X flew full speed onto Blake's back, knocking him to the ground for a moment.

"Vero, look!" Kane shouted, as he flew down from the tree.

Vero whipped around and saw Duff whispering into Danny's ear. Vero's heart nearly stopped as he watched Danny pull the red marble back in the elastic part of the slingshot. At that same moment, Davina burst through the thicket of trees. But Danny didn't see her, just like in Vero's daydream.

"Danny, no!" Vero shouted.

Blake jumped to his feet and swung his scythe at Vero who retreated from the blade. Just as Danny was about to release the marble into the air, Vero screamed with every ounce of his being, "Danny, we are here! You are not alone!"

Danny hesitated for a moment. He didn't release the marble.

"God loves you!" Vero shouted.

The maltures grew more enraged at the mention of God. They hissed and charged at Vero with scythes raised. Vero braced himself for the worst; but in that split second, Vero read Danny's mind. And he saw that Danny was having his own epiphany. Danny remembered how when he was a little kid, his mother would tuck him into bed and shower him with kisses. He remembered how his father spent hours with him carving a car out of wood that they hoped would win the Cub Scouts' Pinewood Derby. Danny remembered carefree days spent riding bikes with his older brother. But most of all, he remembered that he was loved.

Danny slowly lowered the slingshot. He felt ashamed of what he'd become. Out of a pure and simple desperation, he uttered the words, "Please, God, help me."

In that moment Vero learned just how powerful simple prayers can be. For in that precise moment, gold streaks appeared on Vero's forearm and shot up to his fingers. A magnificent sword blade sprang forth from Vero's right hand. From the inside of his palm, the sword continued to grow until a handle appeared, and Vero clutched it in his grasp. The sleek, solid-gold blade with its handle covered in vibrant gems fit Vero's hand so perfectly that it seemed as if his hand and the sword were one. The other angels looked on with their mouths hanging wide open in astonishment.

"Get them!" Greer shouted to Vero. "You are a warrior!"

Blake and Duff charged at Vero in a blind fury, and in

one clean swipe, Vero blocked both of their thrusts with the scythes. The maltures exchanged confused looks, obviously surprised by Vero's prowess. They charged Vero again, slicing at him. Vero fended off their blows with an agility he didn't know he possessed. Then he swung his sword and met their every thrust. The sound of clanking metal reverberated throughout the air. It was a sound Vero had heard while Uriel was sparring with the maltures on the rooftop while Vero hung from the ledge.

Pax and Ada flew over to Danny and stood on either side of him, creating a buffer between Danny and the maltures. Greer and X flew to Davina's side as Kane stood and watched Vero in stunned awe.

"Awesome ... " Kane muttered, his mouth agape.

Vero deflected their every stab. And as his confidence grew, Vero was no longer dodging jabs, but thrusting forward, slashing at the maltures, and forcing them to back away from Danny and head toward the house.

"Release Danny!" Vero demanded as he continued to advance.

After he'd backed them all the way to the house, he kept them both at bay, parrying blow for blow.

"Release him!" Vero shouted.

"If we release him, what will you do to us, Vero?" Blake asked. "Kill us?"

Blake's question threw Vero. A flicker of uncertainty came to his mind. Did he really have it in him to finish them off?

"Vero Leland ... track star, loyal friend, dutiful son, guardian angel ... *killer*!" Blake snarled.

The word *killer* resonated through Vero's head. He could never imagine himself killing anyone. But these were maltures. As his confidence wavered, his concentration broke.

In that moment of confusion, Duff spun away from the house and his blade sliced Vero's shoulder with great precision as Duff tried to jump clear of the fray. Vero was overcome with excruciating pain, and he slumped to the ground.

"Vero!" Kane yelled. He ran over to help Vero, but the hissing creatures swung violently at him, stopping him in his tracks. Vero clutched his shoulder, his energy was starting to drain right along with the blood that was now seeping from his gash.

"Vero! Behind you!" Greer screamed.

Vero turned and saw Duff charging at him with a raised scythe. The curved blade swung at Vero with deadly force. But with incredible swiftness, Vero rolled out of its path. The maltures shrieked.

Vero had allowed those fiends to distract him! *You fool!* he thought, and his anger brought him strength. Vero rose from the ground and held his sword out in front of him.

"Release Danny!" he said, unflinching.

His voice echoed voluminously, deep and commanding. He no longer feared. He no longer felt pain. His only thought was of Danny. If Vero died, so be it. He would fight for Danny and Davina to the death.

Blake and Duff went back on the offensive and charged Vero, but Vero was ready for them. He effortlessly somersaulted over their heads and landed squarely on his feet behind them.

The maltures turned around and engaged Vero, scythes against sword. Vero was equal to their challenge, thwarting each and every slice of their blades.

Then Blake's blade cut close to Vero's chest, but Vero pulled back quickly so the blade only caught his shirt, ripping the red material. Vero recoiled, and that little step back helped him avoid an erratic swipe from Duff. The swing went wide missing Vero completely, and instead it found Blake and cut off his arm at the elbow.

Blake shrieked in pain and fury. His scythe clanged to the ground where it instantly withered. Blake hissed at Duff who showed no concern for his fellow malture.

Defeated and with his scythe gone, Blake turned to run. But Kane flew right at him and knocked him to the driveway. "Not so fast!" Kane put his foot on Blake's chest as the beaten malture whimpered.

"One down!" Greer shouted.

Vero and Duff circled each other — waiting for someone to make a move.

"Yes, Vero, you are a real prize, and you know it, don't you?" Duff said.

Vero was curious, but he didn't let down his guard. Vero continued circling, never taking his eyes off of Duff.

"They're setting you up, Vero. Do your friends know about you?" Duff continued. "They'll tell you that it's all for the greater good, that it's *his* will. But you'll be the one to pay the price, not him."

"Light, Vero. You are light!" Ada called.

"Don't let him get up in your head, Vero. You've got this!" Pax shouted.

Yet, Duff's words bothered Vero.

"If you're not just a pawn, why haven't they told you everything? What are their plans for you, Vero ..., hmmm?"

Duff's malicious words found their mark. Vero wondered

why he was special and what the plan for him was. Why did the maltures seem to know more about him than Vero did? Vero was wrestling with his doubt. His hands began trembling. Duff smiled.

Vero caught his own reflection in his blade, and in his eyes he no longer saw a timid young angel. Uriel's words came rushing back to him: *"The opposite of faith is not doubt. The opposite of faith is fear."* Vero would not give in to his fear. He wielded his sword at the demonic creature with such conviction that Duff fell backward to the ground.

"Release Danny!" Vero said, his blade pointed at Duff's chest.

"You understand nothing. We can't release Danny. We have no authority."

Duff rolled out from underneath Vero's sword and jumped to his feet. As he swiped at Vero's head with his scythe, Vero ducked, spun around, and sliced his sword blade clear through Duff's wrist.

Duff looked down, and as he watched his scythe wither, he let out a screeching howl.

And then the earth around them began to rumble. Between the two miserable maltures, a mound of earth rose up.

"No!" Duff screamed. "It's not our fault!"

As the mound continued to grow, Vero and Kane backed away. Vero held his sword in front of him, shielding the other angels. A resounding clicking sound began to emanate from the mound until it finally burst open, and millions of insect-like creatures emerged.

They had the heads of men, the bodies and wings of locusts, and the tails of scorpions. They grabbed the flailing maltures and dragged them, kicking and screaming, down into the hole.

Their shrieks made Vero think of the cries of wild beasts' prey, as they're being dismembered by their predators.

Once the maltures disappeared into the ground, a few remaining locust-men buzzed around the entrance to the hole. The wind from their wings picked up a huge cloud of dirt all around them, and a face flashed through the haze — a face Vero recognized. Abaddon. Then the buzzing stopped.

A moment later, the dirt settled. The hole had sealed itself shut, and Abaddon and his locust creatures were gone.

Then everything flashed white.

29

THE WHITE LIGHT

Vero was sitting under a shade tree on the banks of a sparkling river in the Ether. He blinked his eyes and massaged his temples, trying to focus on something, anything. After a few moments, he could make out a figure. A powerfully built angel with handsome, rugged features and penetrating violet eyes came into view. He was enormous! At least ten feet tall. His stature was completely intimidating, but there was a kindness to his face that put Vero at ease.

"Hello, Vero. I'm Michael."

The mightiest of all of God's warriors walked over and placed his massive hand on Vero's shoulder. Vero didn't feel worthy of the gesture.

"The others?" Vero asked.

"They're fine."

Vero sighed with relief.

"You were very brave. Look at what your actions have done."

Michael waved his hand, and an image appeared in midair of Davina running up the porch steps of that new home being built on Fairburn.

"Danny! Danny!" she shouted.

Danny turned and saw her. He dropped the slingshot to the ground, and the red marble rolled away. Davina was safe. She sat on the top step with Danny.

"I want to explain ... " she began.

Danny looked at her.

"I really wanted to go to the dance with you. But my dad came back from his trip this afternoon, and when he found out about the dance, he wouldn't let me go. It's not that he doesn't like you; he just thinks I'm too young to go to a dance with a boy."

Danny looked relieved. "Really?" he whispered.

"Yes, Danny," Davina said. "I really do like you. And I'll save a dance for you someday."

A smile broke over Danny's face. He had a nice smile. It was the second time Vero had seen it.

"It's like a miracle that you found me here," Danny said, as he took Davina's hand in his own.

She nodded and laid her head on his shoulder.

"All of your efforts paid off," Michael told Vero.

"I guess," Vero said, feeling a strange mix of emotions.

He was happy for Danny, but a piece of his own heart was breaking. Vero thought of his journey through the belly of the Leviathan, his battle with the maltures—he did all of that to get Danny to lower his hand ... a tiny gesture that had saved Davina's life.

Michael read his mind. "You were able to fight through it all to reach the goodness in Danny's heart. Tonight you helped turn the direction of that boy's life. You brought him a step closer to God." Michael paused thoughtfully. "And he was able to help you."

"What do you mean? How did Danny help me?" Vero asked.

"A guardian angel's purpose is to protect humans. But we can only do so much on our own. God gives humans free will, and we can never dictate to them what they should or must do. However, when a person asks God for help, they are inviting us into their lives. And in return, we become empowered by their hope, their belief. As our power strengthens, we will stop at nothing to help them."

"That's where the extra strength comes from when we're answering prayers?"

"Yes. You grew your sword at the exact same moment that Danny asked God for help. All of you young angels received more strength today."

Vero tried to make sense of it all, but he was still confused.

"If God hears everyone's prayers, then why didn't Danny's guardian angel show up to help him?" Vero asked.

Michael smiled. "He did. And he fought magnificently."

And suddenly, Vero understood.

"I'm Danny's guardian angel."

Michael nodded.

Vero watched as Davina held Danny's hand and the two of them walked away from the house. Michael swept his hands, and Danny and Davina disappeared. Michael understood what Vero was feeling.

"Jealousy is never a good thing, Vero," Michael said

gently. "We have such great love for humans; but Vero, we are not to fall in love with them."

"I can't just turn off my feelings."

"That's because you still live in the earthly world. But I promise you, it will get easier the more time you spend in the Ether. It has to, because, Vero, we have high hopes for you."

Vero looked at Michael.

"Only a handful of beings since the beginning of time have ever been able to get past the golems and the Leviathan and the behemoths. They are there to stop beings from reaching the lake of fire. They may seem like horrible creatures, but God placed them there to prevent fledglings like yourself from reaching Abaddon and his pit."

"But I *did* reach the pit. I saw Abaddon. What happened when I got there? Was I in real danger?"

"Abaddon guards the pit and the lake of fire within. That is his domain. You were standing at the entrance. Not even *I* can enter that pit—not even to rescue someone because once a being is thrown in, there is no return from that pit of despair. The entrance is as far as I'm allowed to go."

Vero became frightened as Michael's words sunk in. "So it was you? You rescued me that day?"

Michael nodded, his face serious.

"Raziel didn't tell us the whole truth," Vero realized. "He said that if we fail in our training, we'll wind up in the choir of angels. He neglected to tell us that we could also wind up in the lake of fire for all eternity."

Michael sighed. "No one likes to think about that. It's too painful. You were never supposed to get that far."

"But then why would God let me get past the Leviathan and the golems and put the other angels in danger?"

"Because apparently God gave you the skills to handle them." Michael sat down next to Vero under the tree, and together they gazed at the fields and flowers before them. "In time you will discover, Vero, that you have been given much more than most angels ... so much more is expected of you."

The gravity of Michael's words hit Vero hard.

"And because you have been entrusted with much," Michael continued, "Lucifer and his maltures will come after you relentlessly."

"Is Lucifer the one who chased me in the grocery store when I was a baby?"

"Yes. He suspects that you are special. And those first few hours when an infant guardian is placed upon the earth are when he or she is the most vulnerable. But we had you covered. The produce deliveryman showing up when he did was no coincidence."

"And the old man who died in the ER?"

"Not an angel. That was Mr. Jenkins. He'd recently passed away, and we asked him if he'd go back to earth for a few moments and deliver a message to your mother."

Vero smiled at the explanation, but then another thought worried him. "Michael, why do they think I'm special?"

"You know of Raziel's book?"

Vero nodded.

"In the book there is a mention of an angel who will tip the scales for good in the final war between good and evil. The identity of the angel was hidden even from the archangels, but the date in which he or she would come down to earth is ... the same night that you were delivered to the ER."

Vero's head sunk to his chest. It was all too much.

"But you were not the only angel delivered that night. A few others came down to earth on that same day. So that is why we were not sure of your identity at first. But now we are."

"But how does Lucifer know?"

"Raziel's book did not always fall into the right hands. Lucifer still doesn't know for certain that it is you. But he suspects and that is enough. He will stop at nothing to thwart God's plan for you. He'll attack you any way he can. And as you saw with Davina, the ones you love the most are now the most vulnerable."

Vero was scared. Michael placed his hand under Vero's chin, making sure Vero didn't miss out on what he was about to say.

"But just like humans, Vero, we angels are never alone."

The blinding white light flashed, and Michael was gone. Vero now realized that he'd seen that white flash before—many times before. When he saw the face of Abaddon, the white light was Michael rescuing him. When he was on the school bus, he thought heavy snow had covered the windshield, but it was Michael protecting him from the malture in that oncoming car. When he was a baby and his mother ran through the grocery store with him, it was Michael who'd saved them. And Vero realized it was true. He would never be alone.

After the light vanished completely, Vero saw something glistening before his eyes. It was a single jewel—a simple yet exquisite gemstone that sparkled radiantly. Vero looked closer and saw it was inlaid on a golden crown, his crown. The crown that Raziel said they all had waiting for them in heaven. He reached out to touch it, and it disappeared.

❖

The water crashed over the three waterfalls and into the serene pool below. As Vero stood off in the distance, he listened to the thunderous, yet calming roar of the cascading water. He turned his face up to the sky, soaking in its warmth as he silently prayed, thanking God for safely delivering him from the maltures.

"Hey, Vero!" Greer yelled.

Greer, Pax, X, and Ada ran toward Vero, and Vero smiled at the sight of them. They were cleaned up, no ripped clothes, no cuts or bruises. No one would have ever guessed that only a short time ago, they'd trekked through the gut of a sea monster and battled maltures. Vero looked down at his own clothes. His jeans and red T-shirt also looked freshly washed.

"And you said you had nothing up your sleeve," Pax chuckled.

Vero shrugged and smiled. "And hey, I was able to communicate with you mind to mind."

"Pretty cool," Pax answered. "It only gets easier."

"How's your shoulder?" X asked Vero.

Vero had forgotten all about his injury. He put his hand on his shoulder and examined it. He rotated his arm, and to his surprise, there was no pain.

"All healed."

"Where did you learn to sword fight like that?" X asked.

"I don't know," Vero said. "Probably the same place I learned to speak Hebrew. But when I get back to earth, I think I may take up fencing. Seems like I might have a knack for it."

"Did you get a vision of your crown? Was there a jewel in it?" Pax asked.

"Yeah," Vero said.

"Pretty cool," Pax said.

Vero noticed Kane was standing away from them, looking nervous. They briefly locked eyes, and then Kane looked away. Vero understood. He walked over to him as the others watched.

"Are you okay?" Vero asked.

Kane nodded.

"Are you sure?"

Kane shook his head.

"I'm the weak link. Everyone got a vision of their crown but me. I guess it's because I've messed up twice now." Kane looked at his feet. "I'm not as strong as the rest of you."

Vero knew how that felt. He'd had plenty of his own failures during training. He couldn't fly at first. He'd humiliated Danny. In the caverns, Vero had refused to listen to his inner voice and wound up in the golems' cavern. "All I can say is that you saved me from the maltures. If you hadn't been there, I doubt it would have turned out so well."

"Thanks," Kane said. "And I'm sorry I attacked you."

Vero knew there would be many more tests to come. Their faith would be challenged at every turn. No one wanted to fail.

"My grandmother says faith takes practice. So maybe the more we do this, the easier it'll get," Pax offered.

Uriel walked up to the fledglings. "I'm very proud of all of you," he said, making sure to extend his gaze to Kane and intentionally include him. "Few fledglings have ever come up against what you five have encountered. And despite a few setbacks, you learned well to rely on your *Vox Dei*. It is the greatest gift you possess. As you progress with your training, listening to the voice should eventually become as natural as breathing ... because dark times are coming."

The group flashed anxious looks at Uriel.

"But for now, you will go back and enjoy your time on earth," Uriel said.

"Usually I hate leaving the Ether, but this time I'm okay with it," Ada said. "I want to go home and do nothing for a few days."

"Agreed," X said.

"In a big way," said Greer. "After seeing a malture, my latest foster mom doesn't seem so bad."

One by one, they closed their eyes and disappeared. As Vero closed his eyes, he felt a hand on his shoulder.

"Hold up a minute," Uriel said. He removed his hand and looked at Vero with those intense violet eyes. "Take a walk with me. I want to show you something."

Uriel and Vero walked over the rolling hills toward the waterfalls.

"I'm extremely proud of you, Vero, " Uriel said. "You don't realize it yet, but every action in the world, no matter how small or seemingly trivial, produces a ripple effect. Even when one person smiles at another, that tiny gesture isn't wasted. It gets passed along. Saving Davina's life has far-reaching implications that you cannot even begin to fathom, and the heavens are grateful to you."

"I'm sorry, Uriel," Vero said, and then paused to choose his words. "I'm sorry for blaming you for that whole garden of Eden thing. It's not so easy, is it?"

"No, it's not."

As they got closer to the waterfalls' shore, Uriel held out his arm and stopped Vero.

"You won't be able to go any farther. I wouldn't want you to bang your head."

"Thanks for the heads-up."

Uriel took a few steps closer to the pool. He bent down and stuck his hand into the still water of the lake. And then he walked back to Vero.

"Close your eyes."

Vero did as he was told. Just as Raphael had done to him in New York City, Uriel placed his thumbs — now wet with the waterfalls' water — on Vero's eyelids. After a moment, Uriel removed his thumbs, and Vero opened his eyes.

The sight before him caused Vero to take a step back. There in the lake, scores of humans were frolicking in the water. They splashed one another, some cupped the water into their hands and let it drip over their heads, others laid on their backs and just floated in it. The humans were of all nationalities and all ages, from little children to the elderly. They were laughing, smiling, and radiating pure joy. Their bodies were shimmering, glowing even. Scores of angels lined the shore and watched their humans proudly, the joy evident on their faces as well.

"Who are those people?" Vero asked.

"The recently deceased. They're being bathed. All souls must be purified before they meet God."

"They're going to heaven?"

Uriel nodded. Vero watched as one by one, the humans walked out of the water and clasped hands with a waiting angel.

"Those are their guardian angels?" Vero asked.

"Yes. This is the greatest moment of a guardian angel's life, when we take our humans to be with God."

Vero, his eyes misty, was overcome with emotion. He knew why Uriel had shown this to him. It was to remind him of what he must do—to one day be standing on that shore with Danny.

With hands still clasped, the angels and humans walked through the waterfall; and one by one, they vanished from sight.

Uriel closed Vero's eyelids with his thumbs, and when Vero opened his eyes again, the humans and angels had disappeared.

"It's time for you to return to earth," Uriel said.

Vero nodded.

"Oh, and when you get back, Vero, I think your sister will finally be ready to talk to you. You're not the only one with secrets in the Leland household. And you can talk openly with her. I won't send any ambulances racing past this time."

Uriel disappeared in a blur. Vero took in one last view of the Ether. He wasn't sure when he would return, but he never doubted that he would be back someday. Something flew past him and landed on a tree branch. It was a dove. The dove stared at him for a moment, and Vero could have sworn that it smiled at him.

30

❖

A SISTER'S
CONFESSION

Vero found himself wearing an Elvis jumpsuit and standing on the curb where the fire truck had hit him. For a moment, he thought time had stood still while he'd been in the Ether, but then he noticed he was the only person outside the gym, and there was no fire truck anywhere. Music blasted through the gym windows, and Vero looked at his watch. Time had not stood still. He'd traveled through the Leviathan and had battled the maltures all in the course of an evening. The fire drill was over, and the dance was back in full swing.

Vero peered through a gym window. Kids were dancing up a storm and having a blast. He spotted Davina dancing with Danny. It was bittersweet for him. Danny looked up and caught Vero staring at them. He flashed Vero a haughty smile. Vero sighed. Being Danny's guardian angel was really going to be a challenge.

"Vero!"

Vero whipped around to see Clover running full force at him. She grabbed him and hugged him tight. In fact, she squeezed Vero so tightly that he thought his head would pop off.

"Are you all right?" she asked.

"Yeah, I'm fine."

"But what happened? I mean, where were you?"

Vero wanted so badly to tell her the truth. And Uriel had given him permission to do so. And yet, he was afraid. How could he expect her to accept who he really was? What if she freaked? Or worse, what if it pushed her even farther away?

"I just went for a walk."

"No, you fell in front of the fire truck. I saw it!"

Vero looked down, not wanting to answer. Clover realized that if she was going to earn her brother's trust, she could no longer lie to him. She'd been just as deceitful as him. So she mustered up her courage and faced him.

"I remember the man who twisted your ankle. I remember everything about him. And I saw you sprout wings that day when you were making a snow angel. And even though Tack couldn't see them, I saw Blake and Duff. I know they're real. And my dreams, they seem like they're really happening. I can't shake them the next morning. Vero, I see things that normal people can't. For years, I thought if I denied seeing all that stuff, then it would just go away, but it hasn't. And I actually think it's getting stronger."

Vero looked at her, completely surprised. He hadn't been expecting to hear this.

"They're true, aren't they? All the things I see?"

Vero nodded, hoping his limited response would suffice.

"You're an angel, aren't you?"

Vero's first reaction was to lie and call her crazy, but then he remembered Uriel's words to him. "Yes," he said.

Clover's eyes filled with tears—not sad ones, but joyous tears. "Well that explains a lot," she said.

"But not enough," Vero replied. He hesitated for a moment. "Clover, in your dream journal there is a drawing..." Vero began.

"You looked in my diary?"

"It was by accident! But there is a drawing of a man, and he has three other faces: a lion, an ox and an eagle—"

"That's the Cherubim," Clover said. "The angels who guard God's throne."

Vero gave her a curious look.

"You really should pay closer attention during Sunday school," Clover grinned.

"I saw him in my dream too," Vero said.

"Why do you think we got to see him?" Clover asked.

"I don't know. But something tells me we'll know why someday."

"Are you sure? Because even though I see all these things... sometimes it just doesn't make any sense," Clover said. "Sometimes I'm not sure of anything."

"Can you see the wind?" Vero asked.

"What?"

"Can you see the wind?" Vero asked again.

"No."

"But it topples trees, moves oceans, shapes mountains, and even holds birds up in flight. You can feel it, and you can hear it. And even though you can't see it, Clover, you know it's there."

Clover understood that he was talking about God. She nodded and then looked up at the night sky—a sky full of endless wonder.

"Is it as wonderful as they taught us in Sunday school?"

"I haven't been to heaven yet," Vero smiled. "But from what I've seen so far, wonderful doesn't even begin to cover it."

Tack came barreling through the gym doors.

"Hey, you two! There's a dance going on in there!"

"We know," Clover said, rolling her eyes.

"And I promised to save a slow dance for you," Tack said with a wink.

"In your dreams, Tack!" she said.

Vero pulled Clover aside and whispered, "Don't forget . . . around us, dreams have a way of coming true."

Clover's eyes went wide. Then a car horn blared next to them as Nora and Dennis pulled into the school parking lot.

"Sorry, Tack. Ten o'clock curfew. No dance tonight," Clover said with definite glee.

"Ah, man! Why do your parents always have to be on time?"

As they walked over to the car, Nora rolled down her window. "If you hurry, we might be able to get in a game of pajama Twister before bed," she said.

"Yes!" Tack shouted, punching his fist in the air, and he broke into a sprint for the car.

"They are so embarrassing," Clover said to Vero.

Vero smiled. He was determined to savor every single embarrassing moment.

"Race you!" Vero said.

ACKNOWLEDGMENTS

I wish to personally thank the following people for their contributions that were so helpful in creating this book:

For my husband, Chris, who majorly helped me to define the angelic realm of *The Ether* ... he was my story consultant, sounding board, and enthusiastic supporter from day one.

For my daughter, Grace, the best little reader in the City of Angels, who devoured each chapter as I wrote it. And for my son, Luke, from whom I gleaned many of Vero's and Tack's youthful characteristics.

For my mother, Joan Elehwany, who encouraged me as a child to tell stories, especially during long road trips. And for my brothers, David and Michael, who had no choice but to listen to them.

For my Hollywood screenplay manager and friend, David Greenblatt, whose years of support and sage advice have greatly inspired my writings.

For my brother-in-law and attorney, Guy N. Molinari, who gave generously of his time and considerable talents.

For Larry A. Thompson, book packager and producer extraordinaire, who originally read the manuscript and shepherded *The Ether* to market.

For my wonderful agents at DMA, Jan Miller and Nena Madonia, whose enthusiasm and constant encouragement was a true blessing for this neophyte novelist.

And for the wonderful folks at Zondervan, especially my editor, Kim Childress, whose continual guidance, advice, and support helped transform *The Ether* from manuscript to novel.

Thank you, one and all. Your help and assistance has been a true Godsend.

Check out this exclusive bonus chapter from the next
Ether novel, *Pillars of Fire*, available December 2014!

Pillars of Fire

AN ETHER NOVEL

LAURICE E. MOLINARI

1

MEDICAL WONDER

T he moon was nearly full, but no light pierced the canopy of cloud and tree to reach the forest floor. Below the tangled branches, the woods were dark and deadly still. Not even the melodious music of the evening crickets could be heard.

From the center of the forest, a column of heavy black smoke wafted through the trees, choking the life from the surrounding air. A moment later, the eerie silence was broken. Birds screeched, branches snapped, and animals crashed through the underbrush, all fleeing in a widening ring of panic. Something was not right in the woodland.

The smoke came from a bright fire in a small clearing. A hunched figure, cloaked in shadows, slowly stepped into the light of the flames. She was a gaunt woman, and behind her trailed a carpet of coarse black hair that gleamed dully in the light. Longer than a hundred wedding trains sewn together, the hair seemed to have a life of its own, slithering around trees and rocks with the agility of a serpent. It looked endless in the dark.

When she reached the fire, the woman swept aside her ragged robe and dropped to her knees. The flames revealed cavernous wrinkles and deep black eyes. She looked to be thousands of years old.

"I am listening, my prince," the haggard woman snarled to the blaze before her. Her voice sounded like the screech of a hundred hungry owls.

"Our time runs short," said a voice from the fire. The flames rose and fell as it spoke. "The others have disappointed me greatly. But you shall not."

Eighty yards away, next to an abandoned well, a fleeing white-tailed buck unknowingly stepped on the long black mane.

"Are we sure it is one of these fledglings?" screeched the hag.

"His true nature will manifest during the Trials. Then we will know with certainty," the inferno breathed. Despite the intense heat from the flames, its tone was menacing and cold. "The child cannot live."

Suddenly, the end of the woman's hair train rose up like a king cobra readying to strike. The buck's eyes filled with terror, and he tried to bolt, but the hair coiled itself around its body with the speed of a viper. Within seconds, the panicked buck was completely encased by the hair, strangled, devoured, and then just gone.

"Don't offer me creatures of the forest," the fire said. "Offer me the fledgling, for he will be the prize of all prizes."

"I will do as my prince commands," the hag said. A smile cracked her ancient lips. "The child will not be."

As she stood up and turned to leave, the hair gliding with her, the blaze called out. "Do you loathe me?"

The woman stopped and slowly turned to face the fire. Her eyes were hollow. "I despise all that He has created. So you are no different."

Pleased with her answer, the fire let out a wicked laugh, and the hag disappeared once more into the dark forest.

❖

Vero Leland stood with his back against the stark white wall. His gray eyes nervously scanned the room for items that could be used to injure him. There were syringes with long needles, razor-sharp scissors, and pointy scalpels on the counter. The room was filled with the nauseating smell of rubbing alcohol. Looking around at the many dangerous objects, Vero was scared. But he was more scared that the flower-themed, flimsy paper gown he was wearing would fly open and expose his pasty backside. He clutched the opening shut in tight fists.

"Sit down. You're going to rip the gown," his mother, Nora, told him. "Really, Vero, you're too old to be afraid of the doctor."

"Easy for you to say. You're not the one who's getting a shot. Just look at the size of those needles!" Vero said, nodding to a metal tray on the counter.

"I'm sure they're not all for you," Nora winked, her faint laugh lines showing.

Vero looked at his mother skeptically, but Nora's vibrant

green eyes filled with tenderness as she gazed upon her only son. "I remember your first set of shots. You were so tiny. When the doctor pricked you, you cried and cried. Then I joined in," Nora said, tearing up. "It broke my heart. The doctor thought I took it harder than you."

"Knock it off, Mom." Vero rolled his eyes. "You're so embarrassing."

"No more embarrassing than a knobby-kneed thirteen-year-old boy in a flowered paper dress," Nora replied, looking hurt.

"Sorry, but, it's just that I'm old enough to get a physical by myself. You don't need to be here with me."

"But I've always taken you to your physical."

"I'm not a little kid anymore," Vero said. "You treat me like a baby. You won't even let me have a cellphone!"

"You'll get one when you're older, like Clover," Nora said.

"See? Like a baby." Vero pouted.

Nora's expression softened. "What if Dr. Walker has questions, and you can't answer them?"

"I'm sure he could find you in the waiting room."

Nora looked at Vero, her lips pursed. She knew he was right, but it was so hard to let go. Nora had always struggled to give Vero independence. She feared for him more than for her daughter, Clover. Thirteen years later, she still regularly woke up in a cold sweat after reliving the night she had found the abandoned baby Vero in the hospital. The night a figure cloaked in a dark robe chased her through a grocery store while she clutched Vero to her chest. The night she so desperately wanted to shake from her memory, but knew she never would.

"Hello, Vero," the doctor said as he shut the door behind

him, snapping Nora from her thoughts. "How's my medical wonder doing?"

Dr. Walker had known Vero his whole life but usually only saw him once a year for his annual physical because Vero almost never got sick. Nora had brought Vero in a few times to discuss how to put more weight on him, but other than that, Vero rarely saw the doctor.

Nora stood up and opened the door. "I'll be out in the waiting room if you need me," she said.

"You're not staying?" the white-haired doctor questioned.

"No, he can handle himself."

Vero smiled gratefully at his mom. Taking one last look at her son, Nora slipped out, leaving him alone with Dr. Walker.

"So, Vero, how is everything?"

"Pretty good."

"You feeling okay? Any complaints?" Dr. Walker listened to Vero's heart with his metal stethoscope.

"No."

"Breathe."

Vero took a few deep breaths as the doctor checked his lungs.

Dr. Walker smiled. "Very nice. So how's your back?"

The question threw Vero. "Oh, um ... my back?"

"Your mother called a while ago, said you were complaining it hurt?"

"Oh, that thing. Yeah, they bought me a new mattress, and it stopped bugging me after that."

Vero felt guilty about twisting the truth, but there was no way he could be honest. Dr. Walker would never understand that all his back pain had completely disappeared the first time he had sprouted his wings. That the back pain had actually been nothing more than guardian angel growing pains.

"Let's check your vision. Put your hand over your left eye and read the chart."

Vero covered his eye and read the chart hanging on the other side of the room. "E, F, P, T, O, Z ..." he said.

"Just read the lowest line you can see clearly," Dr. Walker interrupted.

Vero squinted as his eye scanned down the chart. "I can make out the last line. F, E, A ..." he read aloud. "R, M, E."

"That's awful, Vero! You got every single letter wrong," Dr. Walker told him. "Try the line above it."

"But I see 'em clearly."

"Remove your hand and read it with both eyes."

Vero dropped his hand from his face. He stared intently at the last line. "F, E ... A, R, M, E," Vero repeated.

Dr. Walker scribbled something on his prescription pad and tore it off with great force.

"It took thirteen years, but we've finally found something wrong with you! You need glasses, Vero," he said as he triumphantly handed the paper to Vero. "This is a prescription to see an eye doctor."

"But I'm sure I'm reading the line right." Vero walked over to the eye chart and put his face right up to it. "See? I'm right. Look. F, E, A, R, M, E."

"Interesting ... not only near sighted, but you're far sighted as well."

Then it hit Vero. The letters, F, E, A, R, M, E—they spelled out "Fear me!" He was getting a message that the doctor could not see—a message from the Ether. *Fear me?* he thought. Was he being threatened from beyond?

It had been several months since he had heard anything from the Ether, and Vero missed it terribly. He longed for the vast fields of wildflowers, so brightly colored he had to shield his eyes. He ached for the warmth of the Ether's eternal light. Most of all, he wanted to sprout his wings and soar into the Ether's brilliant blue sky. In fact, it had been so long since he was there, he had begun to worry that maybe he wasn't actually cut out for angel training, and he had been eliminated from his group of fledglings.

Fear me. A chill ran through Vero, giving him goose bumps. No matter how badly he longed to return there, he knew not everything in the Ether was good.

"Any questions, Vero?" Dr. Walker asked, his kindly eyes twinkling.

"No," Vero answered, relieved that there was no mention of any shots.

"Then I'll see you and your new glasses next year," the doctor said on his way out. "You can get dressed."

After the door closed, Vero reached down to grab his jeans off the blue chair. As he ripped the thin plastic belt from his waist, someone knocked, then entered without waiting for a response. Vero quickly spun around and saw a young pretty nurse holding a small metal tray. His hand instinctively pulled the back of the gown shut to hide his underwear.

"Time for your shot," the nurse smiled, flashing a set of perfect, white teeth.

"But Dr. Walker didn't say I needed one!" Vero panicked. "He said I could go."

"Doctors never like to deliver bad news," the nurse smiled. "They make us nurses be the bad guys. Sorry, sweetie."

Vero looked at the woman. Even though she smiled, no warmth reached her eyes. She didn't seem at all sorry for what she was about to do to him. Perhaps after years of dealing with screaming scared kids her sympathy had turned to indifference or worse—annoyance. Vero carefully jumped up on the examination table, one hand still clutching the gown's back flaps. As the nurse rubbed his arm with a small alcohol swab, he swallowed hard. Now that he was officially a teenager, he would put on a brave face and take his shot without complaint. But deep down, he regretted sending his mom out to the waiting room. He still wanted to hold her hand.

"It'll be over before you know it," the nurse said in a flat, monotonous voice. "Hold still."

Vero looked into her eyes for reassurance, but found none. Instead, he saw red. Glowing little flecks of red. Vero gasped. He knew what those flecks meant. He had seen them before. The nurse clenched his arm, ready to stab the long needle into his soft skin, when Vero leapt off the examination table, grabbing the first thing he could reach on the counter to defend himself. Vero looked at his hand—a stethoscope! It would be about as much help as the Q-Tips that had been lying next to it.

"Tell us who it is!" the nurse gurgled deeply as she backed him into a corner.

"Who are you?" Vero yelled.

She growled, revealing that her sparkling white teeth had turned to rotted fangs, and lunged at Vero. Vero rolled underneath her outstretched legs, narrowly escaping. The nurse spun and wildly jabbed the syringe at Vero. He jumped back against the examination table. As the needle came straight for his eye, he grabbed a pillow and blocked it. The needle punctured the fabric and cotton padding, nearly stabbing his nose.

"Tell us which one of you it is!" she commanded.

Vero bolted to the door, but the enraged nurse slammed into his back before he could open it. Feeling the tip of the needle press against his neck, Vero, turned, grabbed her wrist, and with unexpected strength, twisted it, thrusting the needle deep into her shoulder and compressing the plunger. The nurse snarled, and with a final shriek, she tumbled off his back onto the hard floor. Vero was breathing so heavily, he thought he'd pass out. But he had more pressing worries. How was he going to explain the dead nurse, or whatever creature it was, lying in the middle of the room?

As Vero stared at her, he noticed the stethoscope on the floor. He bent down and quickly picked it up. He wasn't completely sure she was dead, so he grabbed a scalpel with his other hand for protection. Vero then kneeled, put in the earpieces, and placed the listening end over her heart. There was no heartbeat. Relief swept over him, followed quickly by anger. "Fear you?" he spat. "How about 'fear me'?!"

But then he heard something, a faint sound in the stethoscope. It was the distant echo of eerie cackling, and it was growing louder. Vero yanked out the earpieces and chucked the instrument to the floor, holding the scalpel in front of him like a sword. There was a demented smile on the nurse's face that hadn't been there previously. Puffs of black smoke blossomed from her nostrils.

Vero backed away as the nurse's body began to blacken. Soon, all that remained was a scorched mark on the checkered tiled floor. Horrified, Vero dropped the scalpel, ran out the door and raced down the hallway toward the waiting room.

Annual physicals are not supposed to be life threatening! Vero thought. When he saw his mother in the crowded waiting room, casually leafing through some gossip magazine, Vero ran into her arms. Nora was caught off guard by his embrace, and dropped the magazine. Parents and kids looked upon Vero with interest. He was still wearing his pink flowered paper dress.

"Vero, what's wrong?"

"The shot ... She was trying to give me a shot!" he blurted, fumbling over words.

Dr. Walker stood behind the appointment desk reading a patient's file. He overheard. "No shot today, Vero. Your vaccines are all up to date."

Vero let go of his mother, his common sense returning to him.

Nora stared at Vero intently, then she said, "Come on, you need to get to school."

A chubby five-year-old boy walked over to him, laughing and pointing. "I see London. I see France ..." he giggled.

Vero turned beet red.

"I see that kid's underpants!"

Vero hid behind his mom.

Pillars of Fire

Laurice E. Molinari

After Vero Leland discovered his true identity in book one, he must continue to maintain his life on earth as a regular 12-year-old kid, which is hard to do when you are really a fledgling, a guardian angel in training to become one of the fiercest of all angels. At any moment, he could be called to the Ether, the spiritual realm surrounding the earth, where he must face whatever trials come his way in angel school, aka C.A.N.D.L.E. (the Cathedral of Angels for Novice Development, Learning and Edification). In book two, part of Vero's training involves the Angel Trials, a set of three challenges where he and his group of fellow fledglings compete with angels from other realms.

But while he is competing in the Ether, back on earth his sister is in trouble. She has a new friend who is leading her down the wrong path. During the third trial, Vero realizes he must choose between saving his sister or winning his competition. But the attack on Clover is only a means to get to Vero, and he finds himself face-to-face with an evil even greater than what he experienced in the Bottomless Pit. Once again, he is tested beyond what any previous fledgling has endured, and how the battle ends will affect not only his grade in C.A.N.D.L.E., but also the fate of the world.

Available in stores and online!

LOOKING FOR MORE FROM THIS AUTHOR?

Be sure to connect with her
at www.LauriceMolinari.com